Heart Breaker

Katy Berritt

Edgecombe Publishing

Contents

To my friend, Jean Joachim, author of so many wonderful books. I have learned so much from you and couldn't have done it without your support.

ONE

JennGoodwin@MyHeart-2-Heart

I don't care what you heard. I don't care what anybody tells you. IT WAS NOT MY FAULT!

It was official; Jenn Goodwin was crazy.

Because trusting the groom's ring bearer to not pee on the bride's dress during the ceremony was crazy. Riding ten miles in the middle of nowhere in search of something to replace the bride's pee-stained gown was crazy. Believing she'd find a replacement, per the bride's demand that the replacement must be pink, was definitely crazy.

After securing the plastic shopping bag holding her purchase to the handlebars of her bike, Jenn hiked up the skirt of her pink—yes, it was pink, so what?—bridesmaid dress, she eagerly mounted up. She pressed the ignition button. The motor roared. Her heart roared right along with it.

Putting the bike into gear, she zoomed out onto the road.

All right, all right, so it wasn't exactly a zoom because, even though zooming was the ultimate in attitude, she'd promised her mother she'd be careful and not die. The poor woman wasn't big on the idea of her daughter becoming roadkill.

So, fine, no zooming, more a nice putt-putt for now. Once her mom got used to her daughter owning a death machine, Jenn would work her way up to a zoom.

Green fields slid by. A few cows mooed at her and fled at the sound of her motorcycle. The sun beamed down on her bare shoulders. It was all kinds of fun except the part where a car full of teenage boys whizzed past her and catcalled while ogling her bare legs. She bared her teeth, dared to take one hand off her handlebars and gave them the finger.

See. Attitude.

Even riding cautiously, it only took her fifteen minutes to get to the hotel. Steering the bike into an available spot, she parked and shut off the motor. She looped the strap of the helmet over her arm, grabbed the bag she would deliver to the bride and walked to the hotel. Entering the gorgeous front lobby with all its sparkly things and the lush carpeting, Jenn headed for the restroom where Amy and her sister Lisa, Amy's other bridesmaid, waited.

She opened the door. Amy stood in the middle of the ladies' room in her fancy underclothes, her lovely wedding dress with its pee-stained train piled on a chair. Nearby on the floor was the shredded remnants of Amy's pink reception dress. And lying on her back, surrounded by a sea of pink—reception dress—beads, her long pink tongue lolling out of her doggy grin, three legs waving in the air, was the ring bearer.

"Woof," the ring bearer greeted her.

"Oh, my God, where have you been! The reception started twenty minutes ago, and Nick's been banging on the door, and I'm about to lose my mind," was Amy's greeting.

Huh. No gratitude. So typical of the bridezilla from Heart-2-Heart. Once upon a time, her partner had been normal. Then she decided to get married. "We're in the middle of nowhere. Shopping options were limited." Scowling, Jenn thrust the plastic bag into the bride's hands, who removed the items from the bag.

"Yay!" Amy tore open the bag and yanked out the contents. A sweatpants and sweatshirt. Not silk. Not sexy. Not pink. Gray. She burst into tears. Behind little

Miss Niagara Falls, Lisa wrapped her hands around her own neck and pretended to strangle herself.

"Sorry, I tried, but it was all I could find," Jenn mumbled. She was tempted to stay to comfort Amy, but gah—tears. Leaving the two sisters to sort it out, she walked to the concierge desk and spoke to the attendant who pointed her towards the ballrooms where signs indicated each room's event.

Horowitz Bar Mitzvah.

Maitland Wedding.

Miller Anniversary.

Dennison Wedding.

Hanging a right at the Dennison sign, she entered the enormous ballroom. After locating her assigned table and setting down her helmet, she made a beeline for the bar. Even though she wasn't normally much of a drinker, every nerve in her body was screaming *Give me alcohol or give me death*! It wasn't exactly what that Patrick Henry guy said, but geez, if you're about to commit treason, wouldn't it have made a lot more sense to ask for alcohol?

Bellying up to the bar, she winked at the bartender with the sexy blue eyes and perused the selection.

"Um..."

"Vodka? Gin and tonic. Manhattan, martini?" He leveled those sexy eyes on her and smoldered.

She liked a good smolder as much as the next girl, but even the world's best smolder wouldn't convince her to drink a martini. She wimped out and ordered a strawberry daiquiri.

Okay, so her attitude thing needed work.

She sipped her pink—oh, drat, what was she thinking—drink while she watched the other guests mingle as she examined, not for the first time, the whole attitude thing. It wasn't like she didn't have attitude in the past; she'd had plenty of attitude; it was just the wrong kind of attitude.

Lifting her glass again, she put it to her lips. Whoa. The darned thing was empty. How had that happened? She went back to the bar.

The lights in the ballroom dimmed. The DJ in the corner turned his mic on. Strobe lights flashed, a disco ball dropped from the ceiling, and the ballroom doors opened again.

"Ladies and gentlemen, introducing for the first time, Mr. and Mrs. Nicholas Dennison," the DJ blared. Amid the hoots and hollers and clapping, Amy and Nick sashayed in. That obnoxious dog gallumped behind them on her three legs, grinning and drooling. Unlike the dog, Amy wasn't smiling.

Jenn poked Mr. Smolder. "That bride needs some alcoholic happiness. Oh, some more for me too. I've had a trying day."

With a grin that showed perfect teeth, he set a daiquiri and a beer down on the bar. Jenn grabbed them and made her way to the happy couple—happy being a loose term—and thrust the beer into Amy's hand.

Amy downed it in about thirty seconds flat, handed the bottle back to Jenn and waltzed off.

"She's going to get drunk," Lisa whispered from behind.

"She deserves to," Jenn answered. "What a disaster!"

"Don't say that to my mom. She'll have a cow. She's spent months and thousands of dollars on this do."

Running her hand across her mouth like a zipper, Jenn said, "Mum's the word. Actually, I'm going to avoid your mother like she's poison ivy." Not that Barbara Novak wasn't a nice person, it was that anyone unfortunate enough to drift into her orbit had a tendency to end up married, and not necessarily to the man of their choice.

Lisa gave an exaggerated shiver since she was Barbara's most recent target, although she'd somehow managed to evade her mother's schemes and find her own guy. Her choice, a shaggy-haired guy named Josh, ambled up and draped his arm over her shoulders.

"Having fun?" he asked and kissed the top of her head.

Ugh. Love permeated the air like smog on a hot Los Angeles day. They looked so freakin' happy it almost made her jealous. No, not jealousy. It was that she was weirded out by the idea that being in love inevitably led to marriage, and kids, and eventually old age and OMG—*wrinkles*—and who the heck needed all that.

She sighed. Maybe she'd like a little of that, however, there was no way she was ever going to have it. When your own father betrayed you, it was a little difficult to believe in love.

The music got a little louder. The party got a little wilder. The ballroom got a lot hotter. Eventually, someone threw open the outside doors leading out to the wide lawn and the manmade pond.

Men asked her to dance, so she did. They all looked alike. They all sounded alike. They all stared at her boobs and ran their eyes up and down the amount of leg exposed by her short, short hem. Whatever. It wasn't like she was going to fall for their baloney.

A man ran onto the dance floor. "There's a dog in the pond and it's drowning," he shouted, pointing outside. "And some guy jumped in to save it."

Everyone rushed to the open patio doors. Within minutes, shaggy-haired Josh appeared carrying the shaggy ring bearer, both of them soaking wet.

That seemed to be the highlight of a day that started out crazy and got loonier as time went on. It could only get worse from here. It was time to go home. Jenn tottered her way back to the table where she'd left her stuff. She was feeling *goooood*. But a little loopy. Okay. A lot loopy. Not safe to ride. She would have to take an Uber home and come back for her bike tomorrow.

She grabbed her helmet, holding it with both hands against her stomach because otherwise it might make a break for it—helmets had been known to do that—and wobbled towards the door.

Lisa grabbed her. "Hey," she blurted out rapid-fire. "FYI. Josh and I decided to fly to Vegas tonight to get married, like right now, because otherwise my mother—well, you know—so I'm letting you know, so you'll be prepared for when the shit hits the fan with Amy." She tapped the enormous rock on her finger, looking smug and disheveled and thoroughly compromised in the best possible sense. Next to her, Josh said nothing, just looked pleased with himself.

Jenn's brain wasn't working at full capacity yet even drunk—oops, sorry, she meant tipsy—she was still smarter than the average sober person, so after a bit of mental grappling, she untangled Lisa's sentence well enough to figure out the implications of her desertion.

Uh oh. "Oh, hey, wait. You're supposed to babysit the do—"

Lisa glanced over her shoulder and gasped. "Oops. Gotta go. Bye." Hand-in-hand, she and Josh made a mad dash out the door.

Darn it. Jenn threw a glance over her shoulder, and there was Amy, holding the ring bearer's leash and stalking across the dance floor, a look of determination on her face.

Oh no. Not happening. She spun on her heel and fled out the wide double-doors into the hallway, where she abruptly stopped because the striped carpeting in the hallway was doing funky things like something out of an op-art installation. Oh boy, not good.

She closed one eye. Didn't make any difference; the long hallway still shimmied, the stripes of the carpeting waving up and down like the ocean on a stormy day. She tried closing the other eye, hoping it would steady things a little better, but all it did was focus her attention on the older gray-haired woman talking to another woman outside the ballroom next door, and the good-looking young guy slinking up behind her back. With a wary look at the older woman, he bent over and dipped his hand inside the pocketbook slung over the woman's arm. When his hand left the bag, it held a wallet.

Holy cow. "Hey, you! Stop!"

The pickpocket's eyes lifted. The old woman turned.

Hands outstretched to stop him, Jenn charged. She forgot she was holding her helmet.

It hit the pickpocket square in the face and sent him flying backwards. He hit the carpet with a thud.

Nobody said anything. Except the pickpocket. "What the fuck?" he muttered to the ceiling. "I just wanted to give her back her credit card." His eyes closed, and he was still.

The old woman bent down next to him. "Noah! Noah, are you okay?" She tapped his cheek. When he didn't move, she lifted pale blue eyes to glare at Jenn.

"You killed my grandson!"

Oh. Fudge.

TWO

NoahMaitland@noahmaitlandesq

Researchers estimate 41% of first marriages end in divorce. Hooray for me!

What the hell happened? All Noah remembered was a girl shouting, then something hitting him in the face like a battering ram. Lights out. The next thing he knew, he was being loaded into an ambulance. When they slid the gurney in, he could see over the EMT's shoulders a pair of big blue eyes full of regret and bright red lips mouthing, *I'm sorry, I'm sorry, I'm sorry.*

Sorry? Like that was going to cut it. She'd damned near killed him, and she was sorry? Whoever she was, he'd never forget her face. Not that he ever wanted to see her face again. If he saw her face again, he'd make sure she never forgot him.

When he was a kid, he'd have been thrilled to ride in an ambulance, but the wail of the siren made his headache worse, and the fact they that kept poking and prodding him when all he wanted to do was sleep was supremely annoying, never mind the fact he was too old, and too damned busy for this shit.

A female EMT shone a bright light in his eyes. Holy Christ. "Hey! Cut it out."

"What's your name?" she asked.

"What?"

"Your name? Do you know your name?"

"For Pete's sake. Of course, I know my name. Noah Maitland. Now get that light out of my eyes."

"What's the date?"

"Who knows? Who cares?" He got a scowly look from the EMT. "Fine. It's June sixteenth, my father's wedding day. For the fourth...fifth...whatever...time. Now get this damned collar off and stop with the flashlight in my eyes."

"I guess he isn't going to die," the EMT said and slapped a blood pressure cuff on his arm and pumped it up.

"Ouch, stop. I'm fine. Let me up. In fact, stop somewhere, wherever, and let me out," he growled, batting their hands away.

"You have a broken nose that needs setting, and possibly a concussion. You're going to the hospital to get X-rays."

He continued to complain, however, no matter how he protested, the hospital is where he went. What a pain in the—he wanted to say *ass* but truthfully, it was his head that was the pain—which rang like a Tibetan gong.

Once at the hospital, he got the whole works: another blood pressure thingie, an eye exam, an X-ray and MRI, along with more poking and prodding. And they reset his nose.

Holy hell on a cracker, that fucking hurt. They couldn't give him any heavy-duty painkillers because of the concussion, which meant setting it hurt like a son of a bitch. Speaking of bitches, he wanted to kill the one who beaned him.

He dismissed the possibility since he would never see her again, thank the Lord, because the last thing he needed was another concussion. Or a criminal charge of murder.

His grandmother Tess showed up in the middle of the circus. Despite how it made his entire face hurt, he smiled when he saw her slight form slip past the curtain surrounding his emergency room cubicle. Five-foot nothing and sprier than a twenty-year-old, she was still beautiful at seventy-two years old. Her light blue eyes were shiny with concern. He loved Tess Maitland. She was the only one of his relatives who cared. The rest of his family was nothing but a bunch of bloodsuckers, and he was usually the host. It was a miracle he didn't have anemia from feeding them all.

She slipped her hand into his and squeezed. A feeling of peace washed over him.

"Oh, dear, I was so worried. How are you?" she asked.

"Broken nose. Concussion. I'll live. But I should sue the bit—" He cleared his throat. "Uh, girl who bashed me."

She gave him one of those grandma looks. "Tsk. It was an accident. She saw you take my wallet out of my purse and thought you were robbing me. All she was trying to do was stop you. Unfortunately, she forgot she was holding her motorcycle helmet."

"But—"

"She felt terrible. She couldn't apologize enough."

"But—"

"Young man, I would be very disappointed in you if you sued her."

And there it was. Grandparent disappointment. Damn it.

"Fine. I won't sue her. Obviously, it was simply a misunderstanding. The least she could've done, though, was check to see if I was okay."

He got another one of those looks. "She checked. She was here at the front desk when I arrived; however, when she saw me, she ducked out the door. I'm sure she was embarrassed."

"Hmm." Wincing at the pain still stabbing at his temples, he changed topics. If he wasn't allowed to sue the woman, he didn't want to talk about her. "So, did Dad and his latest get off on their honeymoon okay?" he asked.

An ironic smile appeared. "You know your father. He and Kitty left even before the EMTs got you loaded into the ambulance."

Laying his head back on the gurney, he closed his eyes. The bright lights made his head pound. "What a damned waste of money."

"I don't know why you keep paying for his weddings. You know the marriage will only last a few years before he dumps her."

Yeah, and he would get to handle the divorce—gratis—the same way Noah handled his father's last four, the three divorces for his mother, and the two for Bret, his older brother, who appeared to be currently working on wife number three which meant divorce number three would follow soon after.

That was why he'd decided to become a divorce lawyer. Why waste all that experience on something like corporate law?

Gram sighed. "I don't know where we went wrong with your father. Your grandfather—God rest his wonderful soul—and I were happily married for forty-four years. We tried to teach Roger to be a good shepherd to the money he would inherit, but..."

She didn't finish the sentence. Why bother? It was an old story, oft repeated. His grandmother and grandfather had had only one child, who sadly had been a bitter disappointment to them.

And all the money his father was set to inherit? Roger had almost emptied the Maitland bank account before his grandparents put a stop to it. Noah vowed never to be a disappointment to the grandparents who'd raised him from the age of thirteen. If his new practice didn't succeed, they were all screwed, even his Gram, since Noah took care of her too. Which reminded him...

"Can you find my phone? I need to talk to the caterers about the open house." Tomorrow's open house that was the start of what he hoped was a successful law practice.

His grandmother frowned. "My goodness, let Zach handle it. He's your business manager. It's what you pay him for, to handle stuff like this."

One would think so, however, he barely paid Zach. Instead, he did all his friend's legal work for the chain of restaurants he owned. Zach was more than his business manager. He was Noah's best friend, and most importantly, he was Noah's cross-fit coach.

"I can't. I have to do it myself."

Gram rolled her eyes. "Yeah, yeah, I know...it's your Santa Claus thing; making a list, checking it twice...or more like half a dozen times."

Okay, so he was a little obsessive when it came to controlling his life. If he weren't, his life would go to hell in a handbasket faster than he could blink. In fact, it seemed as if his life was already there.

One of the guys in white coats entered and handed him a stack of papers. "You're good to go. Like I said, just a slight concussion, but you're going to have a hell of a headache. I suggest you not do too much for the next day or so. Let us know if anything changes though, like if the headache gets worse, you have double vision or you can't wake up. Just get lots of rest."

Resting wasn't going to happen. He couldn't afford any delay, not when everything he owned was on the line. Once again, he cursed fate, or luck, or whatever ill-fated wind that landed him in this mess. He'd had no intention of ever leaving his former employers, the law firm of Waldron and DeMatis, in fact, he'd been working towards a partnership when the lead partners were accused of money laundering and arrested. Poof. The firm was gone, his job was gone, and with the scandal tainting his resume, no one would hire him.

Taking the paperwork the doctor handed her, Gram left for the discharge department. Noah made the necessary phone calls to the caterer, the florist and his new assistant and confirmed—for the tenth time—the details, after which he carefully eased himself off the table and pulled on his clothes. He ignored the gore on his shirt from his bloody nose, likewise the cotton packing stuffed up his nostrils, turning him into one of those dopey mouth breathers.

Exiting through the curtains of the ER cubicle where they'd put him, he peered down the hall in search of his grandmother. Another person in scrubs found him standing there, obviously looking confused, shoved him into a wheelchair with the words, 'Sorry, it's required', and wheeled him around until they found his grandmother, who was waiting by the discharge desk.

The nurse rolled him to the exit door and helped him into the front seat of her car. Sadly, he needed the help. This must be what it was like to be old and decrepit. He couldn't wait.

"I'll take you home," Gram told him, pulling out of the parking lot. "We can get your car from the hotel tomorrow."

He grunted as nodding was out of the question. Nodding might make his head explode, or at the very least, fall off. Leaving his car in the hotel parking lot didn't matter. His used Toyota was twelve years old; all he could afford after the Waldron & DeMatis debacle left him unable to afford his BMW payment. Nobody in their right mind would steal the car he currently drove.

Gram helped him into his small two-bedroom apartment and up the stairs. He collapsed onto his bed. He felt her gently remove his shoes and throw a blanket over him. Her sweet talcum- powder smell tickled his nose when she bent to kiss him on the cheek.

"Call me if you don't want me to come over tomorrow morning, otherwise, if I don't hear from you, I'll pick you up at nine and we can retrieve your car." There was a pat on his shoulder. He heard the front door close, and then he didn't know another thing.

His head was still chiming when his grandmother arrived at his apartment the next morning. He didn't feel well enough to go anywhere, yet he went anyway. His car was old and crummy, but he needed it because the big bash celebrating his new practice was set for this afternoon. He hated parties; however, this one was a necessity since the attendees would be other lawyers who didn't do divorce law yet had clients who could use Noah's services.

His grandmother drove him back to the hotel where he'd left his car and dropped him off. He waved goodbye, got into his wreck-mobile, started the engine and headed towards Princeton.

While at Waldron & DeMatis, he'd made a name for himself as an attorney who went that extra step—translation, he went for the jugular—for his clients, which explained why he had always received so many referrals from ex-clients and other lawyers. Unfortunately, with the recent scandal, his reputation was hanging by a thread. Who knew whether he'd continue to get those same referrals. He'd risked everything on his current venture, the only real risk he'd ever taken—although not by choice—so the idea of failing was terrifying.

He made a left onto a narrow side street and pulled over onto the curb to stare at the bungalow he'd rented, a homey-looking Victorian in creams and browns. Homey-looking was important as divorce was sad, at least for most people.

For Noah's family it was a regular occurrence, so there weren't many tears.

He shut off the engine and got out of his car. The tree-lined street was lovely, the houses all old Victorians or Craftsman style, some one story, some two, about half of them still residences, the other half had expensive wooden signs out front announcing their business.

Like the one in front of the pink and purple bungalow next door. Holy shit? Who would commit such a sacrilege, painting a beautiful house those candy-heart colors? How had he not noticed that atrocity before, he wondered, before remembering that both times he'd been here it was after dark. He cocked his head, squinting at the letters on the sign out front.

Heart-2-Heart. What, a heart surgeon? Nah, couldn't be, not with a pink and purple house. Dropping his car keys into his pocket, he strolled across the lawn to get a closer look at the sign.

Heart-2-Heart. Matches Made to Order.

Oh, Christ. He started to laugh. What were the odds—a divorce attorney and a matchmaker, right next to each other?

Well, more power to the matchmakers, because no matter how good they were, about half their clients would ultimately end up in Noah's office. Pretty convenient, if you asked him.

He turned to leave, then heard the roar of a motorcycle. The bike hung a hard left into the driveway of the pink and purple house, whipped past him and stopped. The rider turned off the engine, dismounted and set it up on its stand.

Whoa. A girl. With legs. Long, slender, fantastic legs encased in tight blue jeans. Damn, those legs. It didn't take much creativity to imagine them wrapped around his waist. He wondered if—no, he hoped—the rest of her was as good.

She pulled off the helmet, and a mane of long blonde hair cascaded out, covering her face. She shook it back, tucked the helmet under her arm and looked up to stare straight at him.

"You!" he said, shock jolting through him.

"You!" she said at the same time. Her big blue eyes widened. She turned and ran inside the pink and purple monstrosity.

THREE

♥

JennGoodwin@MyHeart-2-Heart

Roses are red, violets are blue. That guy that I whacked is black and blue too.

OMG, it was him. The guy she bonked with her helmet. What was he doing here? How had he found her? What was he going to do to her?

Kill her, of course, because that was murder she'd seen in his eyes—the ones with enormous black bruises under them from his broken nose, the nose she'd flattened. She was a dead duck. Hands on knees, she bent over, trying to catch her breath.

Someone hammered on the front door. An angry person. An angry person with big fists.

Oh, who was she kidding, it wasn't some random angry person hammering on her door, it was him, and he'd come to kill her.

"Hey. You. I know you're in there. Open the door." Bang, bang, bang. "Answer me."

She shook her head. She realized he couldn't see her, but so what? The point was she answered him, simply not out loud.

He continued hammering on the door. She hesitated for a minute, her heart pounding while she considered her options. Give in, open the door and face the music, or run like a greyhound out the back door? More hammering, louder this time.

"Open the damned door. I want to talk to you."

"No," she yelled, then clapped her hands over her mouth. Oh, shoot, she hadn't meant to say that out loud.

Hearing her, the banging got louder. "Come on, open the door."

Okay, maybe she should open the door, but she wasn't going to because, in her opinion, she shouldn't have to do anything she didn't want to. It was all about attitude. She was an expert when it came to attitude. There was her previous attitude—the smart-alecky teenage attitude, the one that was all talk and no substance—and then there was the other attitude, the adult-type attitude she was currently trying to cultivate. Unfortunately, the attitude winning right now was the teenage thing, and it was telling her to run. She'd save the other attitude for a time when it wasn't going to get her killed. Turning, she dashed through the house to the back door and wrenched it open.

He was standing on the porch. "Hello. Fancy meeting you here."

Wow. Cute guy.

Whoa. Angry guy!

She slammed the door in his face, clicked the lock shut, spun around and dashed back to the front door, grabbing her helmet on the way. Throwing the door open, she bounded off the front porch, bolted across the lawn, pressing the bike's remote starter as she ran. The Harley's engine started with a roar. She threw herself onto the bike, jammed her helmet on, not even buckling the strap, and rocked it off its stand.

"Hey!"

He bolted around the back of the house at a run. She was way ahead of him. With one foot on the ground, she spun the bike in a tight circle and...she was out of there. Her mother would have had a heart attack if she'd seen, but better that than her daughter's death at the hands of an enraged man bent on mayhem.

She reached the stop sign at the corner. Looking in her side mirror, she watched the same silver Toyota she'd observed parked at the curb next door pull away from the curb and begin following her. Holy cow. It had to be him. Because who else would it be? Why was he following her? Yeah, she'd beaned him, however, the hospital told her he would be fine, so did it warrant him tracking her down with intent to murder?

She gave the throttle a twist and sped up, heading south, fortunately hitting all the lights on green. Unfortunately, he did too. Turning right onto Route 1, she throttled the bike until she was doing sixty. She loved the roar of the engine when she asked for more speed, the muted whisper of the tires on the pavement, the sensation of unbridled power between her legs. Holy cow, this was living. It might be she needed to get to the zooming thing a lot sooner than her mom wanted.

He was still on her tail. She kept her eyes on the road, weaving cautiously between the speeding cars because she only wanted to escape, not die. Ahead, she saw a small gap in the concrete barricades separating the north and southbound lanes. She squeezed the brakes. Pulled over to the shoulder and squooched through the gap onto the other side. The instant she was through, she stopped. Feet down, she waited.

His car reached the gap. Pulling up next to the concrete barrier, he cut the engine. The driver's side window rolled down, and one tanned, muscular arm came out to settle on the frame of the window. His head turned until he was staring straight at her.

She pushed up the face shield on her helmet and stared back. And waved.

His jaw visibly clenched. "What's your name?" he asked.

Was he kidding? "Why, so you can sue me? I don't think so."

He snorted. "I am not going to sue you."

"Yeah, right, like I believe that." The guy must be some kind of moron if he believed she would fall into that trap.

His hands fisted on the steering wheel. "I. Am. Not. Going. To. Sue. You," he reiterated, punching out each word separately.

"Hah. Why should I believe you?"

He turned his head to stare out his windshield, not saying anything for a minute while he tapped one of his fists against his chin. "I promised my Gram," he muttered.

Did she hear what she thought she heard? "What? Say again. What did you say?"

Again, there was a long silence before he turned to glower at her and repeated, "I said, I promised my Gram I wouldn't sue you," loud enough for her to hear.

She laughed. His Gram? His Gram made him promise? With all the yelling and door-banging and masculine tough guy stuff, he promised his Gram? What a wuss. The laughter rolled out, unstoppable.

His eyes blazed fire at her. The look sent a thrill down her spine because, despite the black eyes and swollen nose, the guy was seriously cute—lean cheeks, kissable lips and eyes shining pale steely gray from between the puffiness—however, he was also seriously angry. She didn't know if the thrill she felt was a result of the cute or the angry. Still, right now it didn't matter. All that mattered was that she was safely on the other side of a barricade he couldn't cross, and he wasn't going to sue her. Of course, he could always go back to Heart-2-Heart, but what kind of moron would waste his day waiting for her to reappear?

Hopefully not this moron.

Watching her, his fingers drummed a tattoo on his steering wheel. "Since I said I'm not going to sue you, why won't you tell me your name?" he asked.

Persistent sucker, wasn't he? Not that it would do him any good. Just so they were clear, she stuck her tongue out at him.

The light in his eyes flared. She could almost see the steam rising. Thank God for concrete dividers.

"Son of a—"

She shook her index finger at him. "Uh, uh, uh. Be nice."

His jaw visibly clenched. "I am going to make you pay for that," he growled.

Hmph, threats. So much for his promise to his Gram. Time to leave. "Well, Mister Macho Man, it was lovely meeting you." Putting the tips of her fingers to her lips, she blew him a kiss. "Have a nice life."

He yelped. "Hey—"

Throwing him a last grin, she slammed her face shield down over her face, popped the clutch and pulled into traffic, leaving him far behind, hopefully never to be seen again. She headed north towards home instead of back to Heart-2-Heart. One of her New York City clients had asked to meet with Jenn today, but no way was that happening now. She'd text the girl and reschedule. Reaching her condo, she parked her bike in her assigned spot, locked it up then set the alarm. Done, she walked across the parking lot to her condo, texting her client to cancel as she walked.

Tucking her phone into her pocket, she unlocked her front door and opened it.

With a banshee howl, this thing threw itself at her, landing on her chest and knocking her on her butt.

The dog. She'd forgotten that she was taking care of the freakin' dog. She bounced to her feet and spun around to see Trike stumbling across the parking lot towards the playground. Beyond the playground was a busy street. Oh, shoot, the street. Nick and Amy would never forgive her if all that was left of their mutt when they returned from their honeymoon was something scraped off the pavement and buried in a Papa John's box. She started running.

"Trike. Stop!" Arrrgh. She hated dogs. She particularly hated this dog.

The stupid mutt stopped. Wow. Look at that. She must be a dog whisperer or something. Since the dog was no longer running, she slowed down and approached her at a walk. The mutt crouched, stubby tail wagging, tongue lolling out of the doggy grin on her face. Jenn got three feet from the mutt, reached out a hand to grab her collar....

....and the idiotic thing turned and gallumped off again.

Fudge! Too bad she had this non-swearing rule—intelligent people didn't need to use foul language—because if ever there was a time for another word starting with FU, this was it.

More running, this time in a circle around the park. At least the dog wasn't going towards the street. Jenn on her tail, the stupid thing scampered under the slide, ran around the merry-go-round three times then skidded through a mud puddle under the swings.

Jenn was out of breath and by this time had gathered a crowd.

"Don't run," advised one person. "It will scare the dog into running."

Yeah, right, like she didn't already know that.

"Just call the dog. It'll come." Been there, done that, didn't work.

"Go get some dog food in a pan and rattle it. She'll think it's dinner time and come."

Sure, and while she was getting the dog food, the mutt was in the wind. She sent the crowd a glare, because what she needed more than a bunch of advice would be someone helping her catch the stupid thing.

More circles, more running, more advice, plus a lot of laughter when she tripped and fell in a mud puddle.

Okay, that was it. No more chasing; let the darned thing do what she wanted. Did she care? No, she didn't. Picking herself up, she wiped the mud out of her eyes and headed back to her townhouse. She turned the door handle, pushed the door open and something whizzed by her, nearly knocking her over again. Stalking into the kitchen, she found the mutt standing by the refrigerator, dog bowl in her mouth, waiting to be fed.

The dog gazed up at her, pathetic oozing off her.

"Oh, don't give me your sad little puppy dog...uh, eye," she finished lamely because the dog did only have one eye. Still, that one eye managed to do the trick. "Fine, whatever, I get the point. You're hungry." She narrowed her own eyes, trying to inject hate into the glare yet having trouble dredging up the feeling because, weirdly, Trike's one eye was full of doggy devotion. Jenn found herself feeling a sudden twinge—just a twinge—of devotion in return.

Help.

She yanked open the refrigerator door, took out the opened can of dog food and dumped it into the dog bowl.

"Grrrrr," the dog growled, and dropped the bowl on the floor, splattering grease and bits of food all over the immaculate floor. The mutt fell on the food like locust during the biblical plague.

"Grrrrrrr," Jenn responded in return, and went upstairs to change into something not covered with mud. She opened her bedroom door to—

Devastation. Her bedspread was literally a spread, as in spread on the floor, on the bedside lamp, on the dresser, on the shower curtain rod in the adjacent bathroom. The only place it wasn't spread was on her bed.

She threw the bedroom door open again. "Trike," she yelled.

The dog bounded up the stairs and squatted in front of her, a happy, drooly grin on her ugly face. "Woof." She wagged her stubby tail, obviously looking for her approval.

Not happening, animal. Fresh out of devotion. "I hate you," she said flatly.

Going to her computer, she remoted into her office computer and rescheduled the two appointments she'd had this afternoon. After that, she answered a dozen emails, made four appointments for the following day, and finished up the blog she'd promised Amy she'd write. Lastly, she contacted the hotel—not the same hotel where she'd bonked that poor guy—to finalize the details for the singles mingle they were hosting later this month.

Once her work tasks were completed, she turned her attention to the devastation of her house, and discovered that, in addition to her bedspread, Trike had also dismembered her dining room chairs. She spent the afternoon cleaning up the shreds, then ordering new chairs and a new bedspread from an online store. When that was done, she turned the TV on, yet everything she found was either about someone dying or someone falling in love. She wasn't sure which was more depressing. Turning the TV off, she settled onto the couch with a book.

FOUR

NoahMaitland@noahmaitlandesq

You never know a person until you divorce them.

He hurriedly drove back to his office. He had several deliveries coming for his open house this afternoon and needed to make sure he didn't miss them. More importantly he wanted to be there in case the leggy blonde next door returned—he had a few things he wanted to say to her—but the purple and pink monstrosity's driveway remained empty all morning, and there was no sign of a big black Harley. Even as furious as he was about the entire situation, he had to admire her sheer audacity. All he'd wanted was a sincere apology for knocking him for a loop—yeah, he admitted it had been an accident—however, he didn't consider a sad-eyed look and a few *I'm sorries* thrown at him when he was carted away in an ambulance to be an apology.

He deserved a real apology, and he was going to get it, one way or another.

He popped a couple aspirins because his head was still pounding, then wandered around the reception area, making sure the cleaners had done their job. He'd made his office feel welcoming by having painted it in soothing blues and tans, with dark wood wainscoting. A plush oriental rug in the same colors lay under the cadet blue sofa. Adding his own touch, he set a big bowl of colorful

M&Ms, his favorite snack, out on the coffee table. Going outside, he walked across the lawn to remove the paper covering his business sign—a hand-carved sign with a dark brown background and white lettering—to reveal his pride and joy.

Noah Maitland Esq. Attorney at Law.

He ran a loving hand over the carved letters. He'd worked hard for this title, and even harder to be able to put up this sign with only his name on it.

A florist truck pulled up, and he led them inside. Going to work, they set out an arrangement of orange and white flowers on his assistant's desk in reception, a big bouquet of white roses set on the coffee table and a large all-white arrangement in the conference room. They kept sneaking odd looks at him while they worked yet said nothing, only made their delivery and left. The caterers arrived around one and began setting up for the open house at two o'clock. They brought in tables to set the food on, chafing dishes and a large coffee urn.

Very efficient crew yet similar to the florists, they also seemed to find him fascinating. He didn't know why until he went into the bathroom to shave, since he hadn't taken the time this morning as he'd simply fallen out of bed and jumped into jeans and a t-shirt before climbing into his grandmother's car.

Oh, my holy crap. His eyes looked like Tim Curry's in *Rocky Horror Picture Show* and his nose was a beacon of redness ala Rudolph the Red-Nosed Reindeer. Fuck! He had fifty guests coming in half an hour and there would be no hiding this.

Just a few hours ago, he'd told himself he'd accept an apology from Legs, yet after seeing his face, and knowing he'd have to spend the next three hours explaining, an apology wasn't enough.

Still burning with fury, he shaved and changed into the dark gray suit he'd brought along. Guests arrived, and as predicted...

"Very nice place.... Uh, what happened to your..."

"Judo. I won."

"I have a lady client who needs an attorney, but I don't know. I mean, how will you explain...." Vague gesture towards his face.

"New York Giants tryouts." He put on his pouty face. "Probably won't get drafted though."

"Geez, Maitland. What the hell happened?" Some people were more subtle than others. This guy wasn't one of them.

"Rock climbing. Thirty feet. I'm lucky to be alive."

Then there was this one. "Good God, Noah, that's a face even a mother can't love."

"She's the one who did this," he growled.

It got to the point where he gave them an excuse even before they asked.

"Pitched the opening ball at last week's Mets' game. Line drive right into my face."

"Did you hear about the meteor shower over New Jersey on Saturday? Put a hole right through my roof. Kapow!"

"Bird strike."

"You should see the other guy."

After an hour, he started to run out of fun responses. God forbid he tell them the truth. He'd never live it down. Unfortunately, they didn't run out of questions. Finally, after several hours had passed, he gave one of those verbose and totally full of bullshit speeches, thanking them for coming and delicately hinting they send referrals, before forcibly encouraging his guests out the door.

What a shitshow. Legs was going to pay.

After everyone left, he sent an email to the woman he'd hired for his office manager position to verify she would show up in the morning. That accomplished, he wandered around the office for a few more minutes wondering what he should do now. He glanced once more out the window, still hoping like hell he'd see tall blonde Legs. Instead he saw a petite brunette walk up to the front entrance. She tried to open the door, but he knew no one was there so, of course, it didn't open. Stepping down off the porch, she walked around to the back before returning to the front, looking puzzled.

After watching her for a minute, he locked everything up and left his office. Throwing the dirty jeans and T-shirt he'd worn this morning into his car, he crossed the lawn and approached the young woman.

"Hi."

She startled, her big eyes going immediately to his face with a look of trepidation.

"Sorry. I didn't mean to frighten you. I rent the place next door." He pointed over his shoulder so she'd know he was only a friendly neighbor, not the friendly neighborhood serial killer. Necessary because there were those black eyes, and the swollen nose which made him look like Frankenstein. The only thing missing was the neck bolts. "I'm sure they're closed."

"Huh. That's odd. Jenn told me she'd be in today."

Jenn. So that was her name. He tucked the fact into the back of his mind for future use. "Well, she was here earlier however, she left in a big hurry. Something must have come up." He knew for a fact something had come up, a great big yellow stripe up the middle of her back.

"Gee, I wonder what happened." Scrunching up her face in disappointment, the brunette heaved a sigh. "That's too bad. I wanted to show her this." She held out her hand and waggled her fingers.

Okaaay. "Um..."

She peeked up at him from under her bangs, her smile growing wider. "My ring, silly. See? Chris asked me to marry him last night. I wanted to thank her because she was the one who made our match."

Even though it meant nothing to him he did his duty and admired the ring. Because you never could tell; today's bride could be tomorrow's soon-to-be divorcee and tomorrow's soon-to-be divorcee would need a lawyer. Someone like him. Right?

An idea began to percolate in his head. It wasn't a very nice idea. It might even be considered devious. Actually, it delved into the realm of evil, however, he was okay with evil, at least when it came to Legs. He chuckled thinking about it.

"Well, I guess I'll catch her later." The woman turned to leave.

"Wait," he said. "Before you go, let me give you my card." Pulling one from his suit jacket pocket, he handed it to her.

"A lawyer?"

"A divorce lawyer. Hang on to it for when the match she made for you goes belly up. In fact, before you tie the knot, come see me. I'll make sure you have an iron-tight prenup. That way you'll get everything you deserve when the marriage ends."

Her mouth fell open. He grinned, tipped her a two-fingered salute, turned and strolled to his car. Maybe he'd never get his apology. Maybe what he did was wrong. On the other hand, so what? He got a small bit of revenge. Sure, it was stupidly petty revenge, however, he'd never minded being petty, not if it got the job done. Satisfaction achieved. Moving on.

He went home, went upstairs and changed into more comfortable clothes. Returning to his minuscule kitchen, he took two more aspirins and put an ice pack on his nose then went to his computer to check his personal emails.

Hmm. Ad. Ad. Ad. Delete, delete, delete. Message from his brother asking for money. Delete. Another ad, this one promising to give him the erection of a lifetime. Definitely delete. Nothing wrong with his erections.

Oh, look at that. An email with only an attached picture from his dad. No message. Typical. He opened it. A tropical setting. His father with his arm around his young, not-too-bright-but bright-enough-to-be-a-gold-digger bride. She looked happy as a clam.

His dad looked less so. Fuck. Already? He sent an email back, asking what was going on, knowing he wouldn't get an answer.

Slightly depressed, he retreated to the living room to watch a little television, snacking on a small bag of M&Ms while he did. He cozied into his old saggy brown couch, exhausted by the day. At least the open house had gone well despite the irritation of having to invent a million excuses to explain his black eyes. Oh, wait. Speaking of his open house excuse, that reminded him. The Mets had a big game today against Philadelphia.

The game was good yet not good enough that he didn't get on his iPad while he watched and pull up the website for Heart-2-Heart.

Heart-2-Heart. Matches Made to Order. Just like the sign outside their building. Underneath the heading: Partner—Amy Novak, PhD, with a picture of a cute woman with short, dark hair and big brown eyes. A short bio was below. Hmm. He popped a red M&M into his mouth and crunched it up.

Next to Amy Novak's information was a picture of a young blonde woman. Underneath was the description—Partner—Jenn Goodwin, MBA. He recognized her immediately. It was the nose cruncher, the black eye giver, the *it's not my fault* motorcycle babe. also known as Legs.

Hah! Jenn Goodwin was the furthest thing from good he could imagine. Win wasn't in the cards either, not if he had anything to do with it.

He kept reading. Lots of garbage about soul mates and love everlasting. From what he'd seen of love and marriage in his own family, love didn't last any longer than a roll of toilet paper. He certainly hadn't seen much love, or faithfulness in his career.

Of course, there were exceptions, like his grandparents' marriage. God bless his grandparents. They were the ones who proved there could be such a thing as everlasting love.

At an age when they should have been getting ready to retire and enjoy their golden years, they'd taken him in to raise when his mother's second marriage fell apart and she sent him to live with his father. Unfortunately, his father's third marriage was in the process of blowing up, so he bounced Noah right back. By that time his mother had met chump number three and didn't want a kid hanging around and she sent him to his brother Bret, who was only twenty, still single and a complete stoner. Three homes, and three different schools in six months. That's when his grandparents swept in and took him away to live with them.

It seemed to him that love was like a game of archery. Most everyone, sooner or later, shot their arrows at the target. Sadly, most people missed. Between the two of them, his parents had missed the target a total of eight times. Archery was obviously not their game.

Nevertheless, he was not his parents. He didn't want to randomly shoot a bunch of arrows at a bunch of random females, he wanted to shoot one and hit the bullseye. He wanted to have a marriage like his grandparents. It was rare, but all it took was the right person. She was out there, somewhere, and he was going to find her.

He went back to reading the website which also included a bunch of testimonials from happy clients. Well, give it time.

Okay, so he was a little jaded.

He scrolled back to the main page again and studied her picture for a few more minutes. Yeah, she was a knockout—enormous blue eyes, a cupid's bow mouth, and the long blonde hair he'd already admired—and obviously a smart cookie given the MBA degree, yet none of it mattered because the girl was loony. Loony people were crazy.

The good news was he'd gained a little bit of revenge for his injuries which meant there was no reason to speak to her again. They'd most likely see each other on occasion, so he'd give her a friendly wave and make sure he avoided her. Too bad she was crazy pants because she was stunning.

He closed the website then remoted into his work emails. Debra Rich, his new assistant had also remoted in and answered a number of emails and booked two appointments, referrals from an attorney at his open house, for tomorrow. Thank God. Business.

Ten o'clock arrived. Time for bed. Going into the kitchen, he grabbed some kale from the refrigerator and went upstairs to brush his teeth and strip down for bed. He walked over to the terrarium in the corner and adjusted the heat lamp. Disturbed by the noise, his iguana, Iggy, poked his head out from inside his fake log.

"Hey, big guy. How you doing?" He held out a kale leaf. Iggy's long tongue unfurled, snatching the leaf, and curling it back into his mouth.

"Temperature okay? Are you comfortable?" He gave the lizard's scaly head a scratch. Beady black eyes swiveled back and forth.

"Here, buddy, more kale." He dropped in several more leaves. Iggy lunged and gobbled everything up then bobbed his head, an iguana version of thank you. Done, he crawled back inside his log to sleep.

Time for Noah to do the same. He liked to read a little before he went to sleep. Turning on his iPad, he clicked on the iBook app to finish his latest.

He read three sentences then, unable to help himself, switched to the internet and opened up the Heart-2-Heart website one more time. Just to make sure nothing had changed. Just to make sure he hadn't missed anything the last time he looked. Okay. He was sure. Turning out the light, he went to sleep.

FIVE

NoahMaitland@noahmaitlandesq

WWI started in 1914. In 1939 there was WWII. I think WWIII started this week.

Normally he had an early morning training session with Zach, however, this morning he was still so sore he could barely move, plus the idea of possibly getting whacked in the face—again—was enough to send him to work instead.

His new office manager, Debra, was at the front door when he arrived, which impressed him and boded well for their working relationship. Unlocking the door, he observed her gentle smile, noting again her soft, almost black eyes, and her perfect skin, a vibrant coppery brown that indicated she might have Native American somewhere in her African American ancestry. He liked her short, curly hair that highlighted her delicate features and made her look like a very attractive twenty-nine rather than the forty-two she'd written on her job application. Sitting at her desk, she turned on her computer, and after a short discussion of her duties for the day, went to work.

Retreating to his office, he settled in behind his brand-new desk, running his hands across the silky-smooth walnut surface. He loved it partly because it was beautiful, but mostly because it was his, bought with his money, not a desk inherited from the guy who'd occupied his office before Noah. It felt right.

Gripping his computer mouse, he woke up his computer and checked his personal emails, something he did by habit every morning.

Another email from his dad, which was weird. His father, like his mom, wasn't much for communicating unless he needed money. Dreading what he'd find, he opened the email. One word in the subject field—fun—with another picture attached. He studied the photo of his dad with new bride Kitty who scowled at the camera. On his other side, his other arm was flung around the shoulders of a woman he had never seen before. Short, a little on the chunky side with a big grin spread across her broad face.

He examined the picture, wondering why his father sent it. Not sure he would be happy if he found out. Eventually, he deleted it and prepared for his first appointment which was a humdinger. Nice lady, married thirty-six years, husband the CEO of a major publicly traded company, net worth seventy-five million dollars, give or take a few million here or there. He had to clasp his hands in front of him on his desk to keep from rubbing them together in glee.

Of course, the husband would fight to the death any settlement Noah proposed. However, the guy might as well pay the piper now because, even though New Jersey was a no-fault state, it made exceptions for adultery, and Mr. Big-Shot CEO had been regularly dipping his wick in another lady's lamp and the wife had proof. After discussing next steps, his new client wrote him a large retainer and left.

His utter relief when he gave the check to Debra for deposit was enough to make him dizzy. A few cases like this, and he would be able to stop waking up in the morning in a panic, stop the moments when his heart pounded from worrying about what tomorrow might bring.

"The next appointment isn't due for another two hours," he told Debra. "Would you like to get lunch for us both, and deposit this check while you're at it?"

She jumped up. "What can I get you?" she asked, pulling her purse from her desk drawer.

"BLT, lots of mayo, and a grape soda if they have one, otherwise a coke."

Her eyebrows went up. Okay, so the big bad barracuda attorney liked grape soda. So what? He gave her some money and sent her out the door along with the check and a deposit slip. His fingers twitched when she left, grieving the loss of that piece of paper, so attached was he to the idea it represented actual real money.

His cell phone rang. He let it ring several times, staring at the number blinking on the screen, wishing he could ignore it. Sadly, ignoring his mother's phone calls never worked, she kept calling until he answered. If he ignored them long enough, she'd been known to show up at his office.

"Hey, Mom," he answered, biting back the sigh at what was coming.

"Noah, darling, how are you?"

Like she wanted to know. It was more likely, *'how much can you give me?'* "I'm fine. Mom. How are you?" Shit, shouldn't have asked. It was like giving her an engraved invitation to say—

"Well, I'm a little short right now."

He scrunched his eyes closed. "How short are you? Five-one, five-two?" he quipped, wishing his words were actually a joke.

"You know you're not funny, right?"

No, there was nothing funny about his family. "Sorry. It's early. Still getting into the groove."

"Well, get into it a little faster. I need some cash."

Of course, she did. "Mom, I gave you eight thousand dollars two weeks ago. Where did it go?"

"I spent it."

He shouldn't ask. He did anyway. It was almost like he couldn't help himself, it was like self-flagellation. "What did you spend it on?"

"I paid some bills."

"Eight thousand dollars' worth? For crying out loud, Mom, how could you spend eight thousand dollars in two weeks? Are you gambling or something?" He had to clench his jaw to stop his scream.

"Of course I'm not gambling. How can you even ask that? I had some bills."

An ugly possibility wormed its way into his mind. "I don't see how you could have run up bills like that when I pay for most of your expenses. Either you're gambling or..." He took a breath, hating what he was thinking. "Are you giving money to Sam?" Another example of the commonality his parents shared. Sam, soon to be Melanie's husband number four, was a bum, just like her previous husband, what's-his-name, Lorenzo, and the one before whose name escaped him. The last four of his dad's brides had been gold-diggers. Too bad it was Noah's pocket they were digging into.

"Sam proposed. We want to get married right away so we want to fly to Hawaii to get married. They'll marry you in twenty-four hours."

"Mom, you can get married in twenty-four hours in New York. It's right across the river."

"Who in heaven's name gets married in New York?"

"Thousands of people get married in New York."

"Oh, really. Like who?"

"It doesn't matter. I'm not giving you money so you can marry Sam."

"Noah Maitland, I'm an adult and how I spend my funds is my business."

"No," he practically yelled. "It's my money, which means it is my business."

She gasped. "Don't yell at me." Her voice trembled, the prelude to tears, something his mother was a master at.

He took a deep breath, not wanting to yell at her again. He loved his mother. The problem was, the minute a man entered her life, her children were nothing more than a bother, like a pesky fly that buzzed around her head, refusing to shoo.

"I'm sorry I yelled. I'm frustrated. And broke. I don't have anything to give you. Can't you get by until next month?"

She was quiet for quite a long time before saying, "Oh, Noah, I'm sorry. I don't mean to be a burden. I'm sorry I'm such a sorry excuse for a mother."

The sad thing was, she was sorry. Alas, her sorry wouldn't last. "Mom, stop apologizing. You know I'd give you the money if I had it."

"I know. You're a good son. So could you spare a few thousand?"

Oh my god. He hung up. Shaking three aspirins out of their bottle, he swallowed them dry. His headache was back with a vengeance. Next, he tore open a bag of M&M's and tipped the contents into his mouth. He had to do something to get rid of the bad taste of mother.

SIX

JennGoodwin@MyHeart-2-Heart

Never go to bed angry. Stay awake and plot revenge.

Jenn woke up the next morning with the mutt lying on the foot of her bed. Close enough to make her heart pound with anxiety, not close enough to touch, thank God. She carefully edged out from under the covers and went to shower. After getting ready to go to work, she girded her loins, so to speak, and shoved the dog into her car. Taking the mutt to Heart-2-Heart might be a big mistake, yet no way could she leave the beast alone for nine hours with an entire house full of furniture, draperies, linens and clothing. She approached the old Victorian, and slowed down, keeping an eye out for the car that maniac drove when he chased her yesterday. Fortunately, nothing parked on the street even resembled his rattrap of a silver car, so she felt safe pulling into the driveway.

Getting out of her car, she gingerly snapped the leash onto Trike's collar and dragged her towards the back entrance that opened into the kitchen, being careful not to allow the hairy beast close enough to shed brown and white and orange fur all over her new black A-line dress.

Geez, she couldn't wait for Amy and Nick to come home.

Opening the door, she gave the stupid animal a gentle shove inside—okay, it was more a case of sticking a boot under the doggy ass to boost her over the threshold because she didn't want to get any closer to the animal than necessary—and took off the leash. The kitchen was the perfect place to leave her. Like, how much damage could she do in a kitchen, right? The room had a stove, a refrigerator and a microwave. Not a soft, shreddable item anywhere in sight. Stepping into the hallway, she shut the kitchen door behind her and walked to the reception area, a large space originally the house's parlor that they'd recently remodeled using part of her contribution to becoming a partner. The furniture was gray velvet with Lucite legs and a Lucite and mirrored coffee table, while the rest of the décor was in various shades of gray and white with an occasional touch of pink, Amy's favorite color. She considered it a miracle the entire house wasn't done up in pink, pink and more pink.

The assistant she hired to replace herself was already at her sleek white desk. "Hey, Megan, any messages?" she asked, crossing her fingers that none were from Angry Guy telling her she only had days to live.

Megan Murphy was a gem, always ready for anything she could do to make a difference. She had curly red hair and freckles and one of those cute Irish-type noses upon which perched wire-rimmed glasses. She usually came to work in a long loose hippie-style dress—a sort of flower-power look that went out fifty years ago, but now—unfortunately—was back. In addition to her extraordinary efficiency, she was also the one who convinced Jenn and Amy they needed to start a database for gays and lesbians. Maybe Megan hoped it would lead to her Princess Charming walking in the door. Jenn was actively searching.

Her assistant picked up several pink slips from her desk. "Only a couple. Oh, and here's the notes I took for today's appointments," she said, and handed everything over.

Jenn took some time to read the notes before the appointment arrived. The first woman proved to be a corporate executive in her mid-thirties, attractive, smart, with a wonderful sense of humor. Going to be an easy match. Not so the next woman, who had a list of very specific demands.

Demand One—no older than thirty. Demand Two—over six feet tall. Demand Three—athletic, and Demand Four—(seriously?) a Liam Hemsworth clone, thank you very much, versus the woman herself who was definitely over forty, at least forty pounds overweight, and wore enough makeup to stucco the side of a large house.

Jenn listened, took notes, had her assistant take pictures of the woman then ushered Ms. Stucco out the door with a polite "We'll be in touch," while actually thinking *It might be a while—like maybe a century or two*.

Returning to her office, she called the DJ to confirm their playlist for the upcoming singles mingle event, then created an email to all their old clients who'd let their membership lapse, and sent it off, letting them know about the mixer and encouraging them to rejoin and attend.

After that was completed, she got to work on the part of her job she liked best, finding the perfect matches for their candidates. They had a huge database, which meant it was a monumental job, but when she became a partner, one of the first things she did was organize the data making it easier to sort and match people up unlike the manual searching Amy practiced in the past.

Love was so strange. All these people who were sure there was someone special out there for them, who trusted that love would happen, and they would have their happily-ever-after. How did they do it? Even the ones who were divorced still believed. She wished she did too. Once upon a time she thought the same, however, her father had destroyed her ability to believe when he, along with a friend, decided it would be a good idea to rob an armored car which resulted in the two guards being seriously injured. The betrayal was compounded when he killed himself rather than face justice.

Unfortunately, the money was never found. In the aftermath her family was blamed for everything. The town's disloyalty had hurt, however, next she learned her boyfriend told the cops she was involved. She'd loved him with everything in her seventeen-year-old heart, and he'd taken that love and fed everything to the media, all her confidences, only twisting the details making her appeared to be a greedy liar.

Even then, she still believed.

But there was also her college boyfriend. Keith was all the things she wanted in a partner; attractive, fun, adventurous. Sweet. Kind.

Except he wasn't. It turned out the real Keith was greedy, and amoral, and a whiz on the computer, which was how he discovered all the years-old newspaper articles about the robbery and assumed that she had access to millions in ill-gotten gains. The sad truth was, she did have money, however, not the money from the bank robbery. Instead it was money from her father. Her father had been a genius. Before his death, he and his business partner invented some kind of chip thing used in military computers to locate targets. After her father died, the army paid to buy the patent. Unfortunately, their offer was too late to stop her father from committing the biggest mistake of his life, leading to his suicide. With all the notoriety surrounding his death, Jenn's mom warned them never to tell anyone about the money. When she denied having said millions, Keith had dumped her.

After that, she never trusted another guy.

Given her jaundiced viewpoint, a lot of people considered it weird that she was a matchmaker, however what they didn't understand was that it made her happy to make other people happy. It was simply that that kind of happiness wasn't for her. It was like that old saying; once burned, twice shy, only for her it was twice burned thrice shy.

The phone rang. "Heart-2-Heart. Jenn speaking."

"Jenn, hi, it's Amanda Hinkle."

Amanda was one of her first matches, and it had been a super successful one. Both she and Chris, the man Jenn paired her with, opted out of any further matches mere weeks after being set up together and seemed well on their way to a permanent relationship. Hopefully, Amanda wasn't calling because they'd broken up. "Everything okay with you and Chris?"

"Oh yeah. Better than okay." There was a pause. "We're engaged," she squealed.

Like a couple of high school girls, about five minutes of shrieking, giggling and cheering followed. Hearing the noise, Megan poked her head in, grimaced when she heard the reason and retreated back to her desk.

Catching her breath, Jenn asked for some details which Amanda was happy to provide, but once she was done, the other woman added, "I need to tell you something though. I came by yesterday because I didn't see your text canceling our appointment, and there was this guy—two big black eyes—outside. He sneaked up behind me and scared the living daylights out of me."

Geez, what the heck was wrong with the guy? Didn't he have better things to do with his life than to track her down and harass her? Good thing she went home after their encounter because the guy she'd believed was a moron who wouldn't waste his day coming back to her office, actually came back to her office.

"Um," she mumbled because she didn't know what else to say.

"Jenn," her client continued. "You need to have a serious talk with your next-door neighbor because he's going to wreck your business if he does with other people what he did with me."

Her stomach flip-flopped. What? "Next-door neighbor?"

"Yeah, he told me he rented the house next door. He gave me his card. It says he's an attorney."

"Card? Attorney? Next door?" Well, shoot, could she sound any more idiotic?

"Yeah, the guy handed me his card—Noah Maitland, attorney at law—and said when my marriage didn't work out, to call him, he'd handle my divorce. Actually, he said call him before we got married and he'd draft up a prenup, so I'd get everything I deserve. What the hell, Jenn? I have to tell you, it totally pissed me off."

The nausea she'd felt disappeared. Rage rose in its place, red-hot, and blinding, so overwhelming, she had to force the words out from between her teeth. "Don't pay any attention to that jerk. He's a nut. Just throw the card away. And thanks for telling me."

"My pleasure." After adding a goodbye, Amanda hung up.

Fury nearly consuming her, she stood. She stormed out of her office, stomped past Megan with an, "I'll be right back", slammed out of the Victorian, and marched across the driveway to the cream and tan house next door.

She crashed the front door open with the heel of her hand. The pretty African American lady sitting behind the reception desk blinked in surprise, mouth opening to protest. Jenn marched past her, telling her, "Don't get up. I'll only be a minute," as she stalked into the open door of the adjacent office and slammed it shut behind her.

Her black-and-blue moron next door, the victim of her helmet attack, jumped to his feet.

"You," she yelled, and jabbed a finger at him.

A muscle in his jaw bunched. "You," he growled.

"How dare you." She poked a fingernail into his pec.

His mouth fell open briefly then closed. A smirk graced his lips. "How dare I what?" he asked, silky smooth.

The rat. Like he didn't know, but fine, if that was the way it was going to be, whatever.

"You scared the pea-wadding out of my client, sneaking up on her like you did. Then you said her marriage wouldn't last. Then you also told her she needed a prenup. How dare you suggest her marriage was only about money?" Another poke.

His smirk disappeared. "You broke my goddammed nose. You fucking gave me two black eyes, and you didn't even apologize. Instead you ran away like a coward."

Ignoring that the guy was drop-dead gorgeous, even with his black eyes, and that he was right, she crossed her arms over her chest and looked down her nose at him, which wasn't easy to do. He topped six feet and she was five eight, yet she did it anyway because it wasn't a matter of actual feet and inches. It was all a matter of attitude and Jenn had plenty of that.

"Hmmph," she said with all the disdain she could muster. "Profanity. The crutch of the intellectually impaired."

His nostrils flared, which was an impressive feat as his nose was swollen up like a bratwurst sausage. "My IQ is one-thirty-two," he gritted from between his perfect white teeth.

"Big deal. Mine's one-fifty-eight," she sneered then spoiled it by not knowing what to say next. Apparently attitude only got a girl so far when faced with a dude she'd bent, folded and spindled, even if it was accidental.

She huffed, "Don't ever talk to one of my clients again," lamely.

Something in his gorgeous gray eyes flashed, then a slow smile spread across his face. Since his mouth was one of the few areas of his face not black and blue and swollen, the smile was particularly telling. It was malevolent. It was malicious. It promised retribution the likes of which she could only guess. Her stomach did one of those flip-flopping things again.

He waggled an eyebrow. "How are you going to make me?"

Dang it, he had a point. Where was a good retort when you needed one? Fortunately, she had the attitude thing to fall back on. "Don't push me, buster," she told him. "Or you'll find out." She jabbed a defiant finger at him one more time, but she already realized it was going to be war.

She stomped back to Heart-2-Heart—a lot of stomping going on, however, she was so mad she couldn't seem to help herself—and gave her assistant a wave as she passed through the reception area on her way to the kitchen.

"Jenn, wait. I haven't had time to—" Megan yelled in the background right before Jenn opened the kitchen door and saw...

"No. No, no, no, no. NO."

Pots and pans were everywhere, the microwave rested on the floor, the refrigerator door hung open, now empty of all contents. Bits and pieces of lettuce and bread and lunch meat dotted the floor along with crunched up Dorito chips, an empty milk carton surrounded by spilled milk and the wrappers of an entire package of fake cheese slices. No cheese though, only the wrappers. Yogurt, grape jelly, smears of peanut butter and what looked like chocolate milk decorated the walls.

And to top it all off, there was a puddle of vomit in the middle of the floor—green and pink and brown, and that bright orange color cheese manufacturers used to dye their product, thinking it would fool people into believing it was real cheese—all graphically representative of everything the animal had eaten.

Trike gazed up at her, a loopy grin on her ugly face, sitting happily amid the remnants of her destruction, her long pink tongue lolling out.

"Woof," she yipped. Then, with an expression of pure ecstasy, she lifted up. And farted.

"Holy crap." Jenn held her nose, not giving a flying F if she'd broken her own non-swearing rule. Geez, it was like the city dump exploded in their kitchen.

"Megan, please call a cleaning service to clean this up," she yelled. Spinning on her heel, she left the mutt where she was—like, what more could the animal do?—went back to her office, threw herself into her chair and put her one hundred-and-fifty-eight-point IQ to work. She couldn't do anything about that hairy beast in the kitchen, however, nothing was stopping her from avenging herself on the big fat attorney rat next door.

Rat! Of course. It was perfect.

Delight bubbled up inside. "Megan," she hollered. "Can you come here?" Her approach was dramatically different from Amy's. Back in the day, Amy would have called Jenn on the intercom and politely asked her to come in. Jenn liked a slightly more direct approach. Yelling.

Megan came in, pad and pen in one hand, with the other she pushed her glasses up on her nose.

"You don't need to take notes," Jenn said, pointing at the tablet. "Instead, I need you to do a little shopping for me." She handed her the list she'd made along with her credit card.

Reading it, Megan's eyebrows went up. "Are we into art projects now?"

She shrugged. "I'm sure you can get what you need at the Walmart over on Route 1."

Looking puzzled, the girl left and Jenn returned to her task of contacting clients with updates and sending them information on potential matches.

After a few hours, her assistant returned.

"What's this all about?" she wanted to know so Jenn filled her in on the Amanda Hinkle event. Loyal to her employer, Megan was irate and totally up for a little payback. Together, she and Jenn laid everything out on the lush gray carpet and began to put it all together. Megan giggled while she sketched, clearly amused by Jenn's diabolical plan while Jenn worked with an intense focus.

"He's going to kill you, you know," Megan muttered and carefully added another brush stroke to her artwork.

"He's a lawyer. Lawyers don't kill people. They just sue the pants off them. Which he stated he's not going to do."

"I meant metaphorically."

"I can live with metaphorical. You know that writer, what's his name, Thackery wrote, *'Revenge may be wicked, but it's natural'*? Well, I'm a natural kind of girl."

Another giggle. "I'm coming in early tomorrow. I want to be sure to see what happens. I want to see his face when he sees this."

"Sounds good. In the meantime, I need you to stay a little late today to help with the setup."

It was six o'clock when they saw his silver Toyota leave the driveway next door. They smiled at each other. "Ready?" Jenn asked.

"Ready." Staple guns in hand, they retrieved a ladder from the shed behind the house, set it up in front of his front porch and carried out the rest of their plan.

SEVEN

NoahMaitland@noahmaitlandesq

Lions and tigers and RATS. Oh my!

That girl...woman...whatever...was a menace. At two that afternoon, his ears still rang from her yelling and his chest still throbbed from where she'd poked him. Christ, you'd think it would be enough for her to break his nose and give him two black eyes however, apparently not. Apparently, she wouldn't be satisfied until she'd reduced him to a quivering mound of male jelly which was too bad because what a waste of a hot woman. Hot and crazy should never ever come in the same package.

The good thing about the encounter was, it had cleared the air. At least he thought it did, then he recollected their conversation and realized he'd made a ginormous error. 'How are you going to make me?' he'd asked her.

Oh fuck. A girl—woman—whatever, like her would see it as a challenge. Dread turned his skin hot and his chest tight. Goddammit. No telling what she would do next.

Rising, he walked out to the foyer. Debra looked up. "Listen, I want you to make sure that anytime you leave, you lock everything up tight," Noah told her.

She blinked at him. "Well, of course. I would never leave anything unsecured."

He shook his head at himself. It was silly to even say anything because (a) of course Debra would lock up, but (b) more importantly, it was highly unlikely Ms. Crazy Pants next door would break into his office for any reason. She was too smart for that—one fifty-eight IQ, remember? No, her response would be something else, something a little more original—read terrifying.

He retreated back into his office, intent on calling the rest of the people who had attended his open house yesterday to thank them and nudge them towards a referral, still it was heavy going. His mind was barely on the task, too busy trying to imagine what form the crazy lady next door's revenge would take.

Waiting for something to explode, burst into flames or shatter into a million pieces, the feeling of dread only got worse throughout the day.

The day passed, and nothing happened. Maybe this was the end of it, maybe he was projecting his feelings onto her. She'd maimed him, he'd gotten revenge in response, then she'd yelled at him and dug a few dents in his chest. Maybe, after all, she'd decided they were even.

Six o'clock arrived. He was still in one piece, and Debra had packed it in, so he drove home. Pulling into his parking spot, he shut off the engine and undid his seatbelt.

Bam!

He jumped a foot. Jerking his head around, he saw his brother, his moon face pressed to Noah's car window, fist still raised to bang on the glass again.

Shit. Goddamn son of a bitch.

He pushed the car door open, shoving Bret out of the way, and climbed out.

"Hey bro," his brother said, grinning. The grin slipped to be replaced by a frown. "Whoa. Bro, what the fuck happened to your face? I mean, dude."

Noah grabbed his briefcase from his car and started walking up the path to his front door. "Accident," he muttered. "What do you want?"

Bret trailed behind him for a few feet, abruptly reversed direction and jogged to the big red Ford truck parked on the curb. He pulled the door open, and a girl jumped out. At least Noah thought it was a girl. It was hard to tell what with the black boots with six-inch soles, the black leather jacket and the shaved head. The only giveaway was the long earring dangling from her earlobe, although now that he gave his brother a second look maybe the earring wasn't a clue after all because his brother had one like it.

They strolled back to where Noah waited, the girl (?) loudly chewing gum and blowing bubbles.

Closing his eyes, he took a deep breath because this weirdo wasn't the same weirdo Bret dragged over to Noah's a year ago. Which could only mean one thing.

"When's the wedding date?"

His brother followed him inside when he unlocked his front door.

"Fuck, man, there's no wedding date."

Noah cocked an eyebrow.

"No, I mean, for real. I'm done with that shit, ya' know? I got tired of all the bitchin' and moanin' and the no-sex thing and why would I put up with all that crap that I have to because I'm married and, if I want to for real get rid of her, I always end up having to give her money and then, man, I'm fucking broke and I fucking hate being broke."

Noah ground his teeth because it wasn't Bret who was broke since it was Noah's money that was supporting the guy's lazy ass.

"If you're not getting married, why are you here?" *Shit, Noah, shut your stupid mouth.*

"Hey, can't I come visit my little brother without a reason?"

No, there had never been a single occasion in the last ten years when his older brother dropped in simply to visit. "I repeat, what do you want?"

The Goth-Whatever-it-Was popped another bubble. "Come on, Bret baby, ask him so's we can blow this joint and go buy some blow." A grin broke out and she giggled. At least he now knew for sure it was a girl.

"Hey, that was funny," she continued. "Blow the joint. Buy some blow. Funny, right?"

He opened the door again. "As an attorney—someone legally obligated to uphold the law—I'm going to pretend I didn't hear that. So, on that note, you need to leave."

Not waiting for a response, he pushed them out the door and slammed it shut.

Bang. Bang. Bang. "Noah! Come on, man. I only need a few hundred. Fuck, don't be like this, Noah. I'm your brother."

Yeah, unfortunately he was, yet no way was he going to give Bret money to buy drugs. He forced himself to walk away, up the stairs to his bedroom and turned on the lights. Hopefully his brother would see them and realize the discussion was over, although, given Bret's drug-fried brain, there were no guarantees.

The banging continued for a few minutes then stopped. The roar of the truck's engine starting up thundered through the cul-de-sac before fading into the distance.

Taking a deep breath, he sat on the edge of his bed and put his head in his hands. Two bloodsucking family members in two days, three if he included his father.

They were his family, and he loved them. Well, he sort of did, however, he didn't like them much. In fact, sometimes he hated them. They made him feel helpless, and angry about feeling helpless.

He pressed his fingers into his eyes, welcoming the pain because he deserved it. It was his fault they were the way they were. They were selfish, self-absorbed, and lazy and continued to leech off him because he allowed them to. He enabled their selfishness.

The idea of having to fund their selfishness for the rest of his life made him sick.

The possibility of cutting them off, of leaving them to fend for themselves when they were incapable of doing so...made him sick.

The only reason he'd been able to say no to Bret was because he was sure the money would go to buy drugs. Sadly, it was the only time he told his brother no. He paid his brother's rent, so he had a roof over his head and bought the guy food. It needed to end. He simply couldn't afford to continue giving his family thousands of dollars, not under the current circumstances. He needed to find a way to get rid of their constant demands.

He wanted to live his own life.

His stomach in knots, he agonized over the situation for a few more minutes then, with a sigh of resignation, he crossed over to Iggy's terrarium.

"Hey, buddy." He gently tapped on the glass. Iggy's head poked out from the log, his back spikes unfurling. "Have a good day?" Iggy looked up, his eyes following Noah's movement.

He would swear the lizard's eyes were full of sympathy and understanding. Too bad Iggy wasn't a human. It would be nice to have someone who loved him for who he was, not what he could buy for them.

"Yeah, big guy, I love you, and you love me too, right? You and Gram. You're the only ones who love me without wanting anything. You're happy to be with me because I have kale and strawberries. Speaking of strawberries, are you hungry? I've got a nice fat one."

Iggy's head bobbed and his tongue darted out.

"Coming up." He dropped a small red berry inside which was immediately slurped into Iggy's mouth. Done, the lizard looked up at him again. "What, you want out? Okay, give me a minute and I'll get you out."

He changed into shorts and a t-shirt then, reaching into the terrarium, he picked up the lizard. Putting Iggy on his shoulder, he went downstairs to the kitchen to get a beer and a bag of his favorite candy and parked himself in front of the TV with Iggy on his chest. Digging his sharp little claws in, Iggy climbed up Noah's front a few inches and went to sleep, his bristly little body tucked under Noah's chin.

He turned his head a fraction of an inch away from Iggy's spiny body and clicked on the TV, yet his attention wasn't on whatever was on the tube. His attention was all in his head, taking apart all the myriad events of the day, a good deal of them unpleasant.

There was a second when he considered getting drunk to dull the pain, however, that would make him like the rest of his family. Instead, he surfed through the channels until he found a soccer game being televised from Spain. If there was enough action even Iggy enjoyed it, although he preferred the Animal Channel. Iggy especially liked the veterinarian shows because they frequently had lizard patients.

He popped a red M&M into his mouth and turned his thoughts to a more immediate, and interesting, topic, the blonde babe next door—Legs. He found his attention drawn to the iPad he held in his lap, which had mysteriously opened up at the Heart-2-Heart website when he tapped on the screen.

For about the hundredth time, he studied the picture of the gorgeous Jenn Goodwin; crazy lady, breaker of noses and blacker of eyes. She of the wicked fingernails and the equally wicked mouth. The girl who was smarter even than him, and he didn't know too many people who were.

He smiled. Maybe she had lethal fingernails, but she also had this kissable mouth and a body that made him ache to touch her. The feeling they weren't done, like somehow she would find a way to make him pay, filled him with angst. Also anticipation. The idea of those fingernails doing something more erotic than poking him in the chest was enough to make him hard.

Nah, forget that. They were done with each other, although once she'd calmed down, maybe she'd view his little prank with a more reasonable attitude, possibly even think it was funny. Once that happened, he figured they might even get to be friends. Maybe much better than friends.

Whoa. That notion made him break out in a sweat.

After adjusting the fit of his shorts, he went upstairs, put Iggy back in his terrarium and went to bed filled with this bizarre sense of excitement for what tomorrow would bring.

More clients. More money. More opportunities to screw some dirtbag in court.

Maybe a quick sighting of Legs in those tight jeans.

By the time he left the gym the next morning after a session with Zach, he'd almost forgotten about the leggy blonde and the feud that wasn't. Nothing yesterday had exploded, no windows had shattered, and the police hadn't come to his door last night informing him his office had burned down, so it looked like all was forgotten or at least forgiven.

Turning onto the street where his office was, he slowed. What the heck? A crowd stood in the yard outside the brown and cream bungalow, all of them staring up at the roof. He pulled over on the curb and got out to hear the laughter of the crowd. He looked up to where everyone else's eyes were focused.

Son. Of. A. Bitch!

Stretched between the two gables above the porch roof was a huge white banner.

Noah Maitland, was at the top of the banner. Underneath it said in big red letters, *RATtorney-at-law*. And peering over the top of the word RAT was a huge drawing of said rodent, complete with pointy nose, long rodent incisors gnawing on the 'R', and red beady eyes that looked more than slightly maniacal.

He was going to kill her. Right after he ripped that fucking sign down. Striding to the porch, he climbed the steps and pulled himself on top of the porch railing. He stretched. Damn it. His fingers were a good foot away. He edged a little further towards the middle of the railing and stood on his tiptoes.

Crap, no dice. He clenched his fists, thinking, staring up at the sign, aware of the buzz of conversation and laughter behind him. Okay, new strategy. He slipped off his suit jacket and tossed it aside, toed off his loafers, letting them land on the wooden floor of the porch with a thud. Reaching up, he grabbed hold of one of the corbels nailed to an upright post and began to pull himself up.

And the corbel broke off.

Fuck! A few people screamed, a few laughed. He landed in the bushes, which should have been great because they broke his fall and kept him from breaking his neck. Unfortunately they were holly bushes.

Getting out of the bushes was agonizing. He thrashed, trying to escape, but every move caused a prickle to catch on his clothing, securing him even tighter while scratching the shit out of him.

"God damn it!" he yelled. "Someone help me."

Hands reached out and yanked him out of the bushes and set him on his feet. All around him, people stared, some looking sympathetic, most doing their best not to laugh. Across the lawn, Legs and a redhead in a long flowery dress stood, their expressions a mixture of amusement and chagrin.

"Noah?" He turned to see Debra standing nearby holding onto a ladder propped up against the wall of the house. Her face rippled between suppressed laughter and sympathy when she pointed at the banner.

"Yeah. Thanks." Grrr. Taking the ladder, he unfolded it, climbed up to the top rung and ripped the fucking banner down. He turned to climb back down and saw a gaggle of teenage girls standing on the street, giggling and taking pictures with their phones. Seeing his look, they waved and walked away, staring at their phones. Shit. No telling where those pictures would end up.

It was all her fault. He turned to glare at Legs. She spun around, followed by the short redhead. She walked across the lawn towards her front door, those long legs eating up the distance, those enticing hips swaying. Damn, she had a walk that would make a man's tongue fall out of his mouth and follow her all by itself in the hopes of getting a taste of her luscious ass. He grit his teeth. His tongue should mind its own business.

She climbed the stairs to the front door, the redhead right behind her, and disappeared inside that hideous pink and purple house.

Seeing the fun was over, the crowd began to dissipate. Every inch of his body hurting in some fashion, he picked up the banner and began to fold it up. In the process, the rat face appeared, covered with dirt, and torn from snagging on the roof, its beady red eyes staring at him triumphantly, as if to say, *"Up yours, sucker"*.

He scowled at the picture. Not if he could help it.

He finished wadding it into a tight ball, took it to the back of the house and crammed it into a large trash bin then went inside and threw himself into his chair. Popping a handful of M&M's into his mouth, he glared at the opposite wall for a minute. Christ, this was stupid. Why glare at the wall when he could turn his head ninety degrees and glare at the house next door. The house where his nemesis sat. He wanted to strangle her. How could she? This was his business, his lifeline, the only thing keeping him solvent. More importantly, it kept his Gram from being on food stamps. Dollars to donuts, the news of his escapade would be all over Princeton by now and god knows what kind of devastation to his business that would cause.

Work awaited his attention—and he tried, he truly tried—but eventually he gave up in favor of sitting and stewing.

His door opened and Debra poked her head in. "Noah," she mumbled, her voice timid.

He unhinged his locked jaw. "Do you need something?"

She carefully edged in, eyeing him with trepidation, and set her phone on his desk. "You should see this," she told him and tapped the screen.

A YouTube video came up, the title *A Rat gets Cheesed*.

Oh, fuck.

It was all there. The banner across the front of his house, the look on his face when he saw it, his angry stalking across the lawn, his climb up the railing, his spectacular fall into the holly bushes which had been edited so it played in slow motion. Worse, it repeated the fall five times, also in slow motion. They'd even captured his futile attempts to escape the holly bushes.

It had been a little more than an hour and there were already nine thousand, two hundred and twenty views. With snide comments, several from places like Germany and Sweden.

Forgive and forget? No. Fucking. Way.

He was going to kill the woman. He was going to stomp on her flower garden, fill her mailbox with dog poop, let the air out of all the tires on that blue Honda she'd driven to work today.

This was war.

Turning to his computer, he pulled up Google and waited for the results of his search to populate the screen. Holy fucking cow. Line after line after line of dirty tricks someone could play on their neighbor, their ex-whatever, their friends, even their parents. It sure seemed like there were a lot of vengeful people out there. Well, let's see what they came up with.

Hide cold cuts in the person's office and wait for them to smell.

No. Too difficult to accomplish.

Wrap their toilet bowl in Saran wrap.

Nah. Same problem.

Hang a pail of water over their door and tie a string to the doorknob.

He stopped. Fucking hell, what was he doing? He'd never behaved like this in his entire life. Taking revenge? Plotting stupid pranks like some middle-school kid?

This was ridiculous.

This was crazy.

This was really fun.

He snickered and clicked on another selection, idly scratching the spot next to his ear where a particularly vicious holly thorn had caught him. The next thing he knew, his eyes had drifted, and he was now looking out of his window at the house next door.

Okay, this had to stop. He yanked his eyes back to his computer. Jesus, if he wanted to make his business a success, he should be working on filing MaryAnn Potanski's petition for divorce.

He made himself close Google, and open Mrs. Potanski's file. But barely two seconds later, his gaze had drifted to the right and he was again staring at the house next door, hoping for a glimpse of his leggy blonde bomber.

Holy fuck! He needed to stop this, or he was never going to get anything done which meant he'd fail his client, which meant he'd never get another client, which meant his business would fail which meant all the people who leeched off of him for their support would have to find another way to support themselves.

Okay, maybe it wasn't all bad. Which didn't mean he was going to forgive that woman because his nose still throbbed, his new scratches were driving him crazy and the humiliation he'd felt falling into the holly bushes still burned in his chest. But his heart yearned for retribution.

Back to Google. *Wrap their car in Saran Wrap.* Okay, unlike the toilet thing, this one might have possibilities. Unfortunately, it would take too long plus he would run the risk of getting caught.

It did, however, give him an idea. Getting up, he exited the house through the back door and retrieved the banner he'd stuffed into the trash can. Using the supplies he'd bought to create the welcome poster for the open house, it didn't take long to do what he needed to do. Now all he needed was the right opportunity to complete the next step.

"Noah, your appointment is here." Debra opened the door and ushered in a lady in her fifties.

Shutting off his computer, he rose to greet the woman. He spent a few minutes getting to know her by asking some general questions about her family background, her kids and her job, which was with a hedge fund company, none of which she elaborated on, before he got down to business. "I understand this would be no fault."

"Correct," she uttered, giving him a cold stare.

So far he wasn't liking this woman, which for some attorneys wouldn't matter. However, he prided himself on going balls to the walls for his clients and he couldn't do it if he didn't like them. "I understand your children are all grown so there are no custodial issues. So let's talk about the assets. Have the two of you talked about what might be a fair split?"

Her lip curled. "Me, one hundred percent, him nothing."

Wow. What did her husband do to her? He frowned and changed it to an indulgent smile. "I'm afraid the law doesn't allow it so let's find another solution. Did you bring your financial statements?"

With a look, the woman pulled a folder from her tote bag and placed it in front of him. He went through them. It didn't take him long to realize the paperwork regarding the Canadian real estate leasing company she'd recently inherited from an uncle was not among the documents. "Is this everything?"

"Yes, it is."

He leveled a look at her. She was lying. He knew because Gordon, the estate planning attorney who referred her, was a good friend and had given him the entire picture.

"Are you sure?" He could get tough when he needed to negotiate settlements, but one thing he wouldn't put up with was lying in order to cheat the other party.

Her mouth tightened. "This is all I have to show you."

That clinched it. He handed the papers back. "I'm sorry, but I'm afraid I can't take you on," he told her.

Red tinged her cheekbones. "What do you mean you can't take me on? I want the best and Gordon said you were the best."

"I am the best, or at least one of the best." What a pleasure it was to be able to say. "However, I still can't take your case. I'm happy to refer you to someone else." He gave her a bland smile, giving nothing away. Her mouth pursed and he could almost see the insults flying around in her brain, but it was telling that she didn't ask why. She knew why.

Grabbing her folder, she jerked to her feet. "I don't need your referral." Spinning on her heel, she left, spine rigid.

The door slammed behind her. He sighed. Too bad. Like the lady yesterday, she was worth a bundle so the fees would have been extraordinary, however, he wouldn't work with dishonest clients.

He turned back to his computer, his mind again occupied with thoughts of his strategy and how he was going to make it happen without Legs seeing him. He kept an eye on her house. At noon, he saw a man in a suit enter, obviously a client who would keep the woman busy for a while.

Grabbing the banner he'd edited to suit his needs, he left his office through the back door and carefully walked over to his nemesis's car and went to work.

Once he was done, he went back inside and focused on the rest of his day. With all the shit that happened this morning, he'd forgotten to check his personal emails. Crap, another email from his dad.

Clenching his teeth, he opened the attached photo. In the foreground was his father, dancing with that same chunky woman. In the background was the gold-digger, glaring at the dancing couple. A shiver went down his spine. What the heck?

He looked closer at the dancing lady. She wasn't his usual type. He normally liked them young—very young—slender, stupid and malleable. This woman was, at best, in her late thirties, definitely not slender, and had a look in her eye like she ruled the world.

What's going on? he typed and sent the email to his father with no expectations the man would answer. Yet he knew, somehow, that disaster loomed.

EIGHT

JennGoodwin@MyHeart-2-Heart

If the cops didn't see it, I didn't do it.

Oh my God, she didn't think she'd ever forget the sight of Noah Maitland, Rattorney-at-law, falling into the holly bushes. She scuttled into Heart-2-Heart, Megan on her tail, slammed the door and locked it, just to be on the safe side. Noah Maitland might not be dead, however, if he gained access to Heart-2-Heart, she probably would be.

"Oops," Megan said and plopped down on the sofa. Her face rapidly morphed through several expressions in her attempt to look guilty, but all that happened was she giggled.

Jenn carefully drew the curtains aside and peeked out the window, making sure the big bad rat hadn't followed them. "Yeah, oops. That turned out a lot meaner than it was supposed to," she mumbled. A chortle leaked out. "Oh, shoot, sorry. I shouldn't laugh but come on. Who knew the idiot would try to climb the railing instead of using the ladder we left by the corner of the house."

Megan giggled.

Thinking about the incident, she was having a hard time controlling her laughter and she said, "Did you see the expression on his face when he saw—"

"Yeah, and did you hear the screech when he fell?"

"And what about when he couldn't get out of the bushes?"

They exchanged looks and burst into more giggles. Despite how ridiculous he'd looked struggling out of the bushes, she couldn't help remembering how broad his shoulders were, and how he had these long legs and narrow hips, and his butt? OMG, his butt was to die for.

Okay, he was a jerk, but no one said jerks were obligated to be short, fat and ugly.

"I'm sorry," she said, still chuckling. "We're being mean. We shouldn't laugh. But... but... but.... did you see his expression when his assistant showed him the ladder."

They exchanged another look and again laughter erupted.

She clapped a hand over her mouth. "Okay, we need to stop. I feel terrible." It wasn't like she *meant* for him to fall into the holly bushes. "We shouldn't laugh. Really, I feel bad for the poor guy."

Her assistant's face had turned bright red, and her eyes danced. "Yeah, you're right. At least he wasn't hurt. Other than a few scratches, he's okay. Given the black eyes, and the swollen nose, what are a few more scratches?"

Yeah, what were a few more scratches to add to the injuries she'd already gifted him with, right?

Her assistant tilted her head, frowning. "Speaking of black eyes, I wonder how he got those."

Heat flooded Jenn's face. She shoved those images from her mind. Geez, she hated being blonde—well, no, she didn't, because it was a well-known fact blondes had more fun—but she hated the way her face turned beet red every time she was embarrassed.

Behind her glasses, the other woman's eyes widened. "OMG. You did something to him. It's why he did the shitty thing with the business card and the prenup and everything, isn't it? Come on, Jenn, spill. What did you do?"

Jenn could feel the heat spread. Even her ears burned. "Isortofhithimwithmyhelmet," she muttered, looking down so the explanation was delivered to her shuffling feet.

"What? I didn't understand. What did you say?"

She glared at Megan. Her assistant. The girl who worked for her. Who should mind her own business. Who she didn't need to explain herself to.

"Jenn Goodwin, you tell me right now what you did to the poor man that started this whole thing."

Sheesh. Five feet one, a hundred pounds soaking wet and mean as a rabid skunk. It had to be her red hair. "Fine! I whacked him with my motorcycle helmet."

It was hard to believe it was possible, but her assistant's eyes got even wider. "You whacked him with your helmet? Why?"

Good question because, thinking back, she had trouble remembering what had happened. She remembered his hand in the older woman's purse—the one who turned out to be his grandmother—the sly look on his face, the wallet in his hand, but mostly she remembered the four drinks and the muzzy state of her brain.

She was a bad, bad girl, and now that she was done with her fit of giggles, she realized she owed him an apology.

"Come on," Megan interrupted her thoughts. "Tell me what happened."

The guilt still banging at her conscience, she sent her assistant another look from under her bangs, thinking maybe if she stalled long enough the girl would leave her alone. Yet, she knew that there was no way that would happen because, while Jenn might have attitude, her assistant had something better—pigheadedness.

Megan harrumphed. "And if you think giving me one of your ridiculously coy looks from under your bangs is going to charm me into forgetting about this, you'd better think again because it won't work on me. You're not my type. Now tell me what you did to the poor guy."

She opened her mouth to say no, but the girl wasn't falling for any of Jenn's bull. Megan's glare was panty-melting. "Fine. I'll tell you," she grumped, and did.

"Geez. That's terrible. No wonder he was so angry. You'll be lucky if he doesn't sue you."

Like she needed reminding. "I told you, he said he wouldn't." Maybe he should because she was guilty of horrible deeds.

"After today, he could change his mind."

He could, yet, remembering the look on his face when they discussed it, Jenn was willing to bet he wouldn't. "No," she sighed. "He definitely won't."

"How can you be so sure?"

"He promised his Gram," she responded.

Megan's mouth sagged. "His Gram. Like... his grandmother?"

"I assume so."

Her assistant was quiet for a few minutes before saying, "Still, I think you owe him some kind of apology."

She squirmed. Like she didn't already know that.

"Don't you?" the girl repeated, giving her a narrowed-eyed look.

Geez, who did this girl think she was, her mother? Unfortunately, the girl was right. However, even though she had already determined that's what she needed to do, Jenn didn't have a clue what that type of apology entailed other than possibly walking over to his office again, prostrating herself on his gorgeous blue and brown carpeting and kissing his feet while intoning dozens of mea culpas. She didn't want to offer that kind of apology immediately after the whole rat banner, holly bush thing. Being prostrate could end with a certain blonde—her—being trod on by a certain other someone's size eleven Ferragamo oxfords.

"I know I do, but I don't know what. If he was a woman, I could send flowers or candy, but he's a guy. What do you send a guy?"

"How the heck should I know?" Megan retorted, pointing a finger at her chest. "Remember me? Gay person? Which means I don't have to worry about making anyone with a penis happy."

"But—"

"Sheesh, it's your mess, so you figure it out. Just do it soon, or it won't mean anything." With that, she plunked down in her desk chair and pretended to work.

Smart aleck. "Yes, Mom," she growled.

Without looking up from her computer screen, her assistant flipped her the bird.

Well! Spinning on her heel, Jenn retreated to her office where she sat and fretted for a while. That ball of guilt still sat, hot and heavy in her stomach. Why had she done it? Telling one of her clients she was headed for divorce was mean, but almost getting the man hurt went beyond mean. She wasn't normally so cruel, yet somehow, she'd justified it in her mind by telling herself that he'd threatened her livelihood, which meant she needed to pay him back in kind. Anyway, she had left him the ladder so he could safely take down the banner. It wasn't her fault he was so dumb he didn't see it.

Still, it was obvious she had to apologize. She just had to figure out how.

She'd cogitate on it. In the meantime, she had work to do. Picking up the phone, she began calling the list of potential members who had sent questions to Heart-2-Heart through their website.

Prospect One call: "Thank you for your interest. I have all your information I need for our meeting on Thursday at noon." Pause. Okay, why not? "Oh, before you hang up, I do have one more question; if you did something mean to a guy, how would you apologize?"

"Hell's bells, I don't know. I usually say I'm sorry."

Duh. "Right. Well, thanks. See you Thursday."

Prospect Two: "So how would you apologize to a man if you wronged him?"

"Huh, good question. Maybe take him to dinner?"

Oh, sure, that would work, sitting face to face for two excruciating hours, forced to stare at the two black eyes she'd caused. For Jenn, it would be less of an apology and more like torture. Although the angry guy next door might think they were one and the same. "Thanks. Worth considering."

Prospect Three: "If you played a dirty trick on a guy, and it went badly, how would you apologize?"

"Take him to a game, maybe something like a Yankees game. Guys'll forgive about anything if they get sports out of it."

Okay, on the one hand it could be expensive but, conversely, she wouldn't have to go with him. She could just hand him a couple tickets and tell him to have fun. "Hmm. Not a bad idea. Thanks."

Possible client number four: "How do you let a guy know you're sorry about something horrible you did to him?"

"A blow job, honey. Or even better, full horizontal sex. Trust me, it always works."

Her entire body burst into flames even thinking about getting horizontal with the victim of her ruthless prank. "Okaaaay. So, I'll get back to you about when we can schedule an appointment."

She hung up and groaned. Because the last suggestion was tempting. Even with the black eyes and swollen nose, it was clear the guy was super-hot. To make sure, she went online again, for the fourteenth billion time, and pulled up his website. Noah Maitland, Attorney at Law; Hofstra University, BA; Boston University School of Law, JD; Bar Admissions, New Jersey, New York; blah, blah, blah.

And his picture. Yep, definitely hot. Especially without the black eyes.

The day sped by. She made several trips to reception so she could peek out the window at his office. On the other side of his glass window, she could see his silhouette. Seeing him made her stomach do weird things, this nauseating combination of guilt, dread and a tingle that felt suspiciously like arousal.

Nah, it couldn't be arousal. That her entire body tingled like she'd been zapped by a live wire merely meant she was tired, right? Darn it, maybe she should walk the short distance to his office and risk getting trod on. Like, get it over with.

"Darn it, Jenn, go away," her assistant yelled and threw a pen at her. "I have a job to do and you're driving me batty."

Banished, she went back to her office and spent the rest of the afternoon Googling *Ways to Apologize to Men*. Nothing brilliant appeared so she decided to go home. The dog too, of course. Dragging her feet every step of the way, she made her way to the kitchen to retrieve the beast. She pushed the door open. Trike was lying on her back, feet in the air, jowls splayed out to the side. Around her were bits and pieces of wood from the cabinet doors. The only thing left on the cabinet frames was the silver hinges.

She calculated the damage was around fifteen hundred dollars. Added to the cost of her chairs, the bedspread and all the food the dog had eaten, she figured Amy owed her about two thousand bucks.

Turning around, she walked back to reception. "That stupid animal ate the cabinets."

Megan held her phone up. "Look at this. A video from this morning was posted on YouTube."

What? Bending, she watched all five minutes of the disaster titled *A Rat Ate the Cheese*. She made a *save me God* face. "Oops."

Megan let out a breath. "Yeah. Big oops." Shaking her head, she turned off the phone and threw it into her purse.

"I think he's going to kill me," she said.

"Probably," her former partner in crime mumbled, turning off her computer and standing. "I'm going home now. It was nice knowing you."

How cheery. "See you tomorrow," Jenn responded.

"Maybe," her assistant said and left. Returning to the devastated kitchen, Jenn attached the leash to the dog's collar, led the dog outside and loaded her into the back seat.

Glancing over at her neighbor's house, she could see him still in his office.

Had he seen the YouTube video yet? If he had, wouldn't it be likely he would have come roaring over to kill her? For a moment, she considered going over now to apologize. She chickened out. She was in no hurry to die.

She drove towards home, still fretting about the situation, guilt still burning a hole in her chest. A small black car crept up on her tail and toot-tooted his horn and gave her a thumbs up as he drove by. Several more drivers tooted at her on their way past.

Huh, some people. Always in a hurry. She moved to the right lane, so she wasn't blocking traffic. Several more cars passed. A big SUV drove by. This time she got a glare from the passenger. The SUV was soon replaced by a Jeep full of teenagers who insisted on riding alongside her.

The passenger closest to her stuck his head out the window. "You rock, lady," he yelled. Wrinkling up his nose, he snorted several times. Another teen stuck his head out of the rear window and joined the snorting. His buddies in the car laughed loudly, and they sped off with a screech of tires, probably doing eighty miles an hour. They wove around the cars in front of them and disappeared in the distance.

Jerks. Where were the cops when you needed them?

Apparently right behind her because within seconds she heard the sound of a siren. She checked her rearview mirror. Closing in on her was a white sedan with its distinctive red and blue lights flashing. She pulled over into the far-right lane, thinking to let him pass so he could catch those rotten teens. Instead, he edged up right on her bumper and flashed his headlights at her. Holy cow. He was after her. Why? What had she done? She checked her speedometer, however, she was well within the speed limit. So why was she being stopped?

She pulled over onto the verge, and turned off the engine, a flutter of unease roiling her stomach. The patrolman sat in his car for long minutes while her unease ratcheted up to outright fear. Drat, what was taking him so long? Was he waiting because he considered her dangerous? Was he going to arrest her? Her breath caught in her throat. Oh God, what if he had a gun?

Well, duh, of course he had a gun; he was a cop. Her nerves began jangling all over her body at the possibility a gun could be pointed at her. She could die. She was too young to die. She couldn't die now—she still owed two hundred thousand dollars on her mortgage.

On the other hand, at least she'd look great in her coffin, still being young and unwrinkled.

The cop's car door opened, and the cop got out. Eep, he was big, really big, like Big Foot big, only without all the shaggy orange hair.

She could feel herself shrinking into her seat, her shoulders hunching, her body sinking in on itself, instinctively getting smaller and smaller trying to disappear from sight like a trapped animal. Yep, that was her, the helpless—edible—bunny rabbit, and rapidly approaching was the big bad wolf.

He stopped by her opened window. Nothing was said for a moment. He bent to look into the backseat. Trike lay on her back, feet splayed in the air, sound asleep.

Apparently reassured the dog wasn't about to eat him, he said, "License and registration, please."

Wordlessly, she handed them over. He reviewed them, made a few notes in the digital tablet he held and handed them back. "Do you know why I pulled you over?" he asked.

As there was no saliva in her mouth and her tongue was stuck to the roof of her mouth, she couldn't answer him, not that she had an answer, so she shook her head instead.

"Your taillights are covered. It's illegal to cover your taillights."

She blinked at him. Her tongue came unstuck with an audible sucking sound which made her giggle nervously. "My taillights are covered? Uh—"

He narrowed his gorgeous light blue eyes and compressed his lips. He was young and fit and kind of cute. For a cop. For someone who looked like he was capable of breaking her into teeny-tiny pieces with his little finger.

He peered down his nose at her. "I suppose you think all this is funny, don't you?"

Nothing about this was funny. This was like the unfunniest thing that had ever happened to her and if he didn't leave soon, her heart was going to explode in her chest, which would be bad because who would take care of the dog?

Okay, maybe that wasn't the best reason not to die. She swallowed. "No, I don't think covering my taillights is funny. Why would covering my taillights be funny?" And now that she reflected on it, why *were* her taillights covered?

He frowned. Her thundering heart had slowed from a mad gallop to a mild trot, making it easier to think. None of this made sense. "I don't understand. You said my taillights are covered?"

He handed back her license and registration. "Get out of the car."

Yikes! He was going to shoot her now. Her heart leaped in her chest again, and blood drained from her head. She was going to pass out. She wanted to shake her head no, but shaking her head would guarantee lights out.

Grabbing her door handle, he pulled the door open. "Get out."

No. No, no, no. Her breath wheezed in and out of her lungs, burning. All the feeling left her legs, leaving them limp. She couldn't stand if she tried. She was nothing more than a great big pile of mush. Oh, shoot, where was that attitude when she needed it, the big, brash *I've got balls so don't mess with me* attitude?

It was nowhere because the cop's attitude—and of course his balls—were bigger and brasher.

He held out a hand, expecting her to take it. She heard a whine leak from her mouth, like a balloon collapsing.

"For God's sake, come on. I'm not going to hurt you."

So said the big bad wolf right before he ate grandma. Nevertheless, she took his hand and got out of her car only because she didn't have a choice. Placing his hand on her back, he nudged her towards the rear of her car. When she got there, he turned her around, so she was looking at....

...a long white banner—which looked ominously familiar—draped across the entire back of her car, and on the sign in big bold red letters was COPS ARE PIGS, and to make sure the point was made, a huge pig's face, complete with a piggy snout, peered over the top of COPS.

White hot fury surged through her. "Son of a—" She swallowed the rest. "I'm going to kill him."

The cop's eyebrows shot up. "Are we talking murder here?"

She shook her head, her fury still so intense she could barely speak. "Murder would be too good for that son...of a female dog."

He snorted. Maybe it was a laugh. Or maybe he actually was a pig. Who knew? "I should give you a ticket for the covered taillights, you know," he said. Reaching into his coat pocket, he pulled out his ticket book.

A ticket? It was the last thing she needed. "It wasn't my fault, officer. I didn't put it there. It was the jerk attorney next door. Apparently, he thought it would be funny to get me in trouble with the law. Only it's not funny." She dug the toe of her ankle boot through the gravel a few times. "Not like the rat banner. The rat banner was funny. This isn't funny," she mumbled.

"Rat? Attorney?" he asked, now looking intrigued.

She held a finger up—wait—ran to her open car door and grabbed her cell from her purse. The dog poked her head up from the backseat and snuffled, blowing snot all over. Ugh.

"Lie down," she ordered, and amazingly, the mutt did. She trotted back to the waiting officer. Pulling up YouTube, she typed in *A Rat gets Cheesed*, hoping it was still online. Yes! She hit play when the video appeared.

He watched it. Once or twice a muffled sound rumbled from his chest, maybe a laugh yet it was hard to tell because he had put his hand over his mouth, hiding the smile tugging at the corner of his lips.

The video finished playing. He didn't say anything for a minute, merely stood there, looking at the ground, his mouth hidden under his hand. He took a deep breath.

"Play it again."

She laughed out loud. He shot her a look full of amusement. She replayed it and they both watched for a second time. When it reached the end, he turned to watch a half dozen or so cars drive by. "Okay. Well." He scratched his ear. "An attorney, you say?"

"Yep, law degree Boston U, registered in the State of New Jersey and the state of New York. The whole shooting match."

"What was the title of this video again?" he asked.

She told him.

He tucked his ticket book inside his jacket. "You're free to go now, ma'am. Just make sure to remove the banner. And have a nice evening." Done, he walked back to his squad car and drove off.

Tearing the banner off her bumper, she folded it into a small square and pitched it into the bushes. She got back in her car and drove home. That jerk-face. His little prank had scared the bejesus out of her. What if she'd been arrested? How would that look to their clients, their matchmaker ending up in jail? It could ruin their business. Amy would never forgive her.

By the time she got home, she already had a plan in mind.

NINE

NoahMaitland@noahmaitlandesq

Revenge it is a dish best served cold. I'd like mine with a side of fries, please.

He tore open a little bag of M&M's and poured them out onto his desk, at the same time staring out the window at the house next door. Where was she? In the last two days, she'd arrived at the Heart-2-Heart house no later than eight o'clock, however, it was after nine now and she still hadn't appeared. He drummed his fingers nervously, worried she wouldn't show today. He needed her to show. He wanted to know what happened yesterday when she found the sign. Anticipation fizzed in the depths of his stomach while he envisioned her reaction to his retribution. Yeah, his prank was mean, but so what, it wasn't like hanging a sign on the back of her car would hurt her. It wasn't like he'd caused her to fall into a great big ol' holly bush—like someone else he could mention.

Where the hell was the woman?

With one finger, he idly separated the candies by color, blue in one pile, brown and orange in another, yellow the farthest away because he didn't like yellow. Snagging a red one—his favorite—he popped it into his mouth, crunching up the candy coating while he continued to watch for a certain blue Honda.

At that moment, her car pulled into her driveway. He bolted to his feet and bounded over to the window. Once there, he stepped to the side, keeping hidden behind the curtain while he peered around the window frame and watched her exit her car.

First a foot wearing a sexy red heel appeared. A long slim leg followed, then a second leg bared up to mid-thigh. Whoa. He took a deep breath and tried to slow the drumming of his heart, because, damn, those legs. The rest of his nemesis exited the car, wearing a short black skirt that exposed her legs up to mid-thigh, and a close-fitting white blouse. The woman might be the spawn of the devil, however, there was no denying she had a body designed to make the angels weep.

He ran a finger over his lips, hoping he wasn't drooling.

Legs stood in the driveway for a minute, her face expressionless, like she didn't have a care in the world, making him wonder if she hadn't yet seen the sign he'd hung on her car. How was it possible? Surely someone had alerted her. What a bummer if she hadn't seen the sign. All his planning, all his plotting, all his sneaking around, for nothing?

She turned her head until she stared straight at his window. An expression, one-part fury, two parts—okay, it was one hundred percent fury—settled on her previously blank face. Oh joy. She *had* seen the sign.

Even though he was aware she couldn't see him, he took a quick step backwards. Shoulders rigid, hands fisted as she started across the driveway. He popped a couple M&M's into his mouth, ugh, yellow ones, and chewed them up, thinking maybe the chocolate would calm his nervous laughter.

She disappeared around the front of his house. He heard his front door open, and slam shut. Debra bleated something that that didn't stop Legs from slamming into his office, banging his door shut behind her and planting herself two feet in front of him.

"You!" she yelled.

Her hand, complete with long lethal fingernails, went up. He backed up a step because he didn't need any more dents in his chest.

"You dirty rotten son of a—" She stopped, her jaw flexing, took a deep breath and spat, "Toad!"

Toad? He clamped his teeth together. The worst thing he could do right now was laugh at her. Still...toad?

"A policeman stopped me," she shrieked.

Hah. That was what was known as the law of unintended consequences. Sort of like him falling into the holly bushes.

"With his lights flashing. I almost had heart failure. I could have caused an accident. I could've gotten arrested. I was scared to death. Cops have guns. Cops with guns do gun things. How could you? Nothing I did warranted what you did. It was cruel. I could have died from fright. How would you feel, huh? Huh? How would you feel if I had a heart attack and died right in the middle of Route 1?"

She jabbed her finger at him again, and again he took a step back. She had gorgeous hands, long and slender, but it didn't mean he wanted to be speared by one of her nails.

"You big fat dung beetle."

He stared at her gorgeous mouth saying those strangely erotic insults, watched her eyes blaze fire, and her chest heave with anger. Oh, man, she had the most perfect boobs. His cock twitched, which was crazy because who the fuck got turned on when being called a dung beetle?

"Ooohh, I hate you, you miserable piece of excrement on the bottom of my shoe," she ranted, but at this point he wasn't hearing the words anymore. All his attention was focused on her mouth and what her lips did when she uttered the last word. Shoe. Her lips puckered when she uttered the word *shoe*. He almost wanted her to insult him again so he could see those sweet, kissable lips form that word. She had luscious lips, the upper lip slightly fuller than the lower with a little dip in the middle, the lower lip a pillowy fullness. Her lips were naturally a rosy pink. Most importantly, they were fucktastically kissable.

So he kissed her. Wrapping his hands around her arms, he hauled her forward, chest to chest, and kissed her. He bent his head, parted his lips and laid one on. She gasped. Her hands rose to his chest and pushed, but he ignored it, instead he softened his mouth and ran the tip of his tongue along the seam of her mouth, urging her to open, at the same time threading his hand into her silky hair, holding her steady.

She smelled like spice, and vaguely of dog. He happened to love dogs.

Her mouth eased open. She moaned. Her spine relaxed so that her belly pushed forward into his, and his eager cock pushed back. One of her slim hands wrapped around the lapel of his jacket, pulling him closer, crept up his shoulder to the back of his head and burrowed into his hair, grabbing on to the back of his skull, digging her fingers in. Her tongue met his. She sucked his tongue into her mouth. Oh, Christ in the manger, she was sucking on his tongue.

Heat exploded through his veins, his cock went nuts inside his pants, hard as an iron spike, and his balls tightened to the point of pain. He could hardly think he wanted her so bad. Dropping a hand at her waist down to her ass, he squeezed. God almighty, she had the best ass he'd ever seen, ever touched, hoped to see naked one day. And those legs of hers? Someday he wanted them wrapped around his waist while he slid into her wet heat. Maybe someday was today because there was a desk and a closed door. What more could a guy ask for?

He gently bit her lower lip. "Mmm, God, Legs, you taste good."

The crazy hot kissing abruptly stopped. She jerked out of his arms. "What did you call me?"

He gaped at her. He had no idea. He could scarcely remember his own name, much less what he'd called her. "Um—" He squinted, trying to remember. After a second, a light bulb went off. Unfortunately, it turned out to be the wrong bulb. "Legs?"

"My name is Jenn."

He blinked. "Uh. I know."

"Apparently you don't. Apparently, you've reduced me to a few body parts."

Embarrassment heated his face because...what a dope. "Hey, it's not like I called you Boobs," he mumbled.

He didn't see it coming, however, he certainly felt the impact. Now he had a sore jaw to go with the black eyes and the broken nose. Gripping his jaw with one hand, he wiggled it back and forth. "Ow. Geez, uh...Jenn."

She shook her hand, staring at him with rage-filled eyes.

Those same blue eyes narrowed, her expression shifted, and a wicked, slyly insinuating smile broke out. She started with his face, ogling every one of his features starting with his hair, her eyes burning hot as she worked her way down, licking her lips. Her gaze roamed leisurely over his chest, past his waist until she reached the placket of his trousers which unfortunately was still tented out by his cock. Apparently, it hadn't quite gotten the message the fun was over. Holy fuck. Instinctively, his hand dropped down and spread over the front of his pants.

She let loose with a derisive snort. "Awww, does the little fellow want to come out to play?" she asked. "Too bad, so sad."

Having delivered her opinion of his most prized body part, she stalked out the door. Through the window, he watched her come around the side of his house again and stride across the driveway to her car, her swaying hips a siren's call. She opened the car's back door, letting out the ugliest dog he'd ever seen. Standing well back, she snapped a leash to its collar, pulled it up the porch stairs and disappeared inside.

Tugging at his trousers, he stared at the closed door. Fucking cock. It didn't know when to quit. He'd been so overcome by the feel of her, the taste of her, he'd completely lost control, yet as mortifying as her scorn was, he still could only think about how good her lips had tasted, how taut her ass was under his hands, and how much his cock wanted to get between those long, long legs so it could bury itself in her lusciousness because, holy fucking hell, he'd never had a kiss like that in his life.

To think she hated him. Imagine what the kisses would be like if she actually liked him.

Dung beetle. She'd called him a dung beetle. If nothing else, she was creative with her scorn. He chuckled. Damn, the girl had sass.

Realizing she wasn't going to re-emerge from the house, he wandered back to his seat and fell into it. Debra appeared in the doorway. She tilted her head. "Oooh. You have a new *owie*. Right here—" She tapped her own chin.

He rolled his eyes. "Yeah. To go with the black eyes and the busted nose. I'm now complete."

"Well, I'm sure Mrs. Layton will appreciate it. She's here for her appointment."

Wonderful. He stood again and went out to greet his new client who promised to be one of his more interesting clients ever. Jeri Layton was the wife of a world-famous rocker; she had purple hair, tattoos everywhere except her face, and wore leather and chains. She also came equipped with a healthy bank account. The appointment went fine which was a fucking miracle because his mind was in the gutter, not the courtroom. She hired him anyway. It must be the black eyes and the swollen nose. Made him look totally badass.

After seeing her out, he tried to go back to work. But his mind was busy thinking about that kiss with Legs, who he should start to think of as Jenn so he didn't slip again and get himself punched a second time. Getting punched wasn't the way he wanted to start their relationship.

Whoa. Relationship? Was he thinking about a relationship? He shook his head, frowning when he realized, yeah, actually, he was. For some reason he couldn't explain, he liked this woman.

If forced to give an answer, he'd say he liked her gumption, he liked her intelligence, he liked her quick smart-mouthed responses, and let's face it, he liked the luscious lips that delivered those smart responses. Still, there was something more, some undefinable something that nagged at him, tugging at a feeling he couldn't put his finger on.

He wanted her, but how was he going to make that happen?

When he remembered the last week, he realized she'd turned this thing between them—whatever this thing was—into a game. He wasn't really into games, but if he were, he'd make sure he won. He reviewed the recent events:

First day: She broke his nose and blackened his eyes. Point for the black eyes. Point for the broken nose, both to Jenn.

Day two: He tried to get her to apologize for breaking his nose and blackening his eyes by chasing her down Route 1, but she managed to evade him. Hmm. Point for Jenn. However...he ambushed her client, resulting in sabotaging her business to a small degree. Point for Noah. He ground his teeth. Just not a very strong point. So maybe half a point.

Day three: They had an argument. She left two big dents in his chest. Not a big deal. Half a point for her.

Day four: The rat sign and the holly bushes. Crap, that qualified as a two-pointer for her.

Also day four: The PIG sign. A big high five for creativity. Unfortunately, only one point for himself because she weaseled her way out of a ticket. If she'd gotten a ticket, it would have been at least a three-pointer.

This morning: Another confrontation—no points for an argument—but who cared when it resulted in a delicious, mind-blowing, cock-busting kiss. Lips parted, hair fondled, tongues tangled. Score, score, and score. Three points for Noah.

He tallied up the points. Even giving himself three points for the kiss, he was still three and a half points to his rival's five and a half.

Well, shit. He was a total loser.

Pulling the curtains aside, he stared out at the house next door. Yep, he laughed to himself, grinning. Apparently he was a total loser, at least when it came to revenge. Still, so what?

Because who needed revenge when what he really wanted was the girl instead?

In the middle of his ruminations, his cell rang. He glanced at the number appearing on the screen. Crap. Talk about spoiling his day. "Hi, Mom. How are you?"

"Noah, I need—"

"I transferred four thousand dollars into your account this morning. It's enough to get you by for the next couple of weeks," he told her, determined to head her off at the pass.

"But—"

Burying his head in his hands, he sighed. "Take it or leave it, Mom. It's all you're getting."

The phone went dead. Huh. He guessed the hang-up meant she was taking it, at least for now, however, he was sure she'd be back for more at a later date, especially if she married what's-his-name because the guy was a total mooch. Why his parents seemed to always marry partners who were takers rather than givers, he'd never been able to figure out. He'd never been able to figure out how to say no to them either, but with a brand-new business and his reduced income, he had better figure it out, and quickly. He wished he knew where to start.

Shaking his head at his own lack of backbone, he put his mother out of his mind and tried to finish up the paperwork for Mrs. McConnell.

JennGoodwin@MyHeart-2-Heart

Attitude is a little thing that makes a big difference.

Jenn flexed her fingers several times. Her knuckles throbbed from connecting with his jaw. Maybe she shouldn't have punched the man, but calling her Legs reminded her sharply of all those insults in high school, so when he'd made the crack about her boobs, she'd just reacted without thinking. A lady would have slapped him. However, she wasn't that kind of lady. Ladies with attitude didn't slap guys, they punched them, which he deserved.

And to add insult to injury, he'd kissed her. Ick. Yuk. Ugh. Right?

Oh, for heaven's sake, who was she kidding? The kiss had been the best kiss she'd ever had, like head-to-toe totally yummy, and it had been delivered by that rat, Noah Maitland. Imagine what kind of sparks would have flown if she actually liked him.

Pretending she needed to get a client file, she wandered into the front room and oh, so casually meandered over to the filing cabinet placed conveniently next to the window facing his office window. She pulled the curtain aside and peeked out.

"Why don't you step out onto the porch and look your fill," her assistant grumbled. "Because you're not fooling anyone."

"Oh, hush," Jenn snapped, and practically ran back into her office. The confrontation she'd planned out so carefully when she'd gone over there hadn't gone quite the way she'd wanted.

His magic lips had tasted like chocolate. He'd smelled like chocolate. Son of a gun, she was a total sucker for chocolate. If she didn't know better, she'd think she was a total sucker for Noah Maitland. That couldn't be true, could it? Falling for some random guy was simply asking to be hurt again.

Originally, her plan had been to tell him off. Unfortunately, when the moment came, her beautiful plan fell apart because...his lips. Dang! Those lips. Did the man know how to kiss or what?

Evidently, she was a big sap for his *what*, because he'd literally melted her bones. She could still taste him, still feel the strength of his hand on her ass, still feel the warmth of his fingers on the back of her head. Still see the impressive size of him even though it was hidden inside his conservative gray slacks.

She still throbbed between her legs.

Under her desk, her foot jittered while she tried to decide what to do. After he'd fallen trying to remove the RAT sign, she'd felt so bad that she'd wondered if this game needed to end. If nothing else, she figured that she would apologize, they'd shake hands after which they'd both go about their lives, taking pains to avoid each other even though the feud was over.

But that was before he'd hung the PIG sign on her car. That changed everything. Forget about apologizing. Forget about the meek shall inherit the earth. Jenn Goodwin didn't do meek for anyone. If he wanted to play games, they would plan games, only they would play by her rules.

TEN

NoahMaitland@noahmaitlandesq

Revenge sounds so mean. That's why I prefer to call it returning the favor.

The following two days dragged by. He waited for something to happen in retaliation for the PIG banner, but strangely, nothing did. Maybe she was expecting him to make the next move. After all, he was the one who had been called a dung beetle. He was the one who got punched in the jaw. He was the one who'd had his most favorite body part insulted, so maybe she figured it was his turn?

However, he wasn't going to do it. He didn't want to play this game, or at least he didn't want to play it by her rules. The problem was, he wasn't quite sure yet what his rules were going to be.

Debra stuck her head in the door. "Noah? Did you call a plumber?"

What? "No, why?"

"Because there's one here who swears he was called in."

He rose and followed Debra into the reception room. Sure enough, standing by Debra's desk was a tall roly-poly guy, beer belly hanging over the waist of his dirty jeans, face looking like he hadn't shaved in four days. The guy scratched his chest.

"I'm sorry, there must be a mistake. I didn't call a plumber," he told the man.

The plumber reached into the back pocket of his jeans and pulled out a battered notepad. He stared at it for a long time, still scratching. Noah's hands twitched too, almost wanting to scratch in sympathy. "Twenty-nine-eighteen Queens Road?" the plumber asked.

"Yes."

"Which means this is the place."

"No, it's not. I didn't call a plumber," he said, shaking his head.

"Says right here in my appointment book you called a plumber." The plumber returned to scratching his chest.

Noah wondered if the guy had fleas. If so, they didn't need a plumber, they needed an exterminator. "I didn't call a plumber. My plumbing is all fine, I don't need a plumber, and I didn't call one."

"Well, maybe so, but still, I'm gonna hafta charge you for the trip even if you don't want me anymore. Time is money, ya' know."

"I didn't call you. It's a mistake. Someone gave you the wrong address."

The plumber sneered. "Don't matter. I'm here. I'll send you the bill. You better pay it or I'll be back." Turning, he stomped out.

Noah looked at Debra. She returned the look. "Should I not pay him?"

"Only if you want him, and his cooties, back in our office."

"I'll pay him," she responded.

"Good answer," he responded, and went back into his office.

He resumed working, determined to get something done to make some money, however, his mind kept jumping from the kiss—oh, man, that kiss—to the possibility of a truce between him and the leggy blonde next door. He pulled up Mrs. Potanski's file and began a list of the things they would demand from Mr. Sticky Wick.

Debra stuck her head in the door again. "Um. Did you call for an exterminator?"

"No."

She gave him a puzzled look. "Well, there's one here, and he said he had an appointment."

Once more, he stood and followed Debra into the reception room. Sure enough, a guy was in the front room, wearing bright green coveralls with a bag of equipment at his feet.

"I didn't request an exterminator," he interjected before the other man could say anything, although if he had requested an exterminator, he'd have made sure the guy arrived at the same time as the plumber and his fleas.

The green-suited guy frowned, opened a metal form holder and stared at it for a minute before looking up and asking, "Noah Maitland? Rat problem?"

Goddamn son of a bitch! Picking up the equipment bag in one hand, he wrapped his other hand around the guy's arm and practically shoved him out the door. "Sorry, Mac, I didn't call you, I don't have a rat problem—well, actually, I do, but the rat isn't here She's over at the godawful pink and purple thing next door. Sorry to waste your time. Goodbye." Handing the fellow his bag, he slammed the door in the exterminator's face before he could protest.

He went back into his office and sat down in front of his computer. What the fuck? He glanced out his window at the house next door, tapping his fingers. The plumber could have been an honest mistake. But the exterminator? And the comment about a rat problem.

It was possible it was a coincidence, however, he didn't believe in coincidences. Of course it was her.

Just on the off chance he was wrong, he could simply to go next door and ask the woman. But if he was wrong, it would give her more ammunition to humiliate him with.

On the other hand—the hand that mattered—going next door would give him the chance to ogle her legs again and maybe get an even better taste of her mouth, something he could only dream of under normal circumstances. He absentmindedly ran a finger across his lips, imagining her taste was still there.

He was still thinking about Jenn Goodwin's lips and that kiss when Debra appeared in his doorway once again, her brown eyes widened. Oh, crap on a cracker. Now what?

"Help," she pleaded.

No. No way. He jumped up and strode to the door.

"Happy birthday," someone shouted and threw a shower of pink glitter at him. It coated his hair, his suit coat, the rug.

"What the hell!" He tried frantically to wipe it off because glitter was the worst crap in the world to remove. It could take months. He glowered at the glitter thrower. *Holy shit.* Above the waist the guy was all clown, big red foam nose, blue and red and yellow fright wig, white clown makeup with a wide red artificial smile. Below the waist was a different story. Below the waist there was only one item on his tall, lanky body, a star-spangled G-string barely big enough to cover the guy's junk.

"What the hell!" he repeated, yelling this time. "Who the hell are you? What are you doing here?" The clown opened his mouth to answer, but Noah kept going with, "Forget it. I don't care what you're doing here. I want you gone. Get out."

"But it's your birthday," the clown whined. "I mean, you haven't even given me a chance to do my thing. Nobody ever kicks me out before I do my thing," he said and began singing the worst rendition of Happy Birthday he had ever heard, accompanied by an obscene bump and grind. The G-string slipped and things best undiscovered were laid bare.

"It's not my birthday. Get out!" Noah screamed, waving his arms like a maniac.

The singing stopped abruptly. "Well," the clown said in a huffy voice. "If you're going to be like that." Yanking his wig off his closely shaved head, he stuffed it into his G-string, at the same time tugging the G-string pouch back into place, thank God, stormed to the door where he stopped and turned to glare down his nose at Noah.

He gave his head a toss. "I hadn't even gotten to the best part yet," he sniped. "And now you'll never know what you missed." Spinning around, he marched out the door, skinny bare butt swaying.

Debra was quiet for a long time.

"What?" Noah growled.

A corner of her mouth twitched. "It's just that, when my kids moved out on their own, I was convinced my life was going to be boring. But wow, turns out working here is better than the circus. And to think, I'm getting paid for it." With a wave over her shoulder, she walked to the kitchen and disappeared.

JennGoodwin@MyHeart-2-Heart

Kissing burns 6.4 calories per minute. Wanna work out with me?

Jenn lightly ran a finger across her lower lip. Even after two days, it still tingled from that kiss, which irritated the heck out of her. It sucked that the guy was such a good kisser. It sucked that, now that the black eyes were looking more normal that the guy was drool-worthy. If there were any justice in the world, he'd be an ugly toad with bad breath.

Actually, it didn't bother her that he had all the goods—smarts, looks, great lips, because that made it even more satisfying when his comeuppance happened. Any minute now.

She grinned to herself and twitched the curtain aside so she could see the house next door.

A car pulled up in the driveway and a Joan Jett kind of woman driving a white Mercedes got out and went inside. Not one of the visitors she was waiting for. Time passed. Her feet started to hurt from standing, so she grabbed one of the side chairs in the lobby and pulled it over next to the window.

"Oh, for God's sake," Megan mumbled.

"Mind your own business."

"I'd like to, but you aren't including me in on this one. I deserve to know what's going on. I *need* to know what's going on? What if he comes over here and tries to kill you? Who do you think is going to save you? Me, that's who, so the least you can do is let me know what you've done."

Jenn gave her assistant a side-eye. The girl's lip was curled. Apparently, she believed vengeance should be shared. Jenn couldn't disagree. Vengeance was much sweeter when there were two involved in the plotting.

"Come see."

Megan rolled her chair over and they both sat back and stared out the window. "Tell me what's going to happen," Megan said.

Jenn smirked. "Nope. Much more fun if you see for yourself."

Finally, at five after eleven, a dirty pickup truck with the logo Grayson's Plumber emblazoned on the side, arrived. A slovenly guy climbed out and strolled up the sidewalk to Maitland's front door. The man entered. They waited. A few minutes later the plumber stomped out, got back in his truck, slamming the heavy door behind him, and drove away.

She got a confused look from her assistant.

Ten minutes or so passed. A green and white van with a giant plastic ant affixed to the roof drove up. A young man in green coveralls exited, walked up the stairs and entered the house. Within seconds he came scuttling out, looking bewildered and irritated. He stalked to his van and drove away.

Megan's next look was more puzzled than the previous one.

Eleven thirty arrived. A car pulled up. A tall, skinny, nearly naked, man got out and walked up the front walkway, his red, yellow and blue clown wig blazing the way.

Megan's eyes widened. "Oh my God."

Within seconds they heard yelling, then more yelling, then the clown sprinted out the door, down the front stairs and back to his car. He stopped for a minute to adjust his minuscule G-string because a few things had escaped, then climbed into his car and drove away.

Megan turned to look at her, her eyes big behind her glasses. "Maitland must be shitting his pants."

"Yep. Counting on it."

They both turned back to the window. They waited, watching the house next door, waiting for the expected explosion of angry man. The tension in the room was so thick they could almost taste it. Minutes passed and nothing happened.

Jenn idly twirled a strand of blonde hair around a finger. Maitland should be storming across the driveway by now so where was he? More time passed and yet nothing happened.

They waited another fifteen minutes. Still nothing. After another five minutes, her assistant shrugged. "Huh."

"Yeah."

Standing, her assistant wheeled her chair back to her desk and sat. "Go back to your office. If I see him coming, I'll warn you. In the meantime, I've got work to do."

Jenn waited another five minutes before meandering back to her office. What the heck happened? Where was the guy? Why hadn't he responded? It wasn't right. He should be having a cow right about now, yelling at her with those gorgeous lips. Criminy, the clown alone should have been enough. Did he not see them? Did the guys she hired not do their jobs?

Darn it, not knowing was killing her. She needed to know. She had to know. Jumping up from her chair, she strode into the reception room.

"No," Megan growled and sent her a glare hot enough to peel bark off a tree. She pointed a finger at Jenn's office.

Jenn turned around and went back to her desk. Holy cow. Who did the girl think she was? Wasn't Jenn the boss here? Wasn't she supposed to be the one with attitude? Somehow or other, Megan had usurped Jenn's attitude.

This wasn't fair. Her retribution had fallen flat and now her assistant was blatantly declaring a mutiny, and here she believed the girl was on her side.

After drumming her fingers on the arm of her chair for a few minutes, she fell back on an Amy technique. She pressed the intercom button.

"Intercom? Really?" her assistant grouched.

Jenn took a deep breath, attempting to inhale some attitude. More and more it seemed like her attitude thing was closer to Amy's wimpiness than to the badass 'tude Jenn had been trying for. Apparently, her skydiving and scuba diving and riding a motorcycle didn't count as attitude. Apparently, it was more about telling her own assistant who was boss. "Tell me if you see any action next door," she ordered and disconnected. There, that should do it. Straight-forward, decisive, boss-like.

The day gradually passed, but it was the slowest day of her life. She had three appointments which she took care of expediently, enrolling two of the three into memberships. After Megan went home for the day, Jenn still had one last appointment with a woman at six o'clock. By the time her appointment left, she was exhausted. Normally, she and Amy took turns working the evening hours and the weekends so neither one of them had to work more than a forty-hour week, But with Amy gone, she was doing double duty.

She collected the freaking dog from the kitchen and dragged her out to the car. The animal jumped in, not hampered by her three legs. Too bad she wasn't hampered; she'd be less of a pain in the butt.

Starting the car, Jenn gave the house next door one last look. His window was lit, and the silhouette of a man shone against the glass. Still working. Still hadn't reacted to her retribution. This was the third day in the last week that she had left late and seen Noah still in his office.

She frowned. It occurred to her that she'd never seen him smile. She'd seen smirks and curled lips, but no outright smile. Maybe he never had a reason to smile. Or maybe their ongoing war was the only fun the guy ever had. Or maybe she irritated him to the point where he'd never smile again. If so, that would be truly sad.

Regardless, based on what she'd seen so far, the guy was strung tighter than a snare drum. He needed to relax. He needed to have some fun. She got the feeling he didn't consider this game they were playing fun and it should be, even if it was sort of perverse.

She went home, watched a little TV, feeling a tad lonely, and for some reason, a little discombobulated. Sleep had been known to cure almost anything, so she went upstairs, brushed her teeth and slathered on the usual ton of face cream because there was the wrinkle thing. She went to bed and fell instantly asleep.

It was so hot, and she couldn't breathe, because his hand was on her breast, gently plumping it. His lips—magic lips—were on hers, seeking, caressing, making everything tingle.

She moaned when those magic lips descended and trailed down her neck. Good golly Miss Molly, so good. She clenched her thighs. The lips continued downward, kissing her collarbone, her sternum, the fleshy top of her breast. Oh, man, when was he getting to the good part?

She jerked awake. Her arms were around Trike, her lips pressed to the animal's nose.

The dog let out a long, sloppy-sounding snort. Every muscle in Jenn's body froze. The miserable beast was going to eat her. Flat on her back, she stayed rigid, not daring to move in case moving was a signal for death to descend.

Aggghh, she needed to get to work. Unfortunately, there was a sleeping dog on her chest. Wasn't there some saying to the effect, *Let sleeping dogs lie*? She'd always wondered what the phrase meant. Now she knew. Letting a sleeping dog lie meant hopefully not dying.

"Um... move," she ventured, trying her best to sound calm when really, she was freaking out.

The animal groaned, took a deep breath and heaved it out so her jellyfish lips flapped across Jenn's face. Shades of Ghostbusters. She'd been slimed.

Time dragged on. When she'd about given up, Trike lifted her head, yawned and stretched, digging her enormous claws into Jenn's side.

Then it all went to h-e-double hockey sticks. The dog shoved her face into Jenn's and snuffled a wet, slobbery snuffle. Her tongue, this long pink thing the size of a small ocean liner, lapped out and slurped across Jenn's cheek, licking off her face cream. The tongue rolled back into Trike's mouth. With a sigh, the dog slid her head into Jenn's hand lying open on the bed.

Oh my freaking God.

A few seconds passed while the dog lay there gazing blissfully up at Jenn. Reaching out one shaking finger, her heart in an uproar, Jenn touched the top of the animal's head. A loud moan, followed by a friendly woof, made her jump. Yikes! Jerking her hand out from under the dog, she leaped out of bed, went downstairs and opened the door for the beast to go out and do her business in the backyard.

Dear God. Going back to her bedroom, she showered and hurriedly dressed. The dog was waiting for her at the foot of the stairs when she descended. She wasn't even going to ask how she got back into the house. Instead, she leashed the dog and walked the two blocks to her mother's house. Why hadn't she done this sooner?

ELEVEN

NoahMaitland@noahmaitlandesq

The best moments are grandmother moments.

Debra stuck her head into Noah's office. She had that look on her face again, the one signaling trouble, and crooked a finger for him to follow her in the outer office. He sighed. It was barely nine o'clock, and he dreaded the idea that another parade of weirdos sent by Legs was about to descend on his peaceful day. Getting up, he followed her into the front office, not sure what to expect, but what he might have expected was miles from what he saw. Looking out the window, hands behind his back, feet planted a regulation foot and a half apart, shoulders squared, was a young, blond Yeti-sized state trooper.

Oh, fuck. What the hell had he done now? He played the events of the last few days through his mind, trying to find something that would cause the cops to come calling. Nothing came to mind.

The trooper turned to face him and held out a small photo. "Sorry to bother you, sir. There was a break-in down the street and we're looking for the suspect. Fortunately, their door cam got a pic—" The trooper's expression froze. George Washington's face on Mount Rushmore couldn't be any stonier.

Unnerved, Noah darted a quick look towards Debra, but she was no help at all. She shook her head, *'I don't know'*. He jerked his eyes back to the trooper who was now eyeing Debra.

The officer turned his gaze back to Noah then suddenly reached towards his gun.

Seeing the movement, Noah's heart leaped in terror, but instead of drawing his gun, the officer's hand kept going around his waist to his back pocket. He pulled out a cell phone and tapped on the screen. His eyes focused on the phone then glanced up to look at Noah, then back to the screen again.

With a tightening of his lips, the trooper refocused on Noah, his face getting even grimmer, if it was possible. "Sir. Are you the person who hung a *Cops are Pigs* banner on Ms. Goodwin's car?"

What? How did this guy know about that? Enlightenment struck. Crap, this was Jenn's policeman.

"Um."

"Are you also the person who covered Ms. Goodwin's taillights with the afore-mentioned banner, which is a violation and subject to a fine and possibly jail time? Are you that person? Answer me, sir."

He tried, he honestly did, however, he had nothing.

"And is this you?" he asked, once again tapped on the screen. A video began playing. He held it up for Noah to watch.

Noah stared, aghast. His own face, fury written all over it, filled the tiny screen. He watched the video of himself march across his lawn, climb onto the porch, throw off his shoes and coat before reaching for that heinous banner. Then the fall into the bushes. Repeated five times. In slow motion. This time with the music to *Chariots of Fire* playing in accompaniment.

"Are you this person?" the officer asked, jabbing a finger at the video.

What could he say?

A grin broke out on the cop's chiseled face. "Man, I gotta tell you, all us guys at the station think this is about the funniest damned thing we've ever seen. The only thing better would be if you were a politician."

Crap on a cracker. He'd forsworn getting revenge, but the desire to wring Jenn Goodwin's neck was back with a vengeance. He took a deep breath, remembered there was a cop standing two feet away, and the desire to murder subsided a little. Although, only a little.

The trooper shot a look towards Debra and gave her a wink. A corner of Debra's mouth tipped up.

"Oh, man, you should see your face just now," the trooper continued. "Damn, I wish I had a video of that too." He laughed.

"Ha-ha," Noah responded. Oh, yeah. The guy was a riot. Nothing more fun than an amused Bigfoot.

"So, you should know that what you did was illegal. I could arrest you, but because I got a good laugh out of this, I guess I'll let it go."

Well, gee, thanks. Asshole. At least the danger was past, so the dizziness started to recede, and he could almost breathe again. Stretching his mouth into an insincere smile, he tugged his jacket closed and buttoned it. "Thank you, officer. I appreciate it." Oh my God, was his nose brown or what? But crap. The law.

The cop had the nerve to chuckle. "Relax, man. This whole thing is funny, but it's nothing compared to what an ex-girlfriend did to me when we were dating, and she was pissed at me for forgetting her birthday. Women, right?"

Aha. So Mr. State Trooper was capable of making a mistake? He lifted an eyebrow, encouraging the man to share because anything to keep the behemoth laughing rather than writing him a ticket.

"Yeah, she put itching powder in my Jockey shorts. Man, it was brutal. I itched for a week. Believe me, I never forgot the woman's birthday after that in the four years we were together." The guy threw Debra another side-eye that seemed to say something, but he couldn't tell what, although Debra seemed to get it because her smile turned coy.

Noah gave a little shrug. "Okay, I'll admit, it was kind of funny." Not. "Except the part where I got stuck in the bushes. That was painful." He pointed to some of the scratches on the side of his neck.

The cop's grin got wider. His eyes danced with amusement at Noah's expense. Fine. Whatever. At least the atmosphere in the office had almost returned to normal, meaning he no longer wanted to punch the guy's lights out. In fact, he could almost imagine them being friends someday, like maybe a million years from now, after he had murdered the crazy lady next door, when having a cop for a friend might be helpful.

In the meantime, he smiled back, even though he was still thinking about how he was going to make Legs pay. "Can I get you a cup of coffee or a soda before you leave, officer?" He paused, wondering if he dared. Okay, he dared. "You have to be dying for something to drink. I mean, watching that video a dozen times must be exhausting," he said. Sarcastically.

The officer laughed. He got it. "Try fifty times. The guys couldn't get enough of it. Nothing like seeing a lawyer fall on his ass, you know."

Uh huh. Always happy to be the butt of a joke. No pun intended. "I get it. Now, how about a soda?" It never hurt to make nice with the law.

"Only because you insist." The trooper stuck his hand out. "My name's Lance Swenson, by the way." Turning, he held the same hand out to Debra. She took it, only this time, instead of a perfunctory shake, she got a lingering hold and a smile conveying volumes.

Letting go of the man's hand, Debra trotted into the kitchen and returned, carrying two cans of Coke and a box of donuts she'd brought in for Noah's clients. She handed the coke and the donut to Trooper Swenson, gazing up at him through her eyelashes. Eventually she remembered Noah was there too and handed him the second can.

Lance settled a hip on the corner of Debra's desk while he proceeded to tell them all about the many comments his YouTube video got from the other men he worked with, all the while munching on his donut and swigging down his Coke. Every so often his eyes would dart over to check Debra out and he'd smile.

Turned out, the trooper was a pretty good guy.

The topic moved on to the current standing of the Yankees, and they discussed how crappy they were playing this season while Trooper Swenson continued to sneak quick looks at Debra.

Fun times. To be on the safe side, Noah made a contribution to the NJ State Policemen's Benevolent Association. After a bit more chatting, Lance announced he had to get back to work. He walked out the door with a last smile in Debra's direction and another donut for the road.

His morning having been interrupted enough, Noah tried to focus on work. He finished submitting MaryAnn Potanski's petition and closed the file. His next step was to speak with the husband's attorney to see if they could work out something amicable, although he didn't think it would help.

A few calls came in, one of which was a referral whom he contacted immediately and made an appointment with. Each new client he received loosened the vice around his chest a little more, enabling him to breathe a bit better. He wasn't on the gravy train yet by any means, yet he began to feel like he might succeed.

Which didn't mean all his problems were solved. He still had the enormous challenge of his bloodsucking family looming over him. Speaking of his family, there hadn't been an email from his father yesterday. For some reason that made him extremely uneasy because, knowing his father, at some point the other shoe was bound to drop.

At least he couldn't expect any demands from Melanie as he just gave her four thousand dollars. As far as his brother, last he'd heard, Bret had scored some weed from an old buddy and was now holed up in his double-wide almost comatose. However, that could all change in a heartbeat.

And then there was Legs.

What was he going to do about Legs—er, Jenn? He'd vowed retribution yet, despite the additional irritation incited by Trooper Swenson, Noah's appetite for achieving revenge had waned while his appetite for the woman had increased correspondingly.

Of course, there was nothing saying he couldn't have both. He simply needed the right strategy.

Debra knocked on his door and poked her head inside. "It's like Grand Central Station around here. You have another visitor," she announced.

He groaned. "God, no. What is it this time? An earwax cleaner? A stripper, or God forbid, some church missionary type come to convert me? Did you tell them I only worship at the altar of money?" He didn't, however, saying it usually outraged them so much they left. It wasn't like he didn't respect them, but he didn't have time.

She nervously bit her lip. "No. It's your grandmother."

Oh, crap. He jumped up and rushed out to the lobby. His Gram, dressed in gray slacks and a soft, silky blouse, walked into his arms. Bending low, he gave her a gentle hug.

Pushing him away, she reached up to pat his cheek. "How are you, dear boy?"

He grinned. To his Gram, he would always be a boy, which was okay with him. "I'm fine."

"Hmmph. That's not what I hear from Debra."

He turned to stare at his executive assistant, eyes narrowed. Barely a week working for him, and the woman was already under his grandmother's spell. Debra gave him a rueful smile and lifted her hands in an exaggerated shrug.

Ignoring him, Gram walked into his office. She took a seat and pointed at his chair, indicating he should sit, like he was a six-year-old about to be scolded. That was his grandmother; a ninety-eight-pound steam roller. He hurriedly plopped down.

"Now, before we talk about what's going on here in your office, tell me what's happening with Melanie. I hear she's marrying that worthless Sam Erickson."

He heaved a sigh because he hated having people know about his mother's many disasters mostly because he hated talking about them. Saying it out loud meant he couldn't pretend they didn't exist. "Yeah, she called me from the airport. They're on their way to Vegas as we speak."

"And who paid for it, may I ask?"

Shame caused heat to ride up his neck and burn his face. He was tempted to lie yet he never lied to his Gram so... "Um. I did."

"Noah," she said, her tone of voice letting him know of her disappointment.

He ran a hand through his hair in resignation. Judges in court could censor him, clients could give him hell for not getting them what they considered a fair distribution of assets in their divorce, the media could trash him for any number of poor legal decisions, but nothing made him more ashamed than one of Tess Maitland's rebukes.

"I'm sorry. I can't seem to say no." He paused, trying to find the right words. "I don't know how to say no. I open my mouth and yes falls out… but, hey… I didn't give Bret any money the other day even though he begged and banged on my front door for five minutes," he offered up in hopes she'd buy the idea he was making strides.

Her face twisted into a skeptical *'big deal'* kind of expression. "Because he was going to use the money for drugs, right, and you draw the line at paying for him to break the law."

He rubbed a finger across his brow. "Well…"

"You need to stop enabling them." Lips compressed with disapproval, she shook her head. "Your problem is, in a bass-ackwards kind of way, you get more pleasure out of giving them money than they do getting it."

He opened his mouth to deny the accusation, but she talked over him.

"Which is unhealthy. On both sides. This has to stop. You need serious help."

He wanted to deny it, however, he couldn't. Because it was true. He gave her a sheepish look and a half-hearted grin of agreement, which meant within a week there would be some kind of therapist or interventionist here to help. Heck, knowing the lady, he wouldn't be surprised to find Dr. Phil at his door.

"You're right. I know you're right," he told her, however, in the back of his mind was still this image of his father starving to death for lack of money, his mother marrying some abusive asshole because the asshole could keep her in the land of day spas and BMWs, and his brother ending up in prison for selling drugs.

"Now that's settled, I want to hear about the shenanigans going on in your office this week, the one that involves that cute lady next door."

Okay, this was much more along the lines of what he'd like to discuss. He recounted how he and Legs learned they were going to be neighbors, how he'd chased her down Route 1 and the various dirty tricks they'd played on each other. By the time he was finished, she was doubled over with laughter.

"I think I like this girl." She wiped the tears from her eyes. "I want to meet her, officially that is. Introduce me."

His heart jumped into his throat. Because he liked the woman too, actually too much. He stared at his grandmother for a second, not speaking as scenes from their confrontation spun through his mind; the kiss, her fury, the kiss, his stupid stupid comment...

Oh, God, the look he'd seen on her face. Her face, her eyes, had held a look of stark betrayal. Then it had all changed, and she'd adopted her usual mask. He realized now that there were two Jenn Goodwins; the sassy confident woman who reveled in giving him shit, and the vulnerable woman he'd had a glimpse of the other day. Inexplicably, he wanted both of them.

Bullseye! suddenly sang through his brain.

For a second, he felt like he would pass out. Oh, crap. No. Really? *Bullseye?* Like his arrow had hit the mark. Like she was the One? Miss Crazy Pants? She couldn't be. Could she?

Bullseye! rang once again.

Oh fuck. How could she be the One? She hated him. He sighed, remembering the feeling of rightness he'd had when he kissed her, how his body had recognized her, how every bit of brainpower had fled for parts unknown, something that had never happened before. Oh, God, he was sure she was the One yet how was he ever going to know for sure when they seemed to be stuck playing this silly game?

"Gram, I don't see how it's going to happen. She hates my guts. She's more likely to stab me with a fork at this point than to say hi."

She smiled. "Oh, dear boy. You're so young. Haven't you heard—*hate and love are two sides of the same coin?*" She gave him an eyebrow wiggle. "Well?"

Well was right. The subject was so deep he was likely to drown in it, because he wanted to get to know this girl much, much better and he still couldn't figure out how he was going to do it. Of course, he still wanted to get revenge, only his kind of revenge was the kind that included kisses that left her reeling and unable to think about anything but him.

Casting his eyes towards the ceiling, he took the plunge. "I want to get to know the lady," he told her, and shook his head. "No, I want more than that. I want it all, but we seem stuck playing this stupid game."

His Gram laughed. "And you need help coming up with some torture?"

He frowned. "Well, I don't want to torture her."

"Oh, yes, torture. Just the right kind of torture." She rubbed her hands together. "Oh boy, this is going to be fun."

Half an hour later he had all kinds of great ideas for how he was going to torture his next-door nemesis until he had achieved his kind of revenge.

Plans made, he walked Gram to the front door. Once more, he bent and gave her a gentle hug, inhaling deeply. As usual, the smell of her talcum powder tickled his nose and brought up memories of when he was still young enough to sit on her lap and cuddle and how secure he'd felt, how loved and valued. She still gave him that feeling, however, now she also helped him keep his head on straight with her no-nonsense advice.

She patted his cheek. "Let's do lunch next week." With a quick kiss to his cheek and a final wink, she left.

He returned to his office. Sitting, he reviewed their conversation. Trust his grandmother to get right to the heart of the matter. He wanted Jenn in his life, yet he didn't have a clue how to make that happen. Gram's torture ideas would be fun and would make the woman sit up and pay attention, but they wouldn't hold her attention for long. For that, he needed to know who she was, where she came from, what she valued. What made her tick? Why this mask she wore that seemed to be ever present? He could only surmise that, somewhere, somehow, she had been hurt deeply enough that she'd felt the need to hide behind a brash façade.

Going onto his computer, he began a search. Being an attorney, he knew how to mine the internet better than the average person, so it didn't take him long to find something that made him sit up straight in his chair.

Son of a bitch. Her father had robbed an armored car. Taking a deep breath, he stared at the headline for a minute, greatly tempted to read the article and learn more. This had to be the reason for the shield she put up. He wanted desperately to know more, but prying would only make her slam the door shut. He closed the site without reading the details.

Debra poked her head into his office again. Now what?

"Noah, look out your window."

Turning his head, he did, and saw his Gram climb the stairs to the house next door and walk in. Oh. Crap.

TWELVE

JennGoodwin@MyHeart-2-Heart

Never go to bed angry. Stay awake and plot revenge.

She'd dumped the dog on her mom Leah, which was a dirty trick, but she couldn't take it anymore, not after waking up again with the drooly thing draped across her body. The fact that she was starting to like the dog was reason enough to leave Trike with Leah.

She gave herself a mental slap on the head. Knock off the avoidance ploy. Thinking about the animal was a lame excuse for *not* thinking about Mr. Attorney and his magic lips. Annoyingly, he still hadn't responded to her pranks. She didn't get it. Maybe she needed to up her game.

Megan barged into her office. "Jenn, a cop went into Mr. Rattorney's place, and he's been there forever. Great big tall guy with blond hair. Why would a cop visit our next-door neighbor?"

Jenn jumped up and rushed out of her office and over to her lookout post. A white cruiser with the typical red and blue flashers on the roof pulled away from the curb. Whoa. Maybe she didn't need to up her game. Maybe the game had upped itself.

She made room for her assistant by the window. "Whaddaya think?" she asked her. "Do you think he called the cops on us because of the rat banner?"

"No idea."

"How weird is that? Your description sounds like my cop."

"Your cop? You have your own cop?"

Well, poop. She hadn't told Megan about the cop stop. Now she would have to because if she didn't there would be another rebellion in the house of Heart-2-Heart and the business could only take so much rebellion. With Amy gone, the odds were now one against one, and one of those ones possessed a mean streak a mile wide. In essence, a very dangerous proposition.

Knowing she was beaten even before war was declared, she relented and told Megan the entire story of how she'd been stopped and almost ticketed.

Her assistant laughed. "You have to admit Mr. Rattorney putting our own banner on your car was excellent payback, and it certainly explains why you had to retaliate by sending all those weird people to his place." She rubbed her hands together. "So, I have one question. What's next?"

Walking into her office, Jenn crooked a follow-me finger over her shoulder. As her assistant, the girl was a real pain in the patootie, however, as a co-conspirator, she had no equal.

"Sit." Tapping her fingers on her desk, Jenn cast her eyes up to the ceiling, thinking. "Okay, I have an idea," she said and explained the details.

The girl bounced up and down in her seat like a two-year-old. Was Jenn ever that young? Well, yeah, she had been, and still was, because she was doing her own version of bouncing because she was so excited. She loved nothing more than a good dose of revenge.

"Ooh, let me, let me," Megan begged.

"You can do the research. I'll do the rest." Not looking happy about the rebuff, the girl left Jenn's office and came back a half hour later, a befuddled expression on her face.

"You have a walk-in."

"A walk-in?"

Opening the door a little wider, her assistant gestured to the woman standing directly behind her and allowed her to enter. Jenn studied the older lady as she took a seat. She looked vaguely familiar, but then, a lot of old people looked the same. It was that wrinkle thing, which was one reason why Jenn didn't want any.

The woman appeared to be in her sixties—not their usual client—with chin-length champagne blonde hair, light blue eyes and a smile that lit up the room. Dressed modestly, yet expensively, she wore slim tan trousers, a magenta silk blouse and was barely tall enough to qualify as an adult. The wrinkles Jenn was so afraid of were beautiful on this woman's face.

Her guest sat quietly, waiting for Megan to set two bottles of water on Jenn's desk and leave before speaking.

"So. Good morning." The older woman squirmed around in the chair, trying to get comfortable. "I'm Tess. I hope I'm not breaking any rules by coming in without an appointment. I'm a big believer in rules, you know, as well as due process and women's rights. That goes double for truth, justice and the American way. I also believe in taking accountability for one's actions, the ASP-CA, and loving one's children and grandchildren, but not necessarily paying to support them for the rest of their lives. So what do you believe in, young lady?"

"Uh," Jenn stuttered, her brain having gone into low gear, or even possibly reverse, with the deluge of information. She opened her bottle of water and took a sip, hoping to buy some time.

The old lady grinned, and Jenn realized, once again, the woman was strikingly beautiful despite her age and the soft lines on her face.

"Oh, well," Tess said, waving a hand, seeming to dismiss the topic when she still hadn't answered. "We can talk about it later, when you've had time to think."

Swallowing the water, Jenn shifted into first gear. First gear wasn't as good as being full throttle, but at least it was something. "No, it's okay. So what I believe is women is should be entitled to do whatever they want, whether in the workplace or to be a stay-at-home mom, so yeah, I guess women's rights. I believe in the Golden Rule, *do unto others as you would have them do unto you...*"

She sent a prayer upward at that bit of hypocrisy since revenge wasn't part of the Ten Commandments. "...standing up for one's values, and daring to try new things, even if it's a little scary. Like you, I also believe in due process, as well as respecting the law, although, there might be a lawyer...or two...I wouldn't include."

The lady's eyes twinkled. "Very nice. Anything else?"

She believed in every one of the things she listed, however, she'd left out the thing she most wanted for herself but was afraid she'd never have. "I believe in love, true love, that supports the rights of each individual to be who they are and encourages them to be the best they can be. I believe in fidelity and loyalty in relationships and I believe in love in sickness and in health." She paused then finished the last part in a soft whisper. "Until death does them part. That's what I believe, and it's what I want."

Her cheeks heated as blood rushed to her face. How in the world had they gotten into such an intimate topic so quickly and what in heck had made her regurgitate all her deepest, inner-most yearnings to a woman she'd just met? She cleared her throat. "Yeah, it's what I want... uh, for all my clients."

There was a pause then Tess slapped her hands on her knees. "Well, now we've gotten that out of the way, do you have any old farts you can fix me up with?"

Jenn coughed and took another big gulp of water. What a pistol. "I'm not sure. How old are you?"

"Old enough to drink and young enough to still have sex."

Water sprayed everywhere. Pulling a tissue from its dispenser, she mopped the water up off her desk and threw the tissue away. The delay gave her a few minutes to regain her equilibrium. Also, a few of the brain cells she'd spit out along with the water.

"Ohh-kaay. There's a pretty wide range there, like somewhere between twenty-one and Methuselah. Can you narrow it down a tad?"

"Seventy-two, young lady, but the old fart description is a misnomer. I'd prefer a young fart, if you don't mind."

Holy mackerel. She took another sip of water because she was having real trouble talking. "Uh, like how young? Sixty, sixty-five?"

The look of exasperation on Tess's face should win a prize. "Are you kidding me? Why would I want someone that old? I'm thinking more fiftyish. I loved my husband Hayes to pieces, but it's been a long, long time since he died, and if I'm going to go to the bother of having a man in my life, I want one who at least can get it up.'"

It must have been the shock because it didn't even hurt when Jenn's head banged down onto her Lucite desk. She had a sneaking suspicion this lady was going to be her Waterloo; an ignominious defeat resulting in death on a remote island. She stared at the white surface until her lungs worked again, and her tongue decided it had an actual function.

She lifted her head. "Okay. Fifty...ish. Any other preferences?"

Tess's face lit up. "Oh, boy do I," she said and went on to list them; not too tall, not too short (whatever that meant, it was probably in the eye of the beholder), fit, professional, likes sex, kind, generous, adventurous, interested in travel, likes kids, but doesn't want any more, likes sex, honest, good sense of humor, likes sex, supportive, emotionally mature, not rich but not poor. Oh, and he had to like independent women.

Jenn wrote as fast as she could, noticing how her guest slipped in the 'likes sex' thing, probably hoping it would go unnoticed, as if there was even a remote possibility given that the woman had already clearly stated she wanted a man who could 'get it up'. Good heavens.

Tess eventually wound down. "Will you be able to find those qualities?"

She had to smile. Ten minutes with Tess was like a day inside a hurricane but, because she was a girl who liked a wild ride, she was already half in love with this sassy lady. She was going to have so much fun finding her a match.

"I'm going to do my darndest, however, first things first. We need to sign you up, take a few pictures, a five-minute video, as well as filling out a more comprehensive questionnaire."

"Well, let's get to it," was the response.

"Megan," Jenn yelled.

As if she'd been leaning against the door, waiting for the call, the door opened. "Sign her up?" Megan asked, all innocence.

Hah, she had been listening. Sneaky thing. Jenn waved the older woman out towards Megan's desk, leaving Jenn alone. She shook her head. Wow. What a piece of work.

Speaking of work, there were applications in her inbox from at least ten clients expecting a match sometime in the next few days. She opened the first file, a man in his thirties who was seriously interested in marriage with the right woman. He was handsome, well educated—an attorney—and, if she remembered correctly, he had a great sense of humor. Other than the sense of humor, he was a lot like the guy next door.

Of course, Mr. Rattorney might also have a sense of humor, but after having his nose broken, his eyes blackened, and falling into the holly bushes, humor might have taken a holiday. With good reason.

Her door opened again, and her assistant entered. The girl's big brown eyes grew even bigger. He mouth hung ajar to catch flies.

"What?"

Saying nothing, Megan handed her the questionnaire she'd completed for Tess.

Jenn looked at Megan, puzzled, then glanced down at the questionnaire. And gasped. Her lovely little sweetheart of a feisty lady? Tess...?

...Maitland. Oh. My. God. Noah's grandmother. No wonder she'd looked familiar.

She stared at Megan. Megan stared back. "We're dead," they said at the same time.

There was a long silence then, looking both intrigued and somewhat amused, her assistant turned and went back to her desk, because why should she worry, she was only the assistant. Unlike Megan, Jenn was not amused. Was it a setup? Had he deliberately sent the woman over to spy?

What should she do? Refund her money? Reject her? The woman had paid the fee to join, plus Jenn liked her. Tess Maitland was adorable. Jenn hoped she was as beautiful and had as much spit and fire when she was over seventy.

On the other hand, maybe this was Noah's way of evening the score because when she added up the events and assigned points to them, Jenn was way ahead.

Three points for yesterday's weirdos plus a point for the rat banner. All Mr. Noah Maitland had to show for their feud was his Pig banner.

Oh. Wait. She'd forgotten about that wicked trick with her client. Did that deserve a point? She thought about it and decided, no, it didn't. That was prewar. The opening salvo, so to speak, so it didn't count. But then there was that kiss. Holy shamoley. How could she forget the kiss?

It shook her right down to her toes. Every part of her body, from her lips to her toes, and all the important parts in between, had ignited with lust. A definite four-pointer. Of course, he didn't know his kiss had rocked her world, so maybe he was still trying to even the score.

This was *so* not good. It seemed, without her knowing, he'd upped the game and declared World War III by bringing in his family.

She needed to get prepared; batten down the hatches, shore up the bulwarks, stock up on ammunition. Having made her decision, she went onto the internet and spent the rest of the afternoon researching more dirty tricks. It didn't make her any money, however, it definitely made her feel more in control of the situation.

She continued to work. Four o'clock arrived and Megan went home. Locking up, Jenn went to her car, keeping an eye on the house next door as she crossed the driveway. She didn't know what she expected, bombs to go off, boogie men to jump out from behind the bushes, but whatever Mr. Rattorney had planned, she needed to have a counterplan.

She drove to her mother's to pick up Trike. Her mom came to the door. At forty-nine, Leah Goodwin was a stunner, with shoulder-length natural blonde hair, a long, lean figure and a nearly perfect complexion she never exposed to the sun. It always gave Jenn a weird feeling to look at her mother. It was like looking at herself in the mirror twenty-some years from now.

Her mother was the strongest woman she knew and she wanted to be like Leah when she grew up. After the disgrace due to her husband's crime, her mother decided she needed to take Jenn out of Colorado. Too many people had heard what Randy Goodwin had done. Too many people had their hands out for the money they believed Leah had hidden away somewhere until the heat was off. Too many cops, FBI and Colorado Bureau of Investigation agents still circling around trying to catch her accessing the money.

Then there were the nasty people who bullied them because of Randy's actions, so they moved to New Jersey where Leah finished getting her degree in psychology and now had a thriving practice she ran out of her house while Jenn's sister, Emma, stayed in Boulder and finished college. The saying was 'living well was the best revenge' and Leah had proved it.

"I'm here to get the dog out of your hair," she told her mother.

Her mother shifted uneasily. "Oh, do you have to? Can't I keep her overnight?" she asked.

Was the lady insane? "Keep her overnight? Are you serious?"

Leah did one of those 'who knew' things with her shoulders. "I like the dog. She's great company."

Now she knew for sure her mother had lost her mind. "Mom, she's not good company, she's a monster. She tried to eat my toe, trapped me in my bed for an hour, knocked me on my butt and made me chase her around the playground until I slipped and fell in a mud puddle. She ate my bedspread. Oh, and my dining room chairs."

"Oh, that's typical dog behavior," Leah told her with a flip of her hand. "What with living in an apartment in Colorado which didn't allow dogs, we couldn't have one, but I've always loved dogs. I was even thinking of getting one of my own now that my new practice is off the ground."

Defeated and befuddled, Jenn threw her hands up. "Fine, keep her. Only don't ask me to buy you new furniture when she eats yours. Oh, and don't wear face cream to bed or you won't have a face left." Having delivered her warning, she drove home.

She got a great night's sleep and woke up refreshed the next morning. For the first time in almost a week she didn't have doggy breath in her face, and doggy drool down her neck and canine teeth nibbling on her toe.

In a scary kind of way, she missed it. Yikes.

Not needing to haul the mutt to work, she could ride her bike. Dressing in a pair of tight black pants, thigh-high boots and a silver knit top, she left her car in its parking spot and walked to her motorcycle. Grasping the tarp, she reverently uncovered her bike. *Oh, Harley, baby, I've missed you.* She wrapped her arms around the handlebars and kissed the glass-covered speedometer.

Once her love-in was done, she mounted up. She loved the steady vibrations between her legs—a feeling almost as good as sex—which brought to mind interesting things like wet kisses with tongue and big masculine hands on her breasts and a certain attorney's big thick male...

Ahem. Enough.

She had a busy day planned. Her first client appointment was with a man in his late thirties looking for a woman who liked opera and water sports and travel. It always surprised her when men sought their services because it seemed to her so much easier for men to meet women than vice-versa, but she'd learned the men who were willing to pay a hefty fee at Heart-2-Heart were past the point of indiscriminate hook-ups. It turned out, like their women clients, they wanted to find their forever love.

Lunch arrived, and so did her assistant. "Jenn, a package was delivered for you."

"What is it?"

The girl lifted her hands, like *no idea.*

Rising, Jenn went out to the front room to see. On Megan's desk was a large brown and pink polka-dotted box tied shut with a pink ribbon. Drat. Pink. Well, whatever.

She untied the bow and opened the box. Inside were several dozen obviously homemade cookies of all varieties: chocolate chip, peanut butter, oatmeal, ginger snaps, even a couple of macaroons.

She studied the box then looked at Megan.

Using a finger, her assistant pushed her glasses more firmly on her nose. "They're from him." She jerked her chin in the direction of Noah Maitland's house and handed Jenn the enclosed card.

Jenn read the card which had nothing written on it other than, 'From Noah'. They both returned to staring at the cookies. "Like...do you think maybe arsenic?" she questioned.

A shrug from Megan. "Could be. Or crushed bugs?"

"I dunno. Possibly. Or an overdose of pepper?"

"Or maybe he licked them and got attorney cooties all over them?"

Jenn curled her upper lip. "Ick."

"Yeah, ick."

They stared at each other for a while longer. Finally Jenn picked up the box and took it outside to the trash. Thanks but no thanks. She returned to her office and went back to work. No reason to take chances.

THIRTEEN

NoahMaitland@noahmaitlandesq

Ice cream is happiness condensed.

It had been a productive day.

Okay, fine, so it hadn't been very productive. Yes, he'd seen two new clients, and also connected with Mrs. Carter, a client from his old firm who had left her latest—fourth—husband and wanted Noah to handle this divorce too, similar to the first three. Try as he might, he couldn't keep his attention on his clients. He was too busy obsessing about the gorgeous woman next door and wondering how she'd reacted to his little gift. He wished he had a spy cam installed. Hell, he'd even settle for a baby monitor that would only transmit the audio. A guy could do a lot of toe-curling fantasizing with only audio.

The question was, would she think his gift was sweet and thoughtful, or would she believe it was another dirty trick? Popping a couple of M&M's in his mouth, he examined the situation as he crunched the candies up. He wasn't saying the cookies were a trick, however, he wasn't saying they weren't either. His Gram, whose idea the cookies were, could be a devious lady when she set her mind to it. Wasn't it good that those genes got passed on to Noah?

Debra left for the day, leaving him with a ton of work to catch up on because he'd been such a jackass, having spent most of the week dealing with bizarre drop-ins and obsessing about the blonde next door. With the office quiet, he made himself concentrate on finishing the paperwork for the Layton petition. Even in the midst of his work, he caught himself smiling as he imagined Jenn's reaction to his gift.

Six-thirty rolled around, time to leave. He shut down his computer, picked up his jacket and left the office, locking it behind him. Walking out to his car, he shot a look at the Heart-2-Heart house and spotted a small flock of birds fluttering around an open pink polka-dotted box sitting on top of a garbage can. He took a few steps closer, close enough that he could see the box was full of cookies.

Okay, that answered at least one of his questions; she thought it was a dirty trick. It must have driven her crazy, wondering if he'd sabotaged the treats, and if so, what form the sabotage took. Did she think he was trying to poison her, or maybe she suspected he'd put laxative in the cookies, or salt instead of sugar?

Or maybe they were simply cookies. He laughed. Damn, he couldn't wait to see how she reacted to his next gift.

Still chuckling, he got into his car and headed for his gym to meet Zach. It was a nice evening, the western horizon a wash of orange and coral and violet as the sun set. If nothing else, New Jersey pollution was good for one thing—great sunsets.

His phone rang. Grabbing it from the dashboard, he squinted at the number. Fuck. It was Melanie.

"Hi, Mom. How'd the wedding go?"

A shriek greeted him in response. He jerked the phone away from his ear until the noise abated to a more human level rather than the previous Tasmanian-devil volume.

"Whoa. Stop. What's going on?"

"That son of a bitch stole everything, my purse with all my money, almost four thousand dollars, and my plane ticket, and left me stranded here in Las Vegas. I can't check out of the hotel because I can't pay the bill. I don't even have enough money to buy lunch," she wailed. "I don't have any way to get home. Noah, please. I'm scared. I don't know what to do."

God damn it. He was sure her relationship with Sam was going to turn out to be a total shitshow. Fury erupted inside, at Sam for putting his mother in this position, at his mother for being so persistently willing to throw everything to the side so she could have a man in her life, at his own inability to help her, all of which made his hands shake so bad he had to pull over to the side of the road and stop. "Were your credit cards in your wallet?" he asked after taking a deep breath.

"Of course they were. Where else would they be?"

Shit. "How long ago did he take off?"

"The hotel said they saw him leave with his suitcase about an hour ago."

"Okay, first thing, I've got to cancel the cards," he told her. After promising he'd call her back even as she protested, he hung up. Because he paid her credit card bills, he had the information and was able to take care of the cancellation. He didn't order new cards. He might never order new cards.

He called her back and gave her the bad news that, without ID, she couldn't fly, so she would have to drive.

"I am not driving home!" she yelled when he told her.

"Too damned bad," he yelled back. He'd had it. "I have a friend in Vegas. He'll make arrangements for you to rent a car and loan you some money to get home. See you in four days."

He hung up, still shaking. God damn it. God damn it all to hell. Fuck. He pounded a fist on the steering wheel, then called his friend in Vegas to make arrangements for him to hire a chauffeur to drive Melanie home. His friend informed him that it was possible to fly without ID under certain circumstances—such as this one—but Noah decided to have her driven home anyway, even though it would cost a fucking fortune. Maybe it would teach her a lesson and keep her busy for the next four days with something other than bugging her son.

He called her back to give her the details of his arrangement, and to caution her to be careful driving as she couldn't afford to be stopped without her license. She was quietly crying. Damn it. He pressed a hand to his chest to ease the ache.

"I'm so sorry. It's my fault. You must hate me. If I hadn't been so stupid. If I hadn't been so stubborn. Why do I keep doing this? There's something wrong with me. I keep hurting you, over and over again. I'm nothing but a burden. Why do I do it? I don't understand." More quiet sobs followed.

He had to bite his tongue to keep from agreeing. "Mom," he said softly. "It's okay. We'll work it out. I'll call my friend back. He'll drive you home so you don't have to." He hoped he could figure out a way to help his mother because Melanie was right, there was something wrong with her. She needed help, professional help, and because he loved her, he'd offered to get her help before. If only she would take the help.

He wished he could change things. He wished she were someone different. He wished she was like other mothers. He wished he didn't love her so much.

Yeah, keep wishing, Noah. His mother was shallow and self-centered, and not terribly bright, yet he knew she honestly loved him—at least when she wasn't wrapped up with a new man—which is why he always forgave her. "It's going to be okay," he reiterated.

"Yes. I know. You always take care of me. You're a good son." She was silent but as he was about to hang up, she added, "If I'm going to spend four days in a car, I'm going to need some more comfortable clothes and money for food. Can you wire me a few thou? Please?"

Son of a bitch. She never quit. His family was killing him. Hanging up, he hurled his phone into the console next to his seat. Putting the car into gear, he pulled back into traffic and drove to the gym, stormed into the locker room and changed into his exercise clothing. He was late and Zach was already on the floor of the gym waiting for him. In the background were loud thuds as kickboxers connected with their opponents and the grunts of the cross-fitters as they moved through their routines.

"Ready?" Zach asked.

"No," he snarled. Turning, he struck a punching bag hanging nearby. A vicious front kick followed that made the bag sway violently.

"Noah. Shit, man, what the hell!"

He ignored his friend, delivering a quick one-two jab. The thuds echoed through the vast hollow space of the gym. He threw another roundhouse, putting all his anger into the motion. Another kick, and another. His breath ripped through his lungs, burning. Curses fell from his mouth.

Zach stepped forward, hands out, "Hey! Stop," his friend pleaded, but Noah continued to pummel the bag, kicking, jabbing, kicking. His heart hammered, his lungs strained, yet he continued the barrage of hits. Wham! Wham! His bare foot connected with the bag again. The bag swung wide, nearly striking someone walking by.

Lunging forward, Zach grabbed Noah's arms and pulled them behind him.

"Let go!" Noah struggled against Zach's hold, the anger inside him still hot and viral. His brain was filled with a red haze, his chest burned. He yanked one arm free, striking backwards, hitting hard bone.

"Fuck!" Zach exclaimed then spun Noah around and slapped him across the face, hard. "Noah! Christ. Whoa. Stop, man, stop! What the hell's the matter with you?"

Noah rocked back on his heels. Oh, fuck. What the hell. What the hell happened? What had he done? Bending, he put his hands on his knees, head hanging while he sucked air into his burning lungs. He could feel the heat of his rage still swirling in his blood. Slowly, eventually, it began to fade, leaving him ice cold, his hands shaking, his head pounding.

"Shit." He closed his eyes, trying to slow his racing heart. "Shit. Sorry. I'm sorry."

"Noah, what the fuck?"

All he could do was shake his head, unable to explain because he didn't know how to talk about the shit that was his life. He straightened and faced his friend. A trickle of blood crept down Zach's chin. Oh, God. Look what he'd done. Regret clutched at his throat.

Zach threw an arm around Noah's shoulders and steered him towards the locker room. "C'mon, man, let's get changed and we'll go get a drink."

Numbly, Noah allowed himself to be bullied into changing and walked out to his car. Numbly, he drove to the designated nearby bar to find his friend waiting, beer in hand.

"What was that back there?"

"I don't know. Honest to God, I don't know. I'm so sorry. Did I hurt you? Are you okay?"

Zach gently fingered his chin. "I'm fine. You know I can take care of myself, but what the hell was that about?"

He shook his head. He wished he had the right words to explain. He let the silence build before the words tumbled out without his volition. "I can't do it anymore, but I don't know how to stop it. I feel like I'm being sucked dry, one drop of blood at a time." He took a deep breath and went on to tell his best friend—other than his Gram—about his mother's situation.

Zach scratched his ear. "Yeah, it's a problem. There's gotta be a solution. Lemme cogitate on it, okay?" The thing about Zach was he listened, and he didn't merely listen with one ear while he was thinking about how much work he had in the office or the fight he'd had with his wife, or the game he was missing on TV. The guy thought about what he was listening to. When he said he would think about it, he would, and maybe he would come up with an answer.

In the meantime, Noah was grateful to be able to vent.

Pulling a package of M&M's out of his pocket, he shook a few onto the table and pushed them in Zach's direction, his way of apologizing. The guy grinned and popped them into his mouth.

His plan had been to treat Zach to a few beers, hopefully get a little drunk. however, now he was rethinking the plan. He wanted to forget about his blood-sucking family, not die. With the mood he was in, getting drunk would put him at serious risk of having an accident that could end in death. When it came to defending his clients, he was willing to risk his all. Physically? He liked all his body parts functioning normally and right where they were.

They spent a half hour or so nursing their beers and talking about the vacation Zach and his family were taking in a few days. Ten o'clock arrived, so they called it a night.

Having worked out some of his anger and frustration, he went home, gave Iggy some kale and spinach, refilled his bowl with pellets, and went to bed.

He woke up the next morning, his eyes burning, a mild headache throbbing in the back of his head, his mouth doing a good imitation of the Mojave Desert, complete with cactus. First thing he did was check his emails for any emails from his dad, because that weird itchy feeling on the back of his neck had been getting itchier as time passed with no communication. Still nothing.

He put those concerns aside in favor of his more present and immediate concern, the woman he couldn't stop thinking about.

It was Saturday, technically not a workday so no real reason to go into the office. His business hadn't reached the level where he needed to work twenty-four/seven.

He wondered if she would show up at work today. He stared at the ceiling for a while, mulling over the *ifs, ands* or *buts* of his question. Should he take a chance and go to work in the hopes of seeing her?

He examined the idea for a few more minutes. Okay, to be completely honest, he would love to see her because of the dreams that he had last night? He was shocked when he woke up this morning and his sheets didn't have scorch marks on them from how hot those dreams were.

Back to the subject, the reason he was considering going into work was because he didn't want a two-day gap between the delivery of cookies and his next surprise. Too much could happen before Monday.

He went to the office.

Given the covert quality of his plan, he parked around the corner and walked the rest of the way. The first thing he saw when he reached his front porch was her sleek black Harley in the driveway. There was also a big SUV parked on the pad out back, but a woman exited the house while he watched, got into the vehicle and left. Her assistant's car wasn't there, which meant his target was alone.

Going immediately to his office, he arranged a delivery, paying them double to guarantee his request would arrive in the next hour. He opened his window so he could hear what was going on outside and waited.

Within thirty minutes, a white minivan pulled up in front of the pink and purple bungalow. He watched a young woman get out carrying a paper sack and knock on the side door. The door opened.

Jenn appeared. Damn, she looked soooo fucking good. Appropriate for riding her bike, she wore tight black jeans that clung to every inch of her spectacular legs, brown ankle boots and a black t-shirt clinging to breasts only marginally behind her legs in terms of spectacular-ness.

Oh, man. His mouth watered simply looking at her. Somewhere lower down, a major inferno ignited, making him break out in a sweat. Fuck, he wanted her. He wanted to kiss those pouty lips, run his hands through her silky blonde hair and be inside of her. The idea of her kisses, her heat, her tight vag gripping his cock, had him running a hand across himself through his jeans. This weird bubble, a combination of excitement, anticipation and lust, filled his chest.

Yeah, he wanted all that. Yet more than the sex, he wanted to spend hours talking with her, getting to know her, learning about her dreams, her fears, and especially the insecurities so he could offer support. He wanted her to trust him enough to talk about her dad.

So far, not so good. He didn't know if teasing her would get her to trust him. He hoped it sent the message, "I'm thinking about you. I care that you're happy," but if nothing else, he hoped it would make sure she remembered him, wondered about him, and maybe it would even motivate her to come stomping over here so they could kiss again.

Even from his window, he could see that she looked confused at the delivery, however, she took the package and disappeared inside.

A few minutes passed. The door opened again, and Legs exited, carrying the quart of ice cream he'd had delivered. Her long legs took her to the large trash bin pushed up against the side of the house. She flung the lid up and lifted the arm carrying the carton, preparing to hurl it inside. She stopped in mid-hurl. Her hand, holding the carton, hung suspended for a few seconds. She lowered it. Her head turned, first to the right towards his window then to the left towards the street where he had parked his first day. Her tongue darted out, and she licked her lips.

Inside his pants, his cock jumped.

She pried the lid off the carton then, probably checking for the bitter almond smell of cyanide or the sweet odor of rat poison, she lifted it to her face and sniffed it with first a look of suspicion on her face which was replaced by a look of total ecstasy.

Oh. My. Holy. Fucking. God. His cock was going to incinerate. Every muscle in his body tensed. He grit his teeth against the urge to release himself from his pants and stroke himself to completion, but he didn't because there was still so much to see. There was no way he'd be able to concentrate on watching her if he was busy jerking off since he generally closed his eyes when he came. His hands shaking, he readjusted himself and continued to spy.

She rubbed her nose against the carton again, the look on her face like a four-year-old afraid of getting caught sneaking into the cookie jar. One more sniff and she jammed two fingers into the ice cream, scooped out a giant blob of the chocolate caramel swirl stuff and shoved it all into her mouth.

He slapped a hand over his mouth to stifle the laughter that threatened.

Her head tilted back, her eyes closed in bliss, her throat moved as she swallowed. Her tongue flicked out and licked her lower lip.

His eyelids slammed shut. He would dream about that look for the rest of his life, or at least until he could cause the same look when he was inside her. He opened his eyes in time to see her bite her lip and stand there for a minute, her hand to her stomach, possibly waiting to see if she was going to fall over dead. When some time passed and she still stood upright, those fingers dipped into the carton again and lifted more of the creamy treat to her mouth. She repeated it again, and again. It was a small container, and soon she was scraping the sides for the last gooey drops.

Lifting the carton, her tongue darted out and licked the inside. He almost had a coronary imagining her little pink tongue on his cock. A few more seconds passed while she stared at the carton in her hand and the look of pleasure on her face morphed into one of exasperation.

"Darn it!" she shouted. "Stupid, stupid, stupid." She stamped her foot and hurled the empty carton into the trash bin. Spinning around, she practically ran to the Harley. Settling her helmet over her gorgeous blonde hair, she started the engine and was gone.

He couldn't remember the last time he'd had so much fun. Which was why he was going to have to wait a while before he walked back to his car.

FOURTEEN

JennGoodwin@MyHeart-2-Heart

Payback's a...female dog.

The next morning Jenn woke up to the dog draped over her neck. Trike opened her one good eye and stared at her. Grimly, Jenn stared back.

"Woof." Drool slithered out of the dog's mouth and landed on Jenn's cheek. Ick. "I hate you," she told the animal. The dog smiled. Dogs weren't supposed to smile, yet this one did, and gah, the stupid beast was kinda cute when she did. Jenn sighed. She was doomed.

Nudging the dog to the floor, she rose, showered then parked her backside on the couch and turned on the TV. Trike draped herself across her lap and watched TV too. The dog seemed to have very particular tastes in TV fare. The Smithsonian Channel got a groan, Investigative TV got a messy sneeze that sprayed goo everywhere, and HGTV Small Interiors got a loud fart. She had to agree with the dog on that one.

The day ground by. Life was not going at all the way she had planned. She couldn't seem to focus on anything except the events of the last few days, especially that kiss. It was almost like the container of chocolate caramel swirl ice cream she'd eaten had something more in it than cream and sugar and chocolate flavoring, like the carton had contained some kind of secret potion intended to cast a mysterious spell over her so all her thoughts would be about what's his name, Mr. Rat.

Nah, that was crazy. There was no such thing as potions or spells, and anyway, who would do something like that? It would take someone completely evil and conniving and totally vengeful.

Come to think of it...

Criminy, the man had sent her stuff, things designed to make her crazy, like he wanted to torture her. First cookies and then the ice cream from Brando's, the shop in Princeton that hand-made all their ice creams and gelatos. Why? What was he after? What did he hope to accomplish? Was he screwing with her? Maybe. It would certainly fit in with the evil and conniving thing. It was like he was purposely trying to make her think about nothing but him when she wanted to think of anything other than him. What was he going to do next? Even the prospect of his next move terrified her. He was screwing up her attitude, him and his hot lips and his sexy body and the come-hither look in his eyes.

Not knowing what else to do, she walked into the kitchen, pulled out the container of chocolate caramel swirl ice cream that she'd picked up on the way home yesterday, dug a spoon in it, pulled out a scoop of the icy goody, and licked it into her mouth. Oh. My. God. Sooo smooth. So rich. Sooo tantalizing on the tongue. Which only made her think about Noah even more. She clenched her thighs together against the throbbing between her legs when the cool stuff slid down her throat.

Trike sat at her feet, staring. She stared back. No way. Dogs didn't get to eat ice cream. Dogs especially didn't get to eat ice cream that might be some new kind of aphrodisiac.

The animal stared some more. Well, shoot. She let the dog lick the spoon after making sure there was no chocolate mixed in, got a fresh spoon and ate a few more spoonsful.

There, see, look what that Noah Maitland had done to her. He'd completely ruined her. She hated ice cream, and here she was eating ice cream. Not just any old ice cream, but the same flavor he'd had delivered from Brando's. And, oh my god, she was even liking it.

Ack! He *had* cast a spell on her. She was doomed.

No, wait. She refused to be doomed. Jamming the lid back on, she opened the trash can and prepared to throw the carton away.

Uh, well....

Shoot. She put it back into the freezer. Who knew? Maybe she'd need it for evidence—or something—at some point in the future.

Exhausted from doing nothing, she plodded upstairs and laid down on her new bedspread. Trike jumped up onto the bed, circled a few times and flopped down with her head on Jenn's chest.

They both fell asleep. Thank god the weekend was over.

Monday morning Trike cried when Jenn dropped her off at Leah's. She walked back to her house, got on her Harley and rode to work.

Her assistant was already at her desk, typing something into her computer when Jenn, attired in her black jeans, strolled in.

"How was Saturday? Anything good happen?" Megan mumbled, her fingers clacking away on the keyboard.

Jenn opened up her mouth, prepared to tell her assistant about Saturday and the chocolate caramel swirl ice cream, from Brando's no less, the most expensive sweet shop in town, but she snapped it shut because she knew how that conversation would go:

"He sent ice cream?" Megan would say accusingly. "Chocolate caramel swirl? Then where is it? What do you mean you ate all of it?" Then desk drawers would slam, and feet would stomp, and someone's assistant would get that mulish expression on her pretty face because she had been treated like...an assistant.

Yep, that's what would happen, and Jenn didn't want to hear it. Megan was a wonderful assistant, however, as a co-conspirator, the girl was messing with Jenn's attitude.

So, the answer to the question was, "Oh, Saturday was fine. Nothing happened."

Megan cocked an eyebrow, her bored expression indicating she wasn't impressed, and kept typing.

Jenn slunk into her office, a little angel on her right shoulder shaking his finger *naughty, naughty* at her, the devil on the left chortling with glee.

The devil knew the deal; Jenn was going to hell.

Her mind still preoccupied with the ice cream and her guilt and thoughts of yummy manly lips, she surveyed the pile of folders on her desk, all of them filled with photos and the four-page questionnaires clients completed so Heart-2-Heart could do the best possible job in finding each person their ideal match. She reached for a file in the pile. And stopped. For some reason, her fingers didn't pick up that file. Instead they moved the pile aside to uncover the one on the bottom.

Tess Maitland.

Should she? She still didn't know if the woman wasn't some kind of trap Noah set for her, a woman who'd been sent to spy or catch them in some kind of chicanery although it didn't seem likely. She had seemed so genuine, so totally who she presented herself to be.

What the heck. If Tess Maitland wanted a man, Jenn was going to find her a man. One that could hopefully *get it up*, although she wasn't positive how she would determine that particular feature.

In no time at all, she found three candidates that might fit the bill. Her number one pick was Bruce Harris—fifty-eight, a radio announcer for a major New York City station that combined music from the sixties through the nineties with talk on topics like the current elections or recent scandals. During his interview, she'd learned that he was energetic, had a great sense of humor and was looking for a mature woman, one who was smart and hadn't stopped growing intellectually. Whether he excelled in the bedroom, she would leave for Tess to discover. She dialed Bruce's number.

"So," she started out. "I may have the perfect person for you, however, I need to ask something first."

"Okay, ask away."

"Um...are you..." Hoo boy, the question, *can you get it up* was burning on the tip of her tongue, but she squashed it and went with, "...okay with an older woman?"

"How old?"

"Early seventies, but she's stunning, fun, smart, and she has some interesting hobbies." She went on to tell him about Tess, still omitting the part about his performance in bed, finishing with, "If I were gay, I'd date her myself."

He laughed. "She sounds intriguing. Can you send me her video and her information? If I like what I see, I'll call her."

Excitement filling her, she sent the file and hung up.

Megan appeared in the doorway. "Uh, Jenn? Can you come out here?"

Oh no. Now what? Pushing her chair aside, she left her office and joined her assistant who stood next to her desk staring at an enormous box opened to reveal row after row of filled chocolates. The box was pink, while the frilly cups holding the delicacies were made of silver foiled paper.

Just like last time, they both stared at the box for long moments, neither saying anything.

Of course they realized who it was from, however, neither wanted to say it. Still, somebody had to say something eventually, so it may as well be her. She was the boss, after all, the one who was supposed to have attitude, although this third delivery was beginning to erode said attitude. "From Mr. Rat?" she asked in a whisper, still sticking with the fiction that Noah Maitland was the guy she wanted to get revenge on.

"Yep."

Side by side, they stared some more. Finally, still being the boss, darn it, she rendered a judgment call. "He's trying to kill us with kindness."

"Yeah. Not fair." Megan's mouth pursed into a tight knot.

"I know. He's changed the rules. It's like he's cheating." Worse than cheating, it was like he'd declared war, only it was an entirely different kind of war than the original one. This was a war of seduction. Totally wrong.

"Do you think it's a trap?" Megan whispered.

She shook her head. "No."

Her criminal cohort shot her a quick look from the corner of her eye. "Okay, then maybe...Do you think...? I mean, we never tested the cookies so...?"

"No, the cookies weren't," she said. She didn't believe the guy was trying to poison her any longer, but he was definitely irritating the heck out of her. He was also making a few unmentionable female parts do the happy dance.

"How do you know for sure?"

"Because neither was the—" She stopped, realizing what she was about to disclose.

Her assistant's eyes zeroed in on Jenn. "Neither was what?"

Jenn could feel her entire body shriveling. She forced her mouth up in a smile, but it was a lousy, half-hearted smile that wouldn't fool a two-year-old.

"What else did he send?" her assistant demanded, eyes narrowed threateningly. "Tell me."

"Ice cream?"

Turns out that thing called an Irish temper was true. The girl let out a shriek. "And you ate it, didn't you! You ate the entire carton and you're still alive and you didn't save any for me! And you hate ice cream."

"No, I don't." She glanced towards the window, avoiding her assistant's eyes.

"Yes, you do. You've said so a million times."

She had. She totally had. "Well, it wasn't like it was just ice cream. It was chocolate ice cream with tons of ooey-gooey caramel swirls and you know I love caramel."

"Really, Jenn? Really?

Jenn hung her head.

"How could you?" Megan jammed her fists onto her hips.

Darn. This girl was *so* not good for her attitude. "I couldn't help myself," she whined. "I smelled it and it smelled like caramel, and I tasted it and it tasted like chocolate, and you know I love chocolate, and then I hit this layer of thick caramel that *ooooozed* off the spoon and it was like something possessed me and I couldn't stop myself and I ate the whole thing." Looking up, she gave Megan a wide-eyed look, hoping for sympathy.

What she got was a gasp. "Oh, my God. You drank the Kool-Aid. You've gone over to the dark side. I'm so ashamed of you."

She was ashamed of herself. Sort of. Alright, she wasn't, however, Megan would never let her forget it if she said so. She drew her shoulders back. "You're right. It was a terrible, terrible thing that I did, and it will never happen again."

Well, dang it, it might, because every lick, every spoonful of that ice cream had been nearly orgasmic.

"Good," Megan said. Picking up the pink lid, she shoved it on over the box, stalked outside to her car, opened the door, put the box inside and slammed the door shut. Using her key fob, she beeped the lock shut and stalked back inside. She threw herself into her chair.

"Now go away, you traitor, and make amends," the girl growled.

So Jenn did, but she had this sneaking suspicion that those chocolates Megan put into her car would somehow end up in Megan's mouth.

She tried to go back to work, however, her mind was filled with images of chocolate bonbons, and ice cream and gray eyes and firm lips that had this delicious smirk right before he kissed her. Those lips, especially, were a distraction. Simply thinking about those hot lips on hers made her heart pound, her blood heat, and certain parts of her body clench and throb in anticipation.

Aggghh. This needed to stop. Think about something else, like whether those candies and the cookies and the ice cream were nothing more than one of those really, really long set-ups to the ultimate practical joke.

For some reason it seemed like he'd decided he wasn't going to take revenge on her. It was more as if he intended to torture her with romantic attention.

Even worse, how could she retaliate? She couldn't, in fact, she didn't want to. Like, was she going to send him flowers or candy, or even, like one of her clients had suggested, deliver a toe-curling blow job?

Wellll...

Okay, no. Even Megan, when Jenn verbalized the options, answered, "I vote for sending him candy. At least that would be tax deductible, but I'm sure there's no line item on your 1040 for blow jobs."

Okay, so Mister Maitland had changed the game.

Fine, she was flexible. No reason she couldn't go with the flow. Why shouldn't she enjoy the hotness that was Noah Maitland? Kissing a hot guy wasn't the same thing as having a relationship, right? In fact, she didn't even have to like the guy. It could be just sex.

Just-sex was exactly what she needed. Just-sex didn't betray a person. Unfortunately, keeping it just-sex could be kind of tricky.

Getting up, she paced around her small office. The problem was that she had started to like him. She didn't want to like him. Liking him meant he could hurt her in the end.

That only left one thing, the original thing—revenge.

The day dragged by. Megan, after delivering her view on the blow job, had retreated back into her turtle shell of silence. Still didn't mean the guy was getting a blow job.

"Megan!"

Her assistant appeared in the doorway, still looking truculent. "Yes, Miss Goodwin?"

"Oh, knock it off. I'll apologize some more, later when I have time to think up a good apology, but right now, I need your brain to help me come up with a way to retaliate. Something really torturous." The image of his reaction made her chortle with glee.

"Oh, good. After taunting us like that, we need to torture the heck out of him."

Maybe yes. Or maybe no. It depended on what one meant by torture. And what the ultimate results of that torture was.

FIFTEEN

NoahMaitland@noahmaitlandesq

Old people love to give good advice, it compensates them for the inability to set a bad example.

He wasn't sure when it would happen, which didn't mean he was ignoring the fact that the shit would hit the fan at some point. Yet several days passed, and nothing had happened. Jenn came and went without even a glance in his direction and still nothing.

Using the tip of a finger to push a yellow M&M to the side, he popped a red one into his mouth. He hated the brown ones. Yeah, yeah, he realized they all tasted the same, so his bias was stupid, but it was his bias, and he was going to keep it.

His office door swung open, hitting the wall behind it and scaring the crap out of him. His Gram sashayed in. There was no other word for it. The woman sashayed. Her arms swung back and forth exuberantly, causing her low-cut peach-colored blouse to inch down even lower, her hips pistoned in a sexy shimmy, a shit-eating grin lit her face and there was this spark in her eyes.

If he didn't know better, he'd think she'd had sex...

Nah. The woman was seventy-two-years-old.

She threw herself into one of his client chairs, crossed her slim legs, and leveled that shit-eating expression on him. "So, what would you say if I told you there's still life after sixty?"

He blinked at her. "Of course there's life after sixty. I mean, look at you. You work out every day, you take classes to keep your mind sharp, you play poker with your friends once a week. Heck, you're even learning to play the drums, not exactly a senior citizen instrument."

She wiggled in her chair, looking inordinately pleased with herself. "Yes, and Susan, Laura, Jean and I plan on starting a band when they get a little better on their guitars, but that's not what I meant."

He lifted a brow. "I see. So what did you mean?"

Casting her eyes up to the ceiling, she pursed her lips. "I'm talking *'life'*."

"Yeah. Okay. You said that. So?" he said.

She threw her hands in the air. "Oh, for heaven's sake. Don't be so dense. I'm not talking quilting bees and gardening and scrapbooking, I'm talking *life*. Life—like there's still pep in my step—"

Sure, his Gram was definitely a peppy lady for a senior citizen.

"—like I still like a bit of the old crumpet—"

Crumpet? When did his Gram start liking crumpets? Did she even know what a crumpet was?

"—as in there's still a lot of gas in my tank—" He frowned. The thought that they weren't discussing his Gram's Chevy Malibu rippled through him.

"—you know, I mean I'm still up for a little afternoon delight—"

He gaped at her.

"—a bit of the horizontal polka."

"Gram!" He jumped up out of his chair. "Are you talking about sex!"

"Well, of course I'm talking about sex."

"Gram!" He stared at her, his mouth hanging open. What the hell? Really. What the hell?

"Well, for heaven's sake, I'm seventy-two, not dead. So, I've met a man, and guess what, he likes a little sumpin' sumpin' too, although we've only gotten as far as the sumpin'."

"I mean...you're you know you're..." He cleared his throat.

His grandmother glared at him. "If you say 'old', I will smack you into next week."

He gulped. She would. She had a mean right hook for a little lady, which she'd never hesitated to use on the back of his head when she was displeased with his behavior back when she could still reach the back of his head.

The idea of his Gram having sex was enough to make him groan, but he didn't want to risk that right hook so all that came out was, "But, Gram, why? I mean, Grandpa," which wasn't even a rational question. Or even a complete sentence, for that matter.

Her expression sobered. "Noah, sweetheart, you know I loved your grandfather, but he's been dead for over ten years. I'm not dead and I don't want to be alone anymore." She paused for a breath. "I don't know how many years I have left on this earth, but while I have them, I want someone of my own to love. I miss having a man, I miss a man holding me, kissing me."

He opened his mouth to say something, he didn't know what, but she didn't let him talk.

"I know you love me, but it's not the same. I miss having a man, a partner. I miss having a man love me."

His eyes burned. How come he didn't know that? What a selfish shit he was. Had she been unhappy all those years? The possibility made his heart ache.

He took a deep breath and marshaled his thoughts. "Okay. Okay. So you met a man. Great. Great. I mean, great. Uh, though, I'm concerned about what kind of man he is. What do you know about him? How did you meet this guy? Did one of your friends introduce you?"

That coy smile reappeared. "Oh, no, that nice girl next door—Jenn—found him for me."

He leaped from his chair. "What?" he bellowed. "Legs matched you up with some random guy? Who could be anyone? Like an axe murderer. A pervert?"

She blinked. "Well, of course. You know I went over there the other day. What did you think I was doing over there, knitting booties?"

His mouth flapped. "I...I...I..." A red haze filled his vision. That woman! He was going to kill her. "Wait here," he ordered and stormed out of his office.

It took him less than thirty seconds to cross over their driveways, thrust their front door open and slam inside the cute pink and purple Victorian house.

"Where is she?" he yelled.

The redhead—the one who was her partner in crime—jumped. Her eyes big, she pointed at the door behind her. "Jenn?" she called, her voice quavering. "Someone here to see you." She snickered.

Jenn appeared in the doorway. Her eyes widened when she saw him.

"What did you do?" he yelled.

"What?"

Oh my God. Her mouth did that thing—that *kiss me now* thing—when she said *what*. Fuck, he should have nicknamed her Lips instead of Legs. "Don't give me that crap, what? You know what I'm talking about."

"I don't," she answered, however, something flickered across her face, and it was totally apparent that she did.

"You fixed my Gram up with a man, some totally random man." His Gram, his sweet, innocent Gram, with a strange man who could harm her, take her away from him. Twenty years of memories with his Gram being the most important woman in his life crowded into his mind.

"Well, yeah—"

"What do you know about this guy? What if he's some kind of kook?" Twenty years of hugs when he was sad, and all the pats on his back when he faltered. It could all be wrecked by her subversive matchmaking.

"Listen—"

"How old is he?" He paced around the small space, running his hands through his hair. "What does he do for a living? What if he's some kind of criminal?" Twenty years of late-night talks simply to touch base.

"I—"

"Where did he come from?" If his grandmother was hurt, it would be his fault. He was the one who decided to rent a house next door to this crazy lady. "How long have you known him?"

She crossed her arms over her chest, looking a little irritated. Her foot tapped. "He could be a pedophile. He could be a con artist." He could be one of those serial killers, although maybe not, they generally liked younger victims.

She was glaring at him now, her eyes shooting darts. Damn, she had the most gorgeous blue eyes. "We do a criminal—"

"They had sex!" he yelled, throwing his hands in the air.

She went still. Then one corner of her mouth rose, almost like she was smiling. "Really? Yay."

He was going to kill her! He reached out, aiming for her neck, determined to choke this crazy woman dead, but his hands didn't seem to care that the only way to get the job done was to wrap around her neck. No, they went right for her slender waist and the next thing he knew, she was in his arms and those lips of hers were under his—and oh, God they tasted good—and her tongue was in his mouth and it was going after his tonsils.

She moaned. Her arms circled his neck, her hips bumped up against his. He hardened. Like a stone. Haze swept through his brain, obliterating every sensible thought he'd ever had. The only thing left in his feeble little mind was an image of those long, long legs of hers wrapped around him like a couple of boa constrictors while he drove into her and made her shout his name.

Her hands tightened in his hair, her mouth devoured his. She ground against him. His hands shook, he locked his knees because all he wanted to do was collapse onto the floor and have wild crazy sex with her.

He heard that little voice again. *Bullseye.*

"Ahem."

Grabbing her ass, he hoisted her a little higher. Holy fuck, what an ass she had. Little love arrows were flying everywhere.

"Ahem."

Where was a bed? He needed a bed. He needed this woman like he'd never needed a woman before.

"Ahem! If you two don't knock it off, I'm going to post this on the internet for the entire world to see." The words were practically shouted in his ear. He and Jenn sprang apart and turned to gawk at Red, holding out her phone with a video of them kissing. Noah's breath was heaving in and out of his chest, that haze still eating up brain cells.

"Not nice, guys," she said. "Contributing to the delinquency of a minor."

Really? Seriously? He gave Jenn a skeptical side-eye. Her eye roll told him she agreed. She swiped a hand across her lips, wiping away all traces of his kiss, yet he noticed she followed the hand swipe with a lick of her tongue that went on way too long.

"First of all, Miss Megan Murphy," she said. "Don't you dare. Secondly, you are not a minor. You're twenty-three."

"Yes, but my ears are virgin ears."

"Oh, for Pete's sake, they are not. I've heard your stories."

"Pfft, those are secondhand stories, not enough to get a rise out of an eighty-year-old. You guys were about to set the area rug on fire, and I forgot to send in the premiums for the homeowner's insurance.

"What? Are you crazy?"

Red stuck her tongue out. "Hah. Fooled ya'."

"You're going to pay for that."

He watched the sassy back and forth, his cock still standing tall, his hands still trembling, his lips still burning to kiss hers, however, Jenn seemed to have moved on. In her opinion, he was nothing, a nobody, invisible because she was busy arguing with Red. Shaking his head, he walked back to his office.

Gram was still sitting in his side chair, a bunch of nail polish shit spread out on his desk, painting her nails. She lifted a brow when he fell heavily into his chair.

"Feel better?" she asked and swiped glossy red polish onto her thumbnail.

No, he didn't feel better. He felt used, abused and thoroughly, irritatingly, passionately seduced. Not that he minded the last part. He glowered at Gram. She grinned back and painted another nail and blew on it. Silence reigned while the grandfather clock in the corner ticked away the seconds and he tapped his fingers, determined to make her speak first.

He should have known better. His grandmother was the queen of pregnant silences.

He gave up. "So tell me about this man."

"Bruce. A widower, has three grown kids, four grandkids."

All right, so far he sounded okay. "What did he do before he retired?"

Gram looked up from her nail painting. "Who said he was retired?"

He blinked. "Uh, I assumed—" he said but stopped because there was that old saying about assuming that Gram would be happy to remind him of. "Okay, so what does he do for a living."

"He's a DJ on a radio station." She continued blowing on her nails to dry the polish.

Crap. Radio was dead. DJs made no money. Probably another asshole he'd end up supporting if this turned into a long-term relationship. He sighed.

"One of those stations in New York City. A combination of talk and music from the sixties through the nineties. You know the one," she finished and recited the call letters for one of the most popular stations in the Metropolitan area.

A pang of nausea invaded the pit of his stomach. He had this weird feeling...

"Um. What does he look like?"

Tipping her purse, she grabbed her cell phone when it slid out, swiped through several screens and tapped on a photo. She pushed it across the desk for him to see.

He closed his eyes, not wanting to look, half knowing what he'd see, yet wanting to delay the seeing. He cracked open one eye and peeked at the screen.

Fuck on a Frito. It was a man, with a capital M. He'd been expecting—no, hoping—he'd see this little old guy, shriveled and shrunken with age, a wisp of gray hair barely noticeable on his age-spotted pate, his pants buckled up under his armpits while he took ten minutes to shuffle from his La-Z Boy to the bathroom.

Crap. Crap, crap, crap, crap, crap. This guy was solid, robust. Healthy. No shuffler here. This was a guy who would want a little sumpin' sumpin' six times a day.

He buried his head in his hands. Fucked, and it was all the crazy lady next door's fault. "How old is this guy?"

"Fifty-eight."

"Okay." He rubbed a hand across his mouth. *Don't say anything, Noah. Don't say a word.* "Well... um, he looks nice."

Gram winked. "Oh, he is. Also very cute. And sexy. And he's got this great big—"

"Ahhh! Don't!" he yelped.

"—Cadillac," she finished with a wicked smile. Stowing her phone back in her purse, she put the cap on the bottle of nail polish and dropped it into her purse. "Oh, by the way, I got an email from your father with an attachment, but I couldn't open it." She stood. "Well, gotta go. Bruce and I have a hot date tonight." With a wave, she sashayed out.

Taking a deep breath, he attempted to slow his rampaging heartbeat. His family was going to be the death of him. He stared at the wall for a while, then went to the radio station's website and stared at the guy who looked like more than his Cadillac was big.

He stared at his computer for a bit longer then, feeling his usual sense of dread, he checked for the email his Gram told him might be in his inbox.

Yep. Two attachments. He opened the first one and gazed at it, puzzled. It was nothing more than a picture of palm trees and beach, taken from the water. Pretty, but nothing special. He opened the second. Same beach, only this time the chunky lady was standing knee deep in the azure-hued water. Her fists set on her hips, she stared at the photographer, presumably his father. The gold-digger was nowhere in sight.

Meet Crystal. She owns the whole damned island! Crystal, meet my son, Noah. He's the best.

Ohh-kay? The email was addressed to him yet his father had also cc'd Melanie, Bret and Gram.

After studying the picture for a few minutes and re-reading the short message trying to figure out what the heck was going on, he moved the email over to his personal inbox and forgot about it. The rest of the day passed in a blur during which he vacillated between bewilderment at his grandmother's sudden entry into the dating world and the memory of the kiss he'd shared with Jenn. The taste of her lips remained a tangible presence in his consciousness. His hands still throbbed with the memory of gripping her firm backside and threading the silk of her long hair through his fingers. Everything that happened this morning left him confused, unsettled, plus horny as hell.

There was the ever-increasing certainty that Jenn was the One.

The day passed. He made a half-hearted stab at working, however, he'd done everything he needed to do for the three divorce cases he was working on, so he sent Debra home a bit early, locked up the office and got into his car. He put the key in the starter and turned it.

Urrrrr, click, click, click. He pumped the gas and turned the key again. Click. Damn it. He got out, went around to the front of the car and popped the hood although he had no idea why as he knew next to nothing about cars, even though he should what with driving the piece of shit sitting useless in front of him.

He stared at the engine. Nothing occurred to him. No big shining lightbulb appeared over his head, telling him what to do, and no mechanic, summoned by the crazy lady next door, happened to swing by to give him a clue.

"God damn son of a bitch piece of crap!" He kicked the tire.

"Need help?"

Oh. Fuck.

SIXTEEN

JennGoodwin@MyHeart-2-Heart

STILL NOT MY FAULT!

Well, well, well. Look at that. It appeared the man was having car problems.

"God damn son of a bitch piece of crap!" He kicked the tire.

She grinned because, can anyone say divine retribution? "Need help?" she asked, only a smidgen of snark in her voice.

He swung around to face her. A bead of sweat trickled down the side of his jaw. Pink bloomed on his face, which could be anger, frustration, or the heat, but was most likely embarrassment at getting caught kicking his car because it was a childish thing to do and wouldn't do any good anyway. Cars were funny that way.

He bared his teeth at her, looking about as friendly as the average junk yard dog. For a minute she seriously considered leaving him to deal with his situation on his own, but right after the snarl, a muscle in his jaw spasmed, and this small spark of vulnerability twitched across his face, and she changed her mind because he looked so cute when he was vulnerable.

Actually, darn it, he looked cute all the time which would be the death of her. Still, what a way to go.

She was so busy swallowing her lust, she almost forgot to ask, "What's the matter with the car?"

Closing his eyes, he heaved a sigh. "It won't start."

Duh. Obvious. "Is the battery dead?" Did he know a few curly chest hairs were poking out of the top of his shirt where he'd unbuttoned it? Did he know what a turn-on that was? Did he know he had a body to die for? He looked so yummy standing there, all undone and sweaty, she wanted to run her tongue along the edge of his collarbone and taste him.

He shrugged. "How would I know? I know zip about cars."

Weren't men supposed to know all things car? Apparently not this man.

"Hang on a second... uh, Noah," she said, his name vibrating off her tongue in a strange way. She'd never said his name before; he'd always been the Rat or Mr. Ratttorney, or simply That Guy Next Door. "I'll be right back." Spinning on her heel, she strode to Heart-2-Heart's back door. Unlocking it, she entered the kitchen, opened up one of the top cabinets, pulled out what she needed and walked back outside to rejoin him.

"Get in the car and turn on the headlights."

He gave her a puzzled look, however, he did as she requested. She set the Multimeter to the right voltage, waited a few minutes before hooking it up. "Start the car," she called.

Click.

The needle on the meter moved, showing the battery was fine, yet the car still hadn't started.

"Try again," she called. He tried a second time. Still nothing. She unhooked the Multimeter. "I don't know. The battery looks fine, so it has to be something else. Maybe the starter."

"Crap. Crap, crap, crap."

Something that vaguely resembled pity squeezed inside her chest. Or maybe it wasn't precisely pity, the man was too virile, too self-assured normally, to engender pity. Maybe it was more of an *I want to eat your face off* kind of feeling.

"You'll need to call someone for a tow."

That got another sigh. "I figured." Opening the door to the front seat, he reached in and pulled out his jacket from which he extracted his cell phone. He scrolled through a few things and selected a number.

"I'm calling one of those road services. You don't have to wait." He began speaking into the phone. She waited, not going anywhere. He quirked a brow at her, his eyes holding a question. She shook her head. Still not going anywhere.

He disconnected. "They'll be here in fifteen minutes or so, no problem, so you can leave."

"And how are you going to get home since they're going to tow your car away?"

He blinked. "Um."

Well, that was informative. She cocked her head, letting him know she still expected an answer.

"I can call someone in my family," he said, then hesitated, his lips compressed. "Well, I'll call a friend." He stopped again, the frown deepening, and sighed. "Shit," he muttered under his breath.

"You've got nothing, right?"

"I've got nothing," he admitted with a sigh. "My best friend's out of town for the week and my grandmother—" At this point, he sent her a red-hot glare. "—is on a date that some person—who shall remain nameless—arranged. I'll pay the driver to take me into town. I think there's a car rental place somewhere in town that I can walk to."

Sheesh. Men. "Have the tow driver take your car to that gas station over on Route 1 near the mall. It's right next door to an Avis rental place. I'll ride you over so you can rent a car once they drop your car off," she told him which resulted in the next five minutes being filled with protests, and lame reasons why it made no sense for her to give him a ride. She didn't mind the craziness; he was adorable when he was upset. He paced a lot which gave her plenty of opportunity to admire his broad shoulders and the fantastic ass that his tailored slacks exhibited to perfection.

He was still muttering and throwing his hands in the air when the tow truck arrived. The driver backed his truck up to Noah's car. She lingered while he filled out a few forms, paid with a credit card and gave the driver instructions to take the car to the station Jenn had recommended. The driver hooked Noah's car up and drove away.

Noah stared after the truck, a forlorn expression on his face.

"Well, that's done, so we should get going," she said, making him jump.

He ran a hand through his thick brown hair, still looking a little lost and glum. Regardless, he followed her when she led him over to the back of Heart-2-Heart's parking pad and stopped in front of her motorcycle.

His eyes bugged. "No."

"No?" She looked at him from the corner of her eye. He was not looking back. Instead, he was staring at her Harley with visible horror.

"I am not getting on that thing. These things are death machines."

Good gravy. He sounded like her mother, and here she believed the guy was a manly man. He looked like a manly man, he moved like a manly man, he kissed like a manly man, (yum), but he sounded like a little girl. Yes! The man had a flaw.

"Chicken?"

A muscle in his jaw clenched. "No. Of course not. It's that... uh..." He licked his lips. "Okay. It's nothing. I'm fine. Whatever. It'll be an adventure, right?" His face said he considered this anything but an adventure.

"We can always call a cab," she said, her voice holding a hint of a taunt.

"Gimme a damned helmet."

She hid her smile. Men were so predictable. Call a girl a coward and she'd say, you bet, and walk away. Tell a man the same thing and he'd take up the challenge, even if it got him killed. Popping the seat up, she retrieved her extra helmet and held it out to him.

Slipping the helmet on, he buckled it. Good golly, the fire in his eyes was enough to set her panties on fire. Her mouth suddenly dry, she swallowed. His eyelids slid down until only a sliver of steely gray showed through his lashes.

"Get on. I promise I'll go slow." Of course she would. She'd promised her mother no zooming, however, he didn't need to know that. She put on her own helmet, slammed the seat down and threw a leg over the bike. "Hop on."

He took a deep breath, slung a leg over the rear of the bike and settled on the seat. She hit the starter, making the engine roar.

His arms flew around her waist. "Yikes," he yelped.

Her heart went into overdrive. She revved the engine again so that it matched the speed of her heart. Her impulse was to give him the ride of his life, but she figured she'd terrified him enough for one day, so she slowly drove out of the parking lot, pulled onto the street and steered south, letting the bike roll smoothly over the pavement as they headed south, timing her speed to hit all green lights. They pulled onto Route 1. Smoothly shifting gears, she sped up, heading towards the car rental shop she was familiar with.

Against her back, she felt him take a deep breath. Then, barely heard for the wind in her ears, "Wow."

His arms tightened around her waist, his hands gripping each other in front of her. His hands stayed at her waist for several minutes, then one of his fingers crept along her stomach and stroked. Stroke. Stroke.

Hoo-eey. Heat filled her chest.

His locked hands inched up closer to her breasts. A whirlwind of emotions rose to the surface, tenderness, sympathy... lust, because she remembered what it was like to have those strong masculine hands holding her tightly when he kissed her socks off. Oh my God, what would it be like to have those long fingers with their short, well-trimmed nails trace the faint blue lines of the veins on her breasts? What would it be like to have one of those fingers inside her? Between that finger stroking her, her thoughts and the vibration of the engine between her legs, she was about to have an orgasm of epic proportions.

Maybe once upon a time she'd wanted to take revenge, but the need for that had ceased to exist somewhere between the kiss and the ice cream delivery. Now it was more about taking him. On her desk. On the floor. Against a wall.

Ahead of her, she could see signs for I-195 South. The late afternoon sun shone in her eyes, making it hard to see. So, why not, right? She veered to the right and took the on-ramp.

His hands tightened around her waist. "Hey!" He poked her with a finger. "Where...going?" he yelled in her ear. "Gas station...car..."

She laughed and kept going. With the wind whistling by, the roar of the cycle in their ears, no one spoke. She enjoyed the scenery, the feel of the machine under her. The feel of his hands under her breast.

Evil thoughts began to percolate. This man needed a good shaking up. And she needed to change their relationship. And, as the man said, this would be an adventure. They roared down the highway.

"Hey!" he yelled into her ear. "Wh.... go... Sto..."

The rest of what he said was whisked away by the wind, although she could make a good guess, however, it wouldn't have mattered anyway because she was ignoring it. She kept going. He kept protesting, and she kept ignoring. Apparently realizing he was wasting his breath, he shut up and hung on. Still, that finger kept poking her, sometimes in an interesting spot right under her nipple.

She was careful to stay in the middle lane, not weaving in and out like she usually would. Cars went around her because she was going too slow, but she had no intention of getting in an accident and killing her sexy attorney friend. She had plans for him.

Twenty minutes later they arrived. She pulled into the parking lot, parked in an available slot towards the back, turned off the engine and turned to face him.

He dismounted. "Wow. That was...sort of scary, but...I could get used to it." With a sly smile, he dropped his gaze to her breasts. Hmph. It was obvious what he could get used to.

Lifting his gaze from her breasts, he glanced up at the entrance a few hundred yards away with the tall loops of the Jersey Devil Coaster in the background. "Where are...? What? Great Adventure?" he asked. "Why?"

"Why not?" She dismounted, set the kickstand and popped the seat up.

He didn't have an answer for that, so he handed his helmet to her, all the while staring at the tall structure leading into the park. She put both helmets under the seat and dropped her keys in her jeans pocket. Grabbing his hand, she hauled him towards the gate. When they arrived at the entrance, she pulled her wallet out of her fanny pack and handed the gate attendant her card.

"Hey! I can pay for myself. I'll pay for your ticket too. Girls don't pay."

Sheesh. Another protest. Did the guy never stop?

"Girls can pay, the same as guys. I dragged you here, so it's my treat." She took the tickets when the attendant handed them to her and pulled a still grumbling Noah through the turnstiles.

"What first?" she asked.

He shook his head.

"Oh, I know, El Toro. I love El Toro. I love the sound it makes. It rattles and rumbles and because it's wooden, you can feel the whole thing shake when the cars go across, and the drop? It's like you leave your stomach at the top, never to be seen again. So freakin' fun!" She turned to take his hand.

He went dead white. She'd seen a friend's uncle in his coffin a few years ago, and Noah was whiter than that.

"Um... roller coasters. Not my thing. How 'bout the swings instead?" he offered.

She sighed. "Boring. How about the Ferris wheel?"

He blanched. "No."

She glowered at him. What the heck? Nothing more inoffensive than a Ferris wheel. "Okay, then you choose."

"The race cars?"

Pulling her phone out, she checked the website. "They're closed for repairs."

"Shit. So..."

She made a face. "How about the Green Lantern Coaster?"

"Look, I don't like heights. I don't like things that flip you upside down. I don't like things that can cause me to die."

Wow. Seriously not into thrill rides. She was going to have to work on that. "Well, gosh, I guess that means the merry-go-round 'cause, gee, I totally love the fake horses and the dopey music. Dibs on the blue horse."

An amused smile crossed his face.

She dragged him across the tarmac, her sense regarding the location of the merry-go-round unerring, but almost immediately she saw a vendor with cotton candy, blue and yellow and pink. She slammed to a halt.

"Ooh, ooh, ooh, cotton candy. I have to have some."

He groaned.

"Aw, c'mon. Cotton candy? What color do you want?"

He made a face, rolled his eyes and ultimately surveyed the choices before pointing at a pink bag.

"Pink? You want pink?" She giggled.

"Hey, it's a form of red, and red's my favorite color."

Shaking her head, she bought the treats and handed Noah his, opened her plastic bag of yellow fluff and stuffed a hunk into her mouth. "Oh, my God, that's so good." She swallowed, then checked out the poor man she'd dragged into her adventure. He still stood there, holding his unopened bag of spun sugar. "Oh, for Pete's sake," she said and grabbed it back, opened it, and pulled out a hunk of the sticky treat. "Hey, guy, where'd you go to college?"

He opened his mouth to answer. She jammed the cotton candy into his mouth. He blinked, chewed, licked his lips. "Oh. Yum. I'd forgotten." Retrieving his bag, he stuck another sticky hunk into his mouth, looking delighted.

Satisfied she had put him on the right path—okay, maybe not the right path, it was simply her path, the path to having fun—she took his hand again and tugged him towards their ride. Within twenty feet she stopped.

"Noah! Hot dogs. I'm starving. I need a hot dog." Pulling out some money, she paid the vendor for two dogs. He handed them to her. Carefully juggling them, she examined the condiments.

"Mustard?" she asked Noah.

"I—"

Not waiting to hear the rest, she slathered a spoonful of the yellow stuff on both dogs. "Yeah, and ketchup." On went the tomato sauce. "And you gotta have relish."

"No, I don't—"

She slathered on relish in spite of his protest.

"And sour kraut." That also went on their dogs. "Open up."

He opened his mouth to say something, knowing him, it was a protest. Regardless, she stuck the end in his mouth, kraut and all.

His cheeks bulged. He chewed. And chewed. Chewed some more. He swallowed. Taking the rest of the hot dog out of her hand, he bit into it until the thing had disappeared.

She grinned at him. "Good, huh?"

He grinned back and stuck a big wad of cotton candy in his mouth for dessert. "I haven't had a hot dog since..." He stopped, frowning while he considered it. "Damn, since college."

"Oh, you poor deprived man. Do you want another one to make up for lost time?"

The question warranted another pause before he shook his head, looking like he'd like to change his mind. Instead, he stuffed another hunk of cotton candy in his mouth. "C'mon, let's do that ride," he mumbled and strode off.

Reaching the carousel, they got in line. With a bunch of four, five-and six-year-olds. Oh, joy. Such fun. When the current ride ended, the attendant allowed their line to enter. She ran around to the other side, beating out a little girl for the blue horse. The little girl's face puckered up until Jenn pointed at the horse in front of her. "Look, a pink one. Like the fairies ride." Ecstatic at her find, the girl mounted with some help from her mother, who was aware of what Jenn had done and threw her a dirty look.

Noah sauntered up, mounted the gold horse to her left and waited for the ride to start. Up. Down. Up. Down. Up. Down. Up. Down.

Geez. Kill me now. At last the ride ended. Thank God. She jumped off, grasped Noah's hand, pulled him off his fake pony and off the carousel platform.

"Whirligig."

He turned green. "Is that the thing that goes round and round until you throw up?"

"Yeah, that. I love to spin super-fast so when I get off, I'm so dizzy I fall down."

He curled a lip, giving her a sour look. "Oh, yeah, so much fun. I just ate that hot dog and cotton candy. I'm not sure I can take a lot of spinning right now. Just imagine the mess."

Well, shoot. For a guy who seemed so macho, he was sure a wuss. He wasn't going to make her job of helping him have fun easy to do. "Okay. Air Safari then. That's kind of a kid's ride. You should be okay."

He nodded reluctantly. Looking at a convenient map, they found the ride, yet somehow they never got there because on the way they saw signs for Justice League: Battle for the Metropolis and he made an abrupt left turn and dragged her down the sidewalk and into the ride. Oh golly gee, Noah. So fun. So guy oriented. A shoot 'em up ride.

Yet it turned out to be a blast, literally, as they shot animatronic characters and 3-D images to save the superheroes. They exited laughing hysterically. His face was alight with joy, smiling. It changed him entirely, taking years off his face, changing his posture from the tense form she was familiar with to a man who strode, loose-limbed like a teenager, down the street.

She was smiling like a maniac. She, Jenn Goodwin, who had hardly ever cracked a smile—wrinkles, remember—had smiled more in the last half hour than she had in the last five years.

"Okay, now it's my pick," she said. She needed something with a little more pizazz but, seeing the joy surrounding him, something that wouldn't make him turn green and upchuck his meal. Although...

"I pick... the Slingshot."

His eyes went so wide it looked like his eyeballs would fall out. "That thing where we fall a bazillion feet and go splat if the ropes break?"

"First of all, there are no ropes, there are cables and a mechanism with springs that controls the ride. And, we don't really fall. Well, we do but then we sort of boomerang. We get shot up then we snap back down."

"Do we...I mean...uh, we go up? Into the sky? And then fall?"

"Yeah, sure, of course we go up. Then we come down."

He blanched and turned an interesting shade of green. Wow, she'd never seen anyone that shade of green before. "Hey, it's okay. We're in a cage, and we're strapped in. It's perfectly safe. Come on, I let you take me on two kiddie rides, now it's my turn."

"But we leave the ground. I don't like leaving the ground. I'm happy when my feet are on the ground. It's safer on the ground. If I fall, it's only a few feet."

Huh. She cocked her head, studying him. To see his face, no one would think he was scared, however, she could feel his fear in the shaking of his hand, in the tension radiating off him. "What's the problem? It's supposed to be scary...for about thirty seconds. Kind of like going to a scary movie, right?"

He shook his head. "I hate heights. I mean, I really hate heights. Heights, you know?" His breath escaped from his lungs in gasps. "I'm...Oh, god, I'm just scared I'll fall." He cleared his throat. "When I was a kid..." He cleared his throat again. "We were on this trip, we were at this old hotel, I don't know, somewhere in Florida? My parents were fighting. They told us—my brother and I—to get lost so we did. We went down the hallway and there was this window and Bret dared me to climb through onto the fire escape." Frowning, he swallowed. "I'm so stupid, I didn't see any problem, but there was a trap door, and it wasn't latched and I stepped on it and fell through. Twenty feet down to the parking lot."

Her heart leaped. "But...you were okay, right?"

He made a face. "More or less. I had to go to the hospital to get checked out. Only a mild concussion. Still, heights, you know. Falling. I...uh... It's...that feeling. You know."

She hesitated for a few moments, debating her next sentence. "Okay, I'm sorry. That's terrible. I understand. I don't want to make you do something that you really don't want to do so you know what, I'll pick—" she said.

But, before she could finish, he said, "I hate being afraid of things like this..." She waited for him to complete his sentence.

Looking scared yet somehow determined, he said, "I hate that I let my fear control me. I should be able to control how I feel. I'm always in control, you know, so I shouldn't be afraid of this one stupid thing but... My whole life..."

He stopped again, letting his head drop down to hide his eyes. "I don't know how to explain. My whole life. I have this thing. About control, you know. I don't like to be out of control. Falling? Totally out of my control." He looked up at her from under his brows, his eyes pleading with her to understand. "Maybe more, it's like I need to be in control, but you know what? This thing, this fear of heights? It's controlling me, not the other way around. The fear is controlling me and that's not how I want to live my life."

Something inside her twisted. The man had ripped open his chest and pulled his beating heart out for her to see him at the most vulnerable level. She wanted to hug him and hold him and tell him not to be afraid. However, that wasn't realistic, and that's not what he needed anyway; what he needed was someone supporting him through his fear.

"It's okay to feel afraid. I'm afraid of a lot of things. For instance..." She swallowed. "I'm afraid of bugs. And dogs. I'm scared of dogs."

He cocked his head, giving her a funny look because Trike, right? However, she rushed on, not letting him speak. "I'll help. I'm here for you." She held her hand out, shooting him a look that was part dare, part understanding.

After another sigh, still looking a little—okay, a lot—apprehensive, he took her hand and let her lead the way. They reached the ride. Looking up, he blanched. "Oh boy. This is nuts."

"No, nuts is riding a motorcycle on I-95 without a helmet. This..." She gestured at the ride. "...is supposed to be fun...in a completely terrifying way, of course." Taking his hand, she pressed a kiss to his knuckles.

His mouth turned up in a wobbly smile, yet it was still a smile. "Oh, sure. Fun. Fun like a prostate exam."

She burst out laughing.

He slapped a hand over his face and muttered through his fingers, "I can't believe I'm saying this but okay, let's do it."

Taking his hand, she led him into the line where only four people waited for their turn. She paid the extra fee for the ride. It was only moments before they were being strapped together. The safety bar was lowered. She could hear his harsh erratic breathing. Her hand in his was crushed by his grip, his eyes had closed, and he was shaking.

Boiingg! They shot up into the sky.

He shrieked like a girl. She screamed, the drop so exhilarating it was like flying. "Oh shit!" he yelled. His hand tightened on hers.

She laughed. They skyrocketed up, up, up. The cage stopped, hanging in mid-air for a split second. And then they fell. Her stomach dropped, and she screamed, half with terror, half with excitement.

They hit the bottom and boomeranged upwards again, the blue, blue sky rushing at them as they rose. "Oh, fuuuuck!" he yelled. Down they went. His hand tightened on hers until her knuckles popped. And she laughed.

They hit bottom.

"Oh god." And they shot up again, only not as fast, not as hard, not as far.

"I think I'm going to be sick."

"No, you're not. I won't let you. I've got you and nothing's going to happen to you." She threaded her arm through his and took his hand again, holding it tightly while they rose again. "Open your eyes, open your eyes."

He opened his eyes. "Oh God."

They bounced upwards one more time. Fell. One more bounce, this one not very high, not as scary. A few more bounces before they stopped, and then simply swayed gently from the left-over momentum.

Gradually the pendulum slowed, the arc getting smaller and smaller, before the ride attendant grabbed the cage and stopped them.

Noah didn't speak, however, Jenn could feel his entire body trembling. The attendant lifted the safety bar, setting them free so they could step off the platform onto the tarmac below.

She could hear Noah breathing, in out, in out, the sound deep and shaky. Suddenly, he grabbed her, picking her up in his arms and twirling her, his face shining with delight, twirling her around and around.

"I did it," he said, wonder in his voice. "I did it. I've never done anything like that before. I hate heights. I hate taking risks, but I did it. Scared the crap out of me, but I did it, and I liked it. Because of you," he finished and cupping the back of her head, he kissed her, hard. It lasted forever.

"Jenn. God, I really, really want to make love to you," he whispered in her ear when he came up for air.

The kiss could have gone on forever and she would have been happy, but there was something better waiting for her. Pulling out her cell phone, she called her mom and told her she wouldn't pick up the dog until tomorrow.

SEVENTEEN

NoahMaitland@noahmaitlandesq

Forget the butterflies. I feel the whole zoo when I'm with you.

That had been the scariest fucking thing he'd ever done in his life, but he'd done it. He'd done something he'd never in his life imagined he could do. He'd taken a risk—a physical risk—and not only survived it, but he'd also kind of loved it. Despite the initial desire to throw up.

His entire childhood, he'd had no control over his life. It had been constant chaos, his existence filled with imagined and unimaginable danger—the possibility of abandonment, the risk that he wouldn't know where he would sleep that night, the threat that one of his parents would withdraw their love in favor of their latest love affair.

Growing up, most kids learned things like table manners, how to read, how to play baseball. He'd learned everything had to be controlled. Everything had to be planned to the smallest degree in order to protect himself. The one and only time he'd done something daring, he'd fallen two stories. He'd learned never to take a risk, to always be in control, always making sure he never upset the status quo, otherwise his world would fall apart.

Until today. Today he'd let it all go.

He twirled her around in his arms, so filled with exhilaration that there was hardly room for air to breathe. He hugged her tighter and kissed her, wildly, joyfully, tasting the inherent goodness of her. She tasted of life and exuberance and freedom. God, this woman. He wanted to inhale her, soak up her delight in life and her bravery and her undaunted outlook.

He wanted to be more like her.

Most especially, he wanted to make love to her. Inside was a driving need to absorb her essence into himself by putting himself inside her body. He'd never had this kind of impulse, this utter need to have sex. In the past, his relationships had only progressed to that level after he'd learned more about the woman, studied the positives and negatives and only when he was sure it was the right move, did he sleep with a woman.

But this. This thing with Jenn. This was different. He felt like he was about to step off a cliff into the unknown, and yet, he wanted, more than anything, to take that leap.

Bullseye.

He didn't want to stop kissing her. He loved the muted moans she made and the feel of her fingers in his hair, yet finally, reluctantly, he ended the kiss, although it wasn't easy since he was busy giving her an intermittent kiss or two when she was pressed against his chest. Still, he found time to smile at her.

A grin spread across her face in response. "Fun, yeah?"

He kissed her chin. Her nose, then, for good measure, her lips once more, where he lingered because the taste of her was so sweet.

"I want to make love to you," he whispered in her ear. Almost begged her. The need for her was a bone-deep ache.

Her smile dissolved. She explored his face, searching his eyes for something. He could sense her questions, however, unlike him, she didn't seem to need to beat a decision to death before she acted. The smile returned. Her lips touched his, once, twice, three times, her tongue lightly tracing the seam of his mouth. His cock, always quick to respond to this woman, leaped to attention.

"Yes," she said.

Setting her onto her feet, he hustled her towards the gate they'd entered not two hours ago.

She giggled. Her laughter was like cool water cascading over his soul. They ran through the exit, across the parking lot until they reached her bike, both of them laughing like the idiots they were. He couldn't remember the last time he'd laughed like that, uninhibited, like a joyful child.

Retrieving the helmets, she passed him the spare while she put on her own before throwing a leg over the bike.

"I'm in South Brunswick which is a hike. Where are you?" she asked.

"Only fifteen minutes from here." He grinned and gave her instructions. "Quick. Get on."

He tossed his leg over the seat and settled. She kicked up the kickstand and started the engine with a roar. Within minutes, they were rolling towards the highway and his apartment.

His hands clutched her waist. Riding a motorcycle still scared him a little but not like before. If he died now, at least he would have known perfect happiness once in his life.

They roared north on the highway until they approached his exit. He nudged her to let her know, and she turned off. He shouted directions into her ear, pointing the way, until they reached his apartment building. Looking at the place, he felt a rush of shame. It wasn't much. For a successful lawyer, he didn't have much to show for it. Everything went into the pockets of his family, however, she didn't seem to notice, or if she did notice, she didn't care. She parked on the curb and killed the engine.

"Off, off, off. Quick, quick, quick," she ordered, already removing her helmet and shaking out the long hair he wanted to wrap around his hands, his body, his cock. He jumped off. He waited while she stowed the helmets and then, unable to wait another second, he dragged her to his front door.

He fumbled with his keys.

Then stopped. Kissed her. Kissed her again. One of those long, long legs wrapped around his hips and her heat pressed up against his leg. Holy fuck on a frijole, he needed this woman now.

More key fumbling. Still missing the keyhole.

She giggled. "Hurry."

"I'm trying, God, I'm trying." Damn it.

Key inserted at last, the door crashed open, they flew inside with it, smashing up against a wall. He kissed her some more, pushing her halfway up the wall. His lips ate up her face, her mouth, her ear, her neck, his hands following suit.

She slammed the front door closed then her hands were everywhere on him, but especially down low. He heard, felt, the slid of his zipper and his cock was free. "Ah, God. Fuck!"

"Yes, please," she whispered in his ear and took him in hand. His heart pounded, breath too fast to sustain life. Heat zinged through his body. He needed her now. Hands trembling, he undid the snap on her jeans and seized the tab of her zipper. *Zzzzz.*

Her jeans fell open. Stooping, he nibbled, licked, tasted his way down her chest, stopping to place tiny kisses on each breast, her stomach, her hips, as he slid her pants down and removed her ankle boot to pull off one pant leg. Lifting his head, he gently licked at the apex of her thighs.

She moaned.

He was ready to go. He didn't need a bed because he had a perfectly good wall. He didn't need an invitation—she'd already offered one—but he did need one thing. He pulled out his wallet, hunting for his one lonely condom.

Crap. It had died months ago, so he'd thrown it away.

"Um..." Pulling back, he gave her a look, letting her see his dismay.

Her eyes widened. "Condom? No?"

Think, think, think. Where? It had been so long, but he vaguely remembered purchasing a new box a few months ago with the distant hope he might need them at some point.

"Upstairs. Bathroom."

"Vroom vroom," she yelled, and elbowing him aside, she bounded up the stairs. She stumbled on her pants hanging from one leg, nearly fell. Hiking up his own pants he leaped up the stairs after her, two steps at a time, then tripped on her dragging pant leg and fell on his face.

"Fuck!" He laughed and rolled onto his butt, still holding onto his pants.

"Yes, the sooner the better."

Somewhere near the top of the stairs, she kicked her jeans completely off, removed her shirt then her bra. He awkwardly leaped over her abandoned clothing, banged into a wall, jumped past her, grabbed her hand, and hauled her down the hall and into the bathroom. A quick acquisition of the necessary equipment and into his bedroom. He yanked off his pants and Fruit of the Looms, tossed them aside then stroked on a condom, all in about three seconds flat. If the Olympics had a Putting-on-a-Condom event, he would have established a new world record. Bending, he scooped her up and threw her onto his mattress. She bounced. So did her glorious boobs.

God damn, she was magnificent. She made him happy, with her weird observations, her utter lust for life and her amazing body that seemed made just for him.

He threw himself on top of her and kissed her. And kissed her. And kissed her.

His kisses sometimes hit her mouth, sometimes landed elsewhere, a series of hungry kisses on her chin, her breasts, especially her breasts, all while he ran his hands over her body, savoring the silkiness of her pale skin, the firm softness of her.

"You maniac." She giggled. Hands batted at him, playfully shoving him away and grabbing him by the ears so she could pull him closer. She bit his lip, ran her tongue along his jaw, down his neck, across his chest and back up to his face, the feel of her tongue sending shivers through his body.

She was laughing, he was laughing, stretching his lungs to their limit, before forcing its way up his throat and erupting from his mouth in a rush of joy.

It was phenomenal, mind-bending, totally insane.

She wrapped her legs, those long, long legs he'd lusted after, around his waist. The laughter stopped. Placing her hands on his cheeks, she held him steady, gazing intently into his eyes.

"Come into me."

His heart beating double time, he positioned himself between her legs, the heat of her setting his mind on fire. "My pleasure. Always and forever, my pleasure," he said, while in his mind he again heard 'She's the One' in a quiet voice. Running a finger through her dampness, he made sure she was ready then slowly, carefully, entered her.

She gasped, threw her head back, her breathing morphing from slow and deep to shallow, quick breaths of excitement.

Closing his eyes, he allowed himself to simply feel the heat of her, the tightness of her, the wonder of her. When he opened his eyes, he slid deeper into the heat of her body, gazing into her eyes, looking for signs. She was quick to arouse, slow to come, maybe prolonging her orgasm to better enjoy the getting there. His balls tightened to the point of pain. He wanted to come, he needed to come, but he wanted her with him.

Reaching between them, he ran a finger along her wet seam, searching for the bud at her core. She gasped, mewled, jerked in his arms.

He stroked with his finger, and his cock in her body. "Come. Come for me."

She jerked again, screamed, "Fuck!"

He laughed out loud at her rude slip, then his body clenched and everything spasmed, and he followed her into blissful darkness.

He spent some time simply existing.

God damn son of a bitch, that was the most amazing.... He rested his forehead on hers, catching his breath before straightening to gaze into her beautiful face.

Her blue eyes were huge with wonder. There weren't words. Once more, he kissed her nose, her cheek, her nose again because he adored her nose—her cute little turned-up nose—tenderness welling, the idea that this thing they had begun was something special galloping through his brain.

There was this feeling exploding in his chest, a dream that maybe he could have it all, that there was such a thing as 'the one' and that she was it.

He slid out of her body, reluctant to leave because it felt so right. However, he couldn't stay there forever—at some point, she'd want her body back. He rolled to the side, wrapped his arms around her, and pulled her against his front so her butt was couched against his groin.

Closing his eyes, he took a deep breath, pressing little kisses on the back of her neck while one hand, which seemed to have a mind of its own, roamed gently over her body, although not seeking titillation. He simply wanted to touch her, absorb her essence, and know that she was there with him.

EIGHTEEN

JennGoodwin@MyHeart-2-Heart

You can't buy love, but you sure as heck can borrow it for a while.

He had spooned himself around her body and draped his arm over her waist, while his hand stroked over her curves. Yet not in a lascivious way. Tiny kisses flitted across her shoulder, her neck, in her hair. His hum of satisfaction sighed into her ear.

The man was a cuddler. Who knew?

She wiggled her butt more snugly against his crotch, gave a matching sigh and, drifting in a warm sea of contentment, fell asleep. She had dreams. She never had them, or at least not that she was aware of, but tonight, man-oh-man, did she dream. They involved roller coasters and twirling teacups and motorcycles and a tall manly man who somehow managed to contort himself enough to make love to her on every single ride.

She woke up in the middle of the night to find that manly man smiling at her in the dim light while he threaded his fingers through her hair. Down below, he was hot and hard and pressing at her entrance while he used a knee to push her legs further apart.

She was wet and ready. Spreading her legs, she wrapped them around his waist and coaxed him in. Exquisite. His lovemaking was slow, tender...

Confusing. Because what the heck was she doing?

Only a few days ago, this man was her enemy. Okay, not quite her enemy, but definitely not someone she'd ever contemplated going to bed with.

Well, that wasn't quite true either, because the man was super-hot which she'd certainly noticed, and certainly admired, and let's be honest, he certainly rocked her boat. He made her heart beat faster. He made the blood in her veins race hotly, he made her female bits sing and dance with happiness, even when he wasn't inside her.

On the other hand, what the heck was she doing?

She didn't know. She'd have to figure it out later because all that tender lovemaking was doing what it was supposed to do, which was to make her come. Criminy, who had enough brainpower left to solve a riddle when their brain had blown up with lust?

There was a grimace on his face as he focused on getting the job done. He groaned, the speed of his thrusts picking up. His hands molded her breasts, gently stroking her nipples, giving them a light pinch, plumping them up for a finale. He nibbled on her lower lip, nuzzled her neck, breathed hot breath into her hair. The man was everywhere, or at least everywhere that counted.

Even after coming once, his thrusts, the touch of his hands on her body, were leading her to another orgasm. Oh sweet Betsy from Pike!

With one final hard push, he followed her into...

Ohhhh boy, oh boy, she hated to call it bliss, because like, how sappy, but actually, it was bliss. The man knew how to make love, and then some. Turns out, he wasn't all looks and snarky attitude.

He collapsed on top of her, panting, sweating. She could feel him smile against her chest.

"Damn. God. Jenn. Really." He kissed her shoulder. Maybe she should get a bullseye tattooed on that spot so he'd have a target. After a long time, he moved to her side, sliding out of her so he could resume his cuddling.

"I want to know all about you. Where did you grow up?" he murmured, his hand gently stroking up and down her side.

"First Colorado. Then here. New Jersey," she answered.

"Parents? Brothers? Sisters?"

She told him about her mom and her sister Emma, and about her father dying, yet not how and why. It was too personal, too close, too soon to let the walls down and totally trust. He wanted to know more about Heart-2-Heart. She described how she'd started as the assistant and became a partner.

"What about you?" she asked.

She heard about his days playing Little League baseball, his involvement in the math club—math, ick—and how he was accepted to Rutgers, and later law school. His favorite food was Italian, and he hadn't had a vacation in eight years.

Gad. Poor man. It was so obvious he needed her to make his life more fun.

Eventually his recitation slowed, the words coming further and further apart before stopping. He sighed.

She lay awake for a few more minutes, simply enjoying the feel of him pressed against her back and the weight of his arm around her waist. Loving how he made her feel; at peace, cherished, loved...

In love.

Oh shit. Was she in love? How? She'd sworn she would never let love into her life again. She loved her mother and her sister, but this...this...feeling now? This wasn't a mom or sister kind of love. This was more like what she'd felt for Keith in college. Which wasn't safe. She took a deep breath to loosen the suffocating feeling that was gripping her throat, and let it out, determined to ignore the feeling.

It's not real. It's only that after-sex glow. It'll go away.

The possibility of opening herself up to love once again and making herself vulnerable was enough to shatter her. Breathe, she told herself. Breathe. It's not love. It can't be love.

She swallowed. She didn't know if she could do it. All she could think about was ten years ago when all her friends had abandoned her when her father's crime was announced, and the boyfriend who lied about her, just because, and later, Keith dating her only because he was sure she had money.

Damn it. Breathe. Breathe. That's right. Just breathe.

All right, yeah, she could do this. All she had to do was keep it light. She could have fun. She could have sex. She just couldn't let emotions overrule her head. That's why a girl needed attitude, so emotions didn't ruin her attitude.

The only answer was what she'd always done, keep her feelings in check so no one could hurt her. She would have a fling and walk away when it was done. It simply meant a little planning. Tomorrow she'd have to make sure he knew the rules. Whatever they were.

One minute she was awake...

...and the next minute the bright sunlight from his window woke her up. Morning. No reason to get up yet. Too comfy. Too much to remember, and relish, from the night. His lovemaking was bliss, yet drifting awake in sheets that smelled of soap and Noah was a close second. In the back of her mind, there was this vague memory lurking, something about being in love, but come on, that was total BS. No way was she in love. This was just sex.

She snuggled closer to his hard, masculine body and breathed deep as she drifted half awake. One of his arms was under her head like a pillow, but his other hand was skittering up her left arm. His hand was cool, a little rough, and seemed to know the right spots to give her a bit of a scratch.

Although, geez, he needed to cut his nails, because now they were giving her more than a gentle scratch, they were digging into her skin, and a little hand cream wouldn't hurt either. His hand scratched its way up her neck and settled in her hair. His nails poked into her scalp.

Weird.

Puzzled, she cracked open one eye and saw...a Thing! A big green Thing!

Eeeek! She leaped out of bed. The Thing—whatever it was—came with her, hooking its little claws into her hair.

"Ohmigod, ohmigod, ohmigod. Eeeeeekkkkk."

"Hey, what's going on?" Noah jumped out of bed,

She stopped dancing, rolled her eyes to the side and saw something hanging along the side of her face. Something long and scaly. A lizard tail. A lizard was in her hair. She didn't want to hurt it by batting it away, but it was in her hair.

His eyes widened. "Don't move," he ordered.

After giving the naked guy a good hard glare, she pointed to the top of her head where the lizard still clung. "What. Is. That?"

He ignored the finger pointing, instead staring at her boobs, his gaze lingering way too long before lifting his gaze to the top of her head. "An Iggy?" He gave her a look of total innocence, like he didn't know why she was freaking out, but there was no way he was innocent because the reason for her freak-out had a name. Iggy.

She crossed her arms over her chest, not because she was embarrassed or ashamed of her boobs because she was the first to admit she had better-than-average boobs to go along with her great legs, but because, *really, that's all you have to say?*

Iggy squirmed around, repositioning himself so his tail disappeared. She rolled her eyes upward. The lizard stared back down at her. His tongue darted out.

Oh, for Pete's sake. Reaching up, she scooped him off her head, losing a few strands of hair since the lizard seemed reluctant to let go. She cupped Iggy in her hands and studied him. He was cute, as lizards went, not as cute as the anole she'd had in third grade, but still cute. Greenish brown, about sixteen inches long, including his tail, with nice healthy upright spines. He stared back at her, his black eyes bright and alert.

Growing up, she'd had almost every kind of pet allowed by their apartment management—rabbits, hamsters, exotic fish, and lizards. She liked them. They were smart, generally affectionate, and mostly easy to care for. However, they didn't usually try to sleep with her. What if she'd rolled over? Think of the disaster. Think of how unhappy all three of them would be, but mostly Iggy.

She leveled another narrow-eyed look on Noah that hopefully said, "You're a jerk" but he didn't read it that way. Stepping forward, he laid a lingering kiss on her lips and reclaimed the lizard.

"Iggy, my man. How's it hangin'?" Using one finger, he tickled it under its chin. It made a noise, almost like it was hissing. He grinned. Placing the lizard in the palm of his hand, he held it out to her. "Jenn, meet Iggy. Iggy, meet Jenn."

"Why is Iggy not in a cage?" She gave the lizard a chin scratch and got another hiss in return.

"He's supposed to be." Glancing towards the window, he rolled his eyes. "Crap, I tossed my pants over my head last night and they landed in the terrarium." He pointed to his slacks that were draped half in, half out of the glass terrarium. "He must have crawled up the pant leg to get out." With a final scratch, he carried the lizard back to his enclosure, removed his trousers, the lizard's escape mechanism, and set him gently inside. "Back to sleep, bud," he said and left his pet to his lizardy life.

He shot her a look, his eyes traveling up and down her body, a grin tugging at his mouth. She gave him a sardonic stare in return yet couldn't help noticing that, interestingly, he was at full flag- salute. She was pretty sure it wasn't because of the lizard.

Seeing the direction of her gaze, he looked down at himself and gave an obviously fake cough. "Um. Sun's up. I guess it's time to go to work, right?" One of his hands dropped, oh so coyly, down to cover his salute.

She laughed because it was way too late to hide the goods. He blushed, laughed and removed his hands.

Darn, he was cute when he blushed, but he turned away and she wondered if she'd made a mistake. Maybe, because here was this guy who she barely knew, who she'd played dirty tricks on for the last week, who had played dirty tricks on her in retribution, and yet somehow she'd fallen into bed with him so quickly it was like he'd vacuum-sucked her onto the mattress.

Schlwooop!

And now? So awkward. This must be why so many guys did the wham, bam and scram routine.

She cleared her throat. "Yep, time to get going." She scurried around, gathering up all the odds and ends of her clothes that had been thrown, helter-skelter, everywhere in their overwhelming rush to find the mattress. "I'll ride you back to the gas station so you can get a rental, okay?"

She declined the offer of his shower, saying she planned to go home before work so she could put on clean clothes.

"Then I hope you don't mind if I take a quick shower?" he asked.

After he finished in the bathroom, they dressed, turning their backs, yet she couldn't help looking over her shoulder every ten seconds, and couldn't help noticing that when she did, he was looking over his shoulder too. He was staring at her legs. He seemed to have a thing for her legs. Like she didn't already know that. Like, Legs, right?

She also couldn't help noticing that the guy had one fine ass, and pecs to die for.

Still awkward though. Until he crept up behind her and laid a slow, sweet kiss on her shoulder. It instantly went from awkward to aww.

After checking under the covers, under the bed and around the room to make sure she hadn't forgotten anything, she followed him downstairs. A knock sounded on the door. Noah opened it.

"Yo, bro. Whassup?" A man stood in the doorway, tall and beefy, with one of those beards that could never claim true beard-status because there simply wasn't enough hair there. Under the scraggly fuzz was a big, white-toothed grin. Further up was a pair of bloodshot eyes. Altogether, an unappealing picture.

Noah's jaw tightened. She could feel the tension radiating off him. "Bret, what are you doing here?"

The man's eyes dropped a little and he stared at his feet shuffling on the welcome mat outside. "C'mon, little brother, aren't you going to invite me in?"

"No. I'm on my way to work. What do you want?"

Instead of answering, his brother's gaze turned to survey Jenn. Except for the fact they were bloodshot, his eyes resembled Noah's to a remarkable degree in their light gray color yet, other than the eyes, the two brothers looked nothing alike. Bret was broad where Noah was broad shouldered but slim, Bret was slovenly where Noah was tidy, Noah had a tight body and muscles, yum, where Bret had a beer gut.

For a split second, she was sure she saw a look, almost like calculation, in Bret's eyes, but whatever the look was, it disappeared to be replaced with a warm, friendly gaze of appreciation.

He held his hand out. "Hi, I'm Bret, Noah's big brother."

Reaching for his hand, she began, "Nice to meet you, Bret. I'm Jenn Go—" but stopped when Noah gave her a sharp poke in the back. She looked back over her shoulder to see him, with gritted teeth, gave a slight head shake. "I'm Jenn," she revised. "Nice to meet you. Like Noah said, we were on our way out."

The calculating gleam returned. He turned his gaze to Noah. "New girlfriend, bro?"

"No, only a friend who was kind enough to swing by on her way to work this morning and pick me up because my car broke down." He threw a quick glance towards her Harley parked across the street.

Bret followed his look. "Wow. Nice. Looks expensive. I'd bet over fifteen thou." He turned a speculative look on Jenn, running his gaze up and down her body, yet not in a lascivious way, more like he was adding up the cost of her clothing. She'd seen that kind of look before—and she didn't like it—but before she could say anything, Noah gave her another poke in the back, nudging her out the front door. He turned and locked it behind him.

"We've got to go, Bret. We both have jobs," he said with a hard emphasis on the word jobs.

He stuck his keys in his pocket then stood there, staring at his brother until his brother gave in with a "Whatever" roll of his eyes, turned and walked towards the big red pickup truck parked on the street. He got in, started the engine and drove away.

She lifted a brow. She didn't want to pry, however, there was definitely a story here. Noah lied about her spending the night. Interesting.

"You don't want to know him," he said, and clamped his mouth shut, done with the story.

Given their history, meaning enemies for over a week with only one brief night of insanely hot sex, she didn't feel she had the right to pry but the interaction with his brother left her feeling vaguely uncomfortable. With a nod, she silently led the way over to her bike.

Forcing the scene from her mind, she mounted up on Harley and made room for Noah behind her after they'd both strapped on their helmets. His arms wrapped around her waist. His thighs cradled hers. Oh. My. God. Instant turn-on. Her lady bits were going crazy.

The wind and the roar of cars and trucks passing them by on the highway made it impossible to talk, thank heavens, yet it did nothing to cancel the feel of his warm body pressed against her back. By the time they pulled into the gas station, she was ready to tear off her clothes and lie herself down on Harley's seat to be taken.

Oh, boy, she was in so much trouble. This wasn't at all what she'd planned. She was an adult, at least that's what she told herself, with that adult attitude that meant she was supposed to be smart, sure of herself, and in control. Yet look what she'd done last night. Talk about out of control. It so wasn't like her, but it had been *soooo* good.

He dismounted and watched while she did the same. Removing his helmet, he handed it to her, staring intently into her eyes. Lifting her helmet's face shield, she took it from him and stowed it under the seat, her eyes never leaving his.

He nodded. She nodded back. His eyes dropped to her mouth. She licked her lips. He took a deep breath. She took a deep breath. His eyes widened.

"Crap," he said, and wrapped his hands around her upper arms and yanked her against his chest. His mouth slammed down on hers, his lips, hot as a summer sidewalk, opened over hers, and he devoured her. There were a few groans, not clear whose, a lot of heavy breathing, a bit of bump and grind of pelvises, and a sudden, "Could you two take that elsewhere? You're offending my customers," from the gas station attendant.

They leaped apart. Stared at each other for a few seconds, both of them breathing like steam engines before he pulled himself together and held out his hand. For her to shake.

Really?

"Thanks for the ride."

Really?

Rolling her eyes, she took his hand and shook it. "You're quite welcome. Any time."

"Okay." He hesitated. Shuffled his feet. His eyes met hers then dropped. "Um. Going to go check on my car and then get a rental. See ya'. Bye," he said, and followed the attendant into the station.

She mounted Harley, slid the face shield down and zoomed—okay, she wasn't zooming because there was still the mom issue—onto the street and headed for work a mile away.

Good God. That kiss. Yummy. She couldn't wait for the next one. Of course, that didn't mean she was in love with him. She didn't do love.

Wait. Back up a sec. What was with the hand shaking? The implications of the short interaction suddenly hit her, making her slam on the brakes so hard she almost went over the handlebars. She pulled over to the side of the road and turned off the engine while she agonized over the last few hours. Yes, he'd given her a toe-curling kiss at the gas station, but then he'd shaken her hand. Like she was a casual friend. Or worse, a business acquaintance. Not like a guy who'd had the most amazing, wonderful, stupendous sex he'd ever had. Not like a guy who planned on have a repeat of that sex.

A small hot ember of fear lodged in her chest. It grew and grew and grew, expanding into her throat, threatening to choke her.

Her thoughts returned once more to those few minutes at the gas station. That kiss had rocked her world. She'd never had a kiss like that ever. She wanted more of the same. Surely that kiss meant he wanted more too. Maybe he simply forgot to say so, or maybe he was too embarrassed to say something in front of the attendant. Or, oh God, was Noah Maitland one of those guys who, once he got what he wanted, he didn't want it anymore?

Or maybe....?

Well, she couldn't come up with any more reasons why he didn't say anything but so what. The bottom line was, she wanted more of those kisses, and yeah, all the other stuff too.

That ember in her chest still burned. She rubbed her sternum. Was she getting an ulcer? No, this burning felt more like something she'd felt before; it felt like fear. Fear of being dumped. Fear of public humiliation. Fear that, even if he did want her at this moment, that, sooner or later, he wouldn't, by which time she would be emotionally involved.

Oh, God, she couldn't handle having her heart broken again. She had to protect herself. Maybe she should forget the last twenty-four hours ever happened. Maybe she should chalk it up to one of those things, a one-night stand. Some women didn't have a problem with the one-night stand thing.

Unfortunately, she did.

Which meant she couldn't let Megan know about last night. Private things should stay private. Private things weren't meant to be discussed with one's assistant.

Private things that stayed private meant the entire world wouldn't learn that Noah Maitland had broken her heart.

Been there, done that already. Twice.

The only solution was to do what she'd decided last night; enjoy it for what it was worth yet not become emotionally invested.

She restarted Harley's engine and headed home where she took a nice long hot shower, washed her hair and blew it dry. Since they hadn't eaten before they left Noah's place, she made herself an omelet and ate in front of the TV in her kitchen while watching the news. Going back upstairs, she changed into a flowery summer dress with a low-cut bodice and a short flouncy skirt. Sandals. No pantyhose because.... Well, because. She looked good. She looked hot, hot as in sexy, not hot as in sweaty.

What would he think when he saw her? Would he jump her bones which is exactly what she wanted. Would he even care anymore now that they'd had sex? Or would he believe she was trying to trick him somehow? Whatever the answer, maybe it was time to give it up. Leave the poor guy alone, let him go back to his life. She was sure he'd be happy to see the last of her and her dirty tricks. Better for her too.

On her way to work, she stopped, per her mother's request, to pick up Trike, shoved him into the back seat of the car and drove the rest of the way into Princeton.

The minute she walked in, Megan bounced out of her chair. "You're late. But that's okay because I had time to make some arrangements about how to get back at Mr. Rat in response to his screwing with us with his so-called 'gifts'," she announced with a big grin.

"Um..." Wait. What? What was Megan talking about? They hadn't talked about playing any more pranks.

"Yeah, you're going to love it," Megan continued even though Jenn hadn't responded. "I arranged to have a big sack full of week-old fish sent to him. It should arrive any time now." Megan rubbed her hands together, her eyes sparkling with glee.

Oh, no. Hadn't she just two minutes ago decided it was time to leave the poor guy alone so he could go back to his life? Hadn't she decided no more dirty tricks?

She shook her head no, yet Megan kept talking.

"He's going to hate it. Serves him right for sending those chocolates and the cookies and stuff, right, and tormenting us." She rubbed her hands together again. "This is so much fun. I love a good revenge, don't you? I can't wait to see what he does in return."

Oh. Nuts

"Megan..." she said weakly.

"What?" Megan responded, her smile fading. "Is something wrong? It's a good idea, right? I mean, you hate him, right? You want to get back at him, right?" she said, looking so hopeful Jenn didn't know how she was going to tell her assistant that their erstwhile enemy was no longer their enemy. She didn't know if he was a friend either, but whatever.

"Can you stop it?"

Megan gaped at her. "Stop it? No, why?"

She didn't have an answer. She didn't know if she wanted to have an answer, however, she knew what she did want—she wanted more kisses, more sex, more

Noah. Jenn yanked on a hank of hair, feeling slightly sick to her stomach, not sure if the wobbly butterflies in her stomach were from excitement or guilt or fear.

Maybe Megan's scheme was fate, like that kismet thing. Maybe having the decision taken out of her hands was the way it should be, merely a game and not a love affair. She could handle that. Just have fun. Don't get involved. Don't feel anything. Maybe, just maybe, if it was only a game nobody—namely her—would get hurt.

"When did you say this delivery was coming?"

"Good news. Like now."

The good news? Oh god, who was she kidding? There was no good news. It was all bad news. He wasn't going to take it well. Maybe she could stop it. "Megan," she said. However, she was too late because at that moment, a small yellow van with the words Grocery-Town painted on the side pulled up in front of Noah's place A man carrying a plastic bag got out, walked up the front walk and entered the bungalow. They both held their breath. Within minutes, the man left and drove away.

Okay. Okay. It was happening. The plan was in motion. She could barely breathe. Her palms were sweaty. Her stomach was twisted in a knot. Within minutes she would know whether this morning's handshake meant they were done or whether there was a chance for more of what she'd enjoyed with Noah.

Returning to her office, she grabbed the dog's collar and dragged her, whining and protesting, into the kitchen and locked the door. She rushed back to her office, her brain rapidly running through the details of how this would play out.

Ready or not, it was showtime.

NINETEEN

NoahMaitland@noahmaitlandesq

Carpe Diem does not mean 'Fish of the Day'.

Very little was getting done at work because no way could he work when all he could think about was Jenn? Too bad life wasn't like that movie, *Groundhog Day*, where the Bill Murray character relived the same twenty-four hours over and over and over. If Noah could pick any time to relive, he would pick the previous twelve hours.

Even now, he could still feel the lurch of his stomach, the hollow, sickening feeling when the Slingshot launched him up into the air and then plummeted him straight down a hundred-and-fifty-foot drop.

He could still feel the exhilaration he'd experienced when his feet touched the ground, and the wild excitement of success thrumming through his veins. His arms still held this phantom sensation of Jenn when he hugged her and swung her in a circle and celebrated the conquering of his fear and the resulting freedom he'd felt.

Even better, he could still taste her on his lips, still hear the beat of her heart as he lay his head on her chest, still feel the warm brush of her hands on his body. He could still faintly smell her. He could still feel her heat and tightness surrounding him when he made love to her.

She had invaded every fiber of his body.

He wanted her. He wanted what they had yesterday and last night, and this morning, especially this morning, because this morning hadn't been about sex; it had been about two people being together and laughing at life's foibles. He wanted it with the depths of his soul. She was the One. Now all he had to do was figure out what he had to do to convince her.

The door opened. One hand over her nose, Debra waved the other hand over her shoulder. "There's this guy here who has a delivery and a message for you. Said you're the only one he can give it to."

Frowning, he got up and followed her into the main reception area. The minute he did, he could tell something wasn't right. There was this smell...

The delivery man handed him a plastic bag and mumbled, "The girl what gave me this order said to tell you Jenn sent it," and practically ran out the door. Noah untied the plastic bag. Inside was a second bag. Even with the second bag still tied shut, the odor emanating from inside nearly knocked him over.

He dropped it on the floor and took a few steps back. "What the hell?"

His office manager shook her head, her hand over her mouth.

"Open it," he told her, pointing at the bag inside the bigger bag.

Debra's brown eyes widened then narrowed in a glare. "I'm not opening it. It's above my pay grade. Anyway, he said it's for you. Not me. You."

Gritting his teeth, he stooped and gingerly untied the second bag. The odor became nauseatingly strong.

Fish. Days-old, over-ripe fish. Son of a bitch. He wondered if there was some kind of oblique message in the fact that it was over-ripe fish, or if she hoped it would bring him running. He smiled. It only took him seconds to answer his own question. This wasn't how he would have arranged their next tryst, but it didn't matter; he'd take what he could get.

He closed the bag, retied the knot and handed it to Debra. "Get rid of it."

Debra gasped. Still, she took the bag, her eyes letting him know that he would eventually get what he deserved.

"I'll be back." Storming out the front door, he marched across both driveways and into the house next door.

"Where is she?" he yelled. His heart slammed in his chest with excitement, but his cock already knew what awaited it and was leading the way, hot and hard in anticipation.

Her eyes wide, Red pointed to the closed door behind her. "In there," she squeaked.

He took a deep breath. She was inside that room, behind that closed door. Jenn, with her long, long legs and her daring spirit and her lips that set him on fire. He suppressed the grin that threatened to break out.

"Fine," he snarled. "I have a few things to say to Miss Stinky Fish. Don't come in unless you're asked to." Turning the knob, he shoved open the door. He slammed it behind him. Then stopped and grinned.

She sat on her desk, legs parted enticingly, wearing only her bra—red, his favorite color—thong panties and high-heeled sandals. Fucking hell in a handbag.

JennGoodwin@MyHeart-2-Heart

Love is the only game that is not called on account of darkness

Sweet Betsy, the man was hot. "Yell at me," she whispered.

He frowned, shaking his head *what?* and looking confused. "Yell at me," she repeated and jerked her chin towards her closed office door, and Megan.

Enlightenment flared in his eyes. He grinned. "How could you?" he shouted, his grin growing bigger. Hopefully, it wasn't the only thing growing bigger.

"What, Mr. Smart-aleck Attorney? How could I what?" she shouted back, at the same time curling a finger to beckon him closer.

Two strides brought him between her legs. "You sent dead fish! My office smells like someone died in there!" he shouted over his shoulder loud enough for her assistant to hear. He unbuckled his belt and unzipped. His cock sprang out and every part of her body jumped up and woofed. Her boobs tightened, her nipples tingled and between her legs there was an ache only he could take care of.

Reaching into his slacks pocket, he pulled out a condom and held it up for her to see.

Saliva gathered in her mouth. She licked her lips. "You deserved it!" she shouted and held her hand out for it. She wanted to do the honors. He tore off the wrapper and placed it in her hand. She loved the feel of him in her hands, big and hard, hot and silky, as she rolled it on.

He groaned. "What! What did I do to you that deserved dead fish!" His voice ended on a tremulous high note. His face was tense, his eyes hotly focused on hers. Reaching behind her back, he unhooked her bra, and he slid the straps off her arms before allowing it to fall to the floor. He dove forward, snagging a breast and sucked it into his mouth.

She squeaked. And forced the next words out. "You sent us cookies! You sent us ice cream!"

He gave up sucking her breast long enough to shout, "So what! I was trying to say I was sorry!" He went back to licking.

Zap! It was as if her breast was a direct link to her vagina. "You were trying to poison us!" No longer able to stay upright, she fell onto her back.

"I was not!" He went with her, leaning over her body to lavish kisses on her neck, rubbing his cock against the crotch of her panties. "It was supposed to be an apology."

"You toad! You rat! You horrible, horrible man!" she shouted. Fire shot through her lady bits. "But don't stop," she whispered. "You amazing piece of male perfection." Dear heaven, how she needed him.

"Never," he whispered back and, pushing aside the delicate piece of fabric covering her mons, he slowly slid into her.

She almost went through the roof. "Oh my God," she mumbled and lifting her hips, she urged him on. She bit her lip, her mind shattering into a thousand shards of wonderfulness.

His face tightened. He drove into her, his hips ramming forward, shoving her across the desk. God, it was good, it hurt, it was fantastic. She almost couldn't stand it.

He fingered her clit. She screamed—oops—then replaced her passionate scream with, "I'll get you for this! I'll pay you back if it's the last thing I do!"

He stroked, he petted, he continued to finger her clit, his body hot against hers. "God, I hope you do. Ten times a day. A hundred times a day" he whispered in her ear. Then, lifted up off her to yell, "Yeah, you think you're so smart. You wait, lady. You'll get what's *coming* to you," loud enough for Megan to hear. He snorted with laughter at his joke.

"I.... ay yi yi," Jenn screamed because he'd hit the right spot. She burst into flames, and shouted again, at the last minute turning her cries of satisfaction into, "I hate you, you dirty rat!" She ran her tongue around his ear and whispered, "But I love what you do. Oh, God."

At her words, he leaned away from her a tad, the smile on his face dissolving. "Jenn. Goddamn, what you do to me." His rhythm slowed, his thrusts becoming slow caresses that reached into the heart of her. He stared into her eyes, his own ablaze. "I love this, what we do together." He slid into her, holding the position for a moment, and withdrew, leaving little tendrils of exquisite delight behind.

"The way your gorgeous long legs hold me so tight. Your hair." He ran his fingers through a few strands. "Like silk. So tantalizing. I want to wrap myself in it like a heavenly shroud. The way you smell drives me wild."

His words settled into her mind, warm and honeyed, and spread through her body, sparking tiny explosions of happiness.

And suddenly shooting little darts of fear. Oh dear.

He stopped moving. Reaching over her head, he curled his fingers around her outstretched hand, using his other arm to prop himself above her. His eyes met hers, his gaze filled with something that both thrilled her and scared her to death. She could feel him trembling.

"Jenn." He stopped, licked his lower lip, took a breath. His hand squeezed hers so tightly, her knuckles ground together. "I think... I feel... I think I'm in—"

She slapped her free hand over his mouth. "Don't!" Oh, God, don't say it. It wasn't right. It wasn't time. It wasn't true. It was a lie. It was always a lie, and it always led to heartbreak.

They stared at each other, neither daring to breathe. She watched something in his eyes shift, swirl, and dissipate into a cold flatness.

Eyes narrowed, he jerked a nod.

He gave a little push with his hips, withdrew and shoved back in, hard, ferociously, a muscle in his jaw clenching under her palm when he pushed into her body, once, twice, three times, the pace relentless, the gentleness gone. Whatever he had been about to say was also gone, for good or bad. She wished she knew which. She wished she understood why she cared. She wished she could figure out why she'd stopped the words. She wished she wasn't afraid. She wished she didn't let fear rule so much of her life. Oh, God, if wishes were horses, she'd have enough to pull an entire stagecoach.

Resigned, she allowed her hand to drop away.

"Fuck," he muttered, his gaze still fierce on her as he drove into her, pushing her across the desktop with the strength of his thrusts.

"Yes, that. Only that. Nothing else. Please."

With a groan, he gave one last hard thrust, one last groan and exploded, his hips driving against her erratically, his breathing harsh in her ear.

Her breath rasped in her chest. Oh God. Yes. That. What were the words? Cataclysmic? Mind-bending? Life-changing. No. No. It can't be.

She tried to gather her spinning thoughts, remembering Keith, her college boyfriend, remembering all the other old hurts, the betrayals, recalling the old ways of coping and finally was able to shout, "Leave me alone!" although she barely had enough energy to breathe.

He shook, panted, adding a few feeble thrusts now that he was done. "Gladly," he tried to shout, but it came out breathy and weak. He tried again. "Gladly," he shouted then, "Not in a million years!" he whispered in her ear,

His hips stopped moving. He inhaled deeply, rested against her for a minute before peeling himself off her body. He looked shaken, confused, smug, all at the same time. Taking a step backwards, backwards, he removed the condom and tossed it into the nearby trash can, then, tucking himself into his pants, he straightened his tie and smoothed down his hair. The perfect attorney was back, yet the look in his eyes was more plundering pirate.

She slid off her desk. Her poor legs wobbled, almost collapsing. She grabbed her dress with nearly numb fingers and slipped it on over her head. Staggering to her chair, she collapsed into the seat. Holy cow. Could a woman die from ecstasy? She inhaled a lungful of air—which, yikes, smelled like sex—prompting her to grab a can of aerosol air freshener and sprayed the heck out of the room.

She tossed the can back into the drawer, sat back and stared at him, sure she looked more confused than he did. Her chest ached. For some reason, she felt like wailing like a child. What had happened? It was more. Way more. It was too much. Her big plan to have a casual affair, enjoy the sex, enjoy his body and his company had just gone wonky in a big way. Tears threatened. She needed to get it back on track.

Like right this minute. "Get out...of my life," she wheezed. She had to grope for the words because her brain, along with her tongue, had melted like that carton of chocolate caramel swirl ice cream. This was supposed to be about sex and what happened today was threatening to ruin it.

"Get out of my life," she repeated, shouting it this time as she regained her breath, her confidence, her attitude. Attitude was supposed to keep her from getting her heart broken. "Until the next time," she whispered, her heart clenching. Those tears were now closer to the surface.

Still holding her gaze, he straightened his spine, pulled back his broad shoulders. She could almost see him rebuilding the shell he kept around himself. Good. That was what they needed. Distance.

He took a deep breath. "My pleasure!" he yelled. He gave himself one last check to make sure everything was where it should be and turned to leave. At the door, he paused. He turned to face her then laid a hand over his heart and tapped several times. Another pause, before he yanked the door open and walked out.

"I'm telling you, Ms. Goodwin," he threw over his shoulder. "Any more of your tricks and you'll be sorry!"

She sat for a second, and then, because she couldn't help herself, she jumped up and followed him. He reached the outer door.

"If you're going to send something, I like truffles," she said.

One of his eyebrows went up. He grinned. "Got it," he said and exited.

Rushing to the door, she watched him stride across their driveways. He reached his front yard. She stepped out onto the porch, watching his gorgeous sexy ass as he rounded the corner and disappeared from view. With a sigh, she turned to go back inside. Out of the corner of her eye, she spotted a truck pull up in front of Noah's house. She stopped. The truck looked vaguely familiar. It had the same dented left front fender as the one she'd seen Noah's brother get into. She examined it. It had the same tiny American flag on the antenna.

None of her business.

She turned and went inside. Megan was standing by her desk, arms folded over her chest, foot tapping. She stared at Jenn.

"What was that?" her assistant asked.

Jenn smiled, trying for one of those nonchalant faces that would throw her assistant off the track. "He was a little upset about the fish."

"Hmm. Sure, I'll bet. What about that thing about the truffles?"

Casting her eyes upwards, she stared at the ceiling. "Oh yeah, that. Um... he said this wasn't over. I had to give him something."

Megan's eyes light up. "So do you think he'll retaliate?"

One could only hope. The sooner the better. "Absolutely, but if he does, I want the retaliation to at least be something I like, right?"

Megan's lower lip went out in a pout. "I don't like truffles. Why didn't you ask him to send something I like, like caramel corn?"

Oh, boy. She sighed. "Okay. Next time." Shaking her head—assistants—she retreated to her office, shut the door behind her and stared into space for a while, tapping a fist against her mouth as she assessed the last ten minutes. It had never been like that. Maybe it was the duality of the situation, making love while they pretended to fight. Maybe it was the fact that they made love in her office while Megan was right outside the door and could walk in at any time—like Jenn had walked in on Nick and Amy. Or maybe it was him, and it could continue to be him if he played by her rules.

Usually she was a woman who didn't mind taking risks, example, her motorcycle. Yet she had never risked her heart. But this thing with Noah, this...this...felt a lot like risking her heart which was why she'd stopped him before anything irretrievable could be said.

She hadn't wanted to know if what Noah had been about to say was an admission of love.

On a more worrisome note, there was this insidious need to know him better. Her thoughts went round and round, like a hamster on a hamster wheel. Too much thinking. Too much feeling. Too much yearning. Too much fear. It was killing her.

The phone rang. Surprise. It was Amy.

"Hey, girl. I need to let you know we aren't coming back until a week from Friday. My *husband*—" She stressed the word husband. "met this woman who owns an island and wants some work done on the house she owns there. Nick wants to go take a look, see if maybe he can get the job. If so, it would be a great way to get some additional time at the lovely ocean. I'm hoping we can leave on the flight we already booked but..."

"Oh."

"Yeah. So...the dog."

Poor Jenn, stuck with Trike, while Amy and Nick enjoy the sunshine. Yet, somehow the prospect wasn't quite as bad as it was two weeks ago, although now that she thought about it, she should call her insurance agent and try to increase her coverage for any additional damage. Would destruction by dog be covered under her policy? Could a three-legged, one-eyed drooly dog be considered a natural disaster? Who knew? Still, no harm in trying.

After a little further discussion hammering out some details, they said good-bye and hung up.

Megan stuck her head through Jenn's doorway. She grinned. "Guess what? You have a VIG visitor."

Jenn lifted a brow.

"A Very Inquisitive Grandmother." Megan retreated and came back with Tess who sashayed into the office and made herself comfortable in Jenn's guest chair.

Tess rubbed her hands together. "Okay. Let's talk about Noah. There are things you need to know starting with his family."

TWENTY

NoahMaitland@noahmaitlandesq

I didn't quit, I just realized the game wasn't worth playing anymore.

Noah strode across the driveways, his heart still pounding, his body on fire. God, it had been even better than last night. The sight of her sitting on her desk clad in nothing more than her panties, bra and strappy little sandals had been enough to send him into orbit. He wanted her like he'd never wanted any other woman before. He wanted those legs. Those gorgeous breasts. Her eyes. God, he loved her eyes. So blue, so intense they dared him to love her harder. So beautiful when they softened into mist when she came. They had made love five minutes ago, and he already wanted her again.

The need for her was like a sharp needle in his chest, pricking and poking him, but it wasn't only her body or her beautiful face he needed. He needed her laughter, her bravery, her in-your-face attitude that somehow added something to his life that he didn't have. He'd lived his entire life trapped behind unseen bars. Jenn Goodwin held the key that would free him.

He'd almost told her so, however, for some reason, she'd stopped him. Didn't every woman want to be told they were beautiful, desirable...loved?

Loved? If not for her hand clapped over his mouth, he would have told her so. The idea that what he was feeling was love was exhilarating, but scary as hell. Love could mean soaring to the heights. It could mean warm arms and a safe place to fall and the possibility of that thing they call happily ever-after, yet, God help him, it also would also mean he would have to let down the barriers he'd crafted so carefully over the years.

It meant letting go of his usual control. Letting go of his need to plan, to make things happen the way he wanted them. To leaving nothing to chance. Yesterday, he'd thrown caution to the winds. He'd let go of his habitual rigid control and trusted that wherever that took him, that in the end, he would be okay. It was like he'd been set free from a cage he had been happy in only because he didn't know there was life outside that cage.

He wanted her, but what about Jenn? Could he convince her he was worth the risk, or was he setting himself up for heartbreak? The possibility was terrifying but everything he was ached to take that plunge because, when he considered it, it wasn't really a risk at all. It was simply right.

He bounded up the front stairs and entered the reception room and stopped dead. Trooper Swenson jumped to his feet from where he'd been sitting on the edge of his assistant's desk. Debra rose too, her big dark eyes widening in alarm.

"What? Why are you here?" He reviewed the last few days in his mind, again wondering what laws he might have broken. Oh, fuck, now that he contemplated it, there were so many.

Swenson waved a hand. "Hey, Mr. Attorney, no worries. I'm here to pick up Debra."

Noah swung his gaze to his assistant. Even with her dusky skin, he could see her blush. He jerked his chin towards the trooper. "You and him?"

Her lips quirked in an embarrassed smile.

Fucking A. Just what he needed, an officer of the law in and out of his office at random, waiting for him to make an ass out of himself. He studied the two of them. Maybe it wouldn't hurt to have an in with the law. He shook his head. What was he supposed to say other than, "Well, have fun."

Debra's face lit up in a smile.

The click of his front door opening reached Noah then the sound of heavy footsteps. He looked over his shoulder to see his brother entering the front room. Damn it.

"Hey, bro," Bret said in jovial tones and threw an arm around Noah's shoulder to give him a bear hug. Double damn it. He side-eyed a look at Swenson, who had discreetly taken a step back into the shadows of the hallway leading to the kitchen.

He returned his gaze to his brother. "Bret, why are you here?"

"C'mon, can't I visit my only brother once in a while?"

Christ, why did he keep asking that same question? "No. What do you want? If it's money, I don't have any to give you right now."

A smile spread across Bret's face, so fake, so conniving, Noah wanted to throw up. "Geez, little brother, you sure have a low opinion of me."

With good reason.

"I wanted to tell you that I broke up with that girl you saw me with the other day. I thought that would make you happy."

It did, however, he wasn't going to tell his brother, it would encourage him to stay. "Okay, now you've told me, so you can leave."

Bret's mouth gaped open, and his eyes popped wide like he was shocked. He wasn't. Nothing about the man was ever what it seemed to be. "Whoa, hold on, bro, that's not the only reason I came."

Gritting his teeth, he waited.

"That girl? You know the one? That woman you were with this morning? I was going to ask you if you had her number so I could ask her out but, hey—"

Noah jammed his hands into his pockets because otherwise he might use them for something other than jingling the coins he found there.

"But I guess I don't need to 'cause I see she's right next door." Bret smirked.

The need to pound his fist into his brother's face was so strong, it made Noah nauseous. Every muscle in his body was trembling. "Leave her alone."

"Aw, c'mon, Noah. She's totally hot, and I kind of dig her, and since you said you're only friends why wouldn't she go out with me?"

Fuck. This was so typical of his brother, act like a total asshole and then wait for Noah to take a swing at which point Bret would feel justified in striking back. That had been their history throughout their childhood. But Noah was now an adult, so he tried to restrain himself.

"I said, leave her alone. She's not for you."

Bret's fake smile disappeared. His mouth thinned and hot anger blazed from his eyes. "Why? Because she's got money, and I don't? Yeah, I know all about her. She owns that business next door, but even better, she's rich. Why wouldn't I want a piece of that sweet little pussy?"

Noah hit him.

Bret staggered back, hitting the wall behind him and bouncing off. Catching his balance, he righted himself and charged at Noah.

Emerging from the shadows, Swenson rushed forward and grabbed Bret in a bear hug.

"Son of a bitch! Let me go, asshole." Bret struggled in the trooper's grip, swearing and swinging his arms.

"Settle down," Swenson said. "Or I'll have to arrest you."

Bret froze. He turned his head to peer over his shoulder at the six-foot-five trooper who was staring grimly at him.

Nothing was said for a few minutes while the trooper continued to hold Bret in a tight hug. Finally, a sneer still gracing his lips, his brother relaxed. "Let me go. I'm fine. I'm leaving."

The trooper opened his arms, leaving his captive free to go. Bret straightened his clothes, not that it made any difference, and stomped out. The outer door slammed behind him.

Damn it. Noah ran a shaking hand through his hair while confusion raged through him. His heart slammed in his chest and sweat covered his body.

Shit. Shit, shit, shit, shit, shit. What did Bret mean, rich? Rich like she made a good living, or rich like Bret found out about the robbery and had leaped to some unfounded assumptions? God, he hoped it wasn't the latter because even a hint that she might have that kind of money could be trouble.

He took a deep breath and let it out. What was he thinking? To Bret, anyone with more than a hundred dollars in their bank account was rich because the guy didn't have a pot to piss in. That Jenn was co-owner of a business and rode an expensive motorcycle would be enough to turn the man on. No way could Bret have learned about her father, right? Even Noah, with his skills honed by years of fact-finding as an attorney, had a hard time digging up the little bit of information he'd found.

Not wanting to invade her privacy, Noah hadn't read more than the headline. Maybe it was time he did.

"I feel like I know that guy," Swenson murmured after a minute.

So did most of New Jersey's finest. "It wouldn't be surprising."

An awkward silence fell over the room. Debra broke it by chirping brightly, "Well, I guess we should go, Lance. Noah, we'll be back in an hour." She grabbed Swenson's hand and practically dragged him from the room.

Noah walked into his office, his mind swirling with thoughts that had no beginning, no end, merely bits and pieces that he tried to make sense of without success. He finally put aside his anger at his brother in favor of the one possibility that continued to rise to the surface—he was falling in love with Jenn, yet she still wanted to play games. He had no desire to play games.

He tore open a new bag of M&M's, shook out a few and popped a couple of red ones into his mouth. How was he going to convince her that love was worth the risk? That *he* was worth the risk?

Fuck. It was almost like his problem with his family. Logically he grasped he had to cut them off, but he hadn't been able to do it. Rubbing his chest against the ache that had lodged there, he gave thought to what Gram had said, that he was as dependent on them accepting his money as they were to receive it. Why couldn't he say no?

He wasn't sure that he liked the answer.

TWENTY-ONE

JennGoodwin@MyHeart-2-Heart

I'm not afraid to fall in love—I'm afraid to fall for the wrong person. AGAIN.

Where was the dratted man? Jenn tapped her fingers on her Lucite desk in frustration. She was sure she'd made it clear what she expected from him during and after the heart-stopping sex on her desk, but if she hadn't been obvious enough, there was his grandmother.

She had to smile, remembering their interview. Poor lady, she was positive she was being so clever with her story about how Bruce didn't want a committed relationship so maybe Jenn should find Tess another match. Still, what the heck was Jenn supposed to believe when someone said they weren't interested in a committed relationship at the same time they were making whoopee with the partner they didn't want to commit to.

Tess said it like that, one big, long sentence she'd blurted out, looking so guilty and embarrassed Jenn realized immediately it was a lie. It wouldn't have mattered anyway; she had already talked to Bruce, and he was crazy about Tess Maitland, but she played along purely to see what would happen, and to have a little fun, then sent the lady back next door with a message for her grandson—it was his turn.

After all that, one would think the object of her obsession would have found the time to respond to her invitation, yet all day yesterday had passed and nothing. Maybe he was one of those fickle guys who were more interested in playing the field. She'd certainly met plenty of guys like that, yet she'd assumed he was different. She'd hoped he was different. He had to be different, because he'd almost said the L word. Hadn't he?

"So where is he?" she asked Trike, who lay at her feet, snoring.

Like she knew she was being addressed, the dog opened her good eye and peered up at her.

"Well?"

The dog wuffled, sighed and closed her eye again.

Megan entered her office and shut the door behind her. "There's this guy in reception who said he wants to see you about joining, but I'm not sure he's our kind of client."

She frowned. "Why's that?"

Her assistant stared at the ceiling, winding a curl around a finger. "Well, he's kind of...uh... He doesn't look like he can afford us, you know? Just jeans and a tee-shirt, both a little grubby."

"So, in other words, he dresses like Mark Zuckerberg."

Megan's expression went flat. "Oh. Yeah. Got it. Okay, whatev. Guess I'll bring him in," she conceded.

Having made her point, Jenn sat back, hoping she was right, that the guy in their waiting room were a Mark Zuckerberg clone, although if he was Mark Zuckerberg rich, he wouldn't need someone else to find him a wife.

The door reopened, and a man walked in. It wasn't Mark Zuckerberg. It wasn't even Murray Zuckerberg, the guy who sold newspapers on the corner of Nassau and Witherspoon in Princeton.

It was Noah's brother. What the heck?

With a veiled look, the guy threw himself into a chair and propped his foot, clad in a heavy boot, on the edge of her desk.

Jenn glared at his foot, a slow burn creeping up her neck. His foot came down with a thump.

"Oops, sorry about that. I was doing some digging out in the yard. Guess I should have cleaned up a little before coming here." He ran a hand through his already disheveled hair, his face reddening.

"What can I do for you, Bret?" she asked.

"Oh, wow, you remember me. I was sure you wouldn't."

"I meet new people all day long. It's my job to remember their names."

His smile deflated a bit. He took a deep breath and came in for a second assault. "Well, then, great, you're so good at the new people thing and all, I bet you remember I'm Noah's brother."

She said nothing, however, what she was thinking was, why was he here, and what did he want? Megan had been right, the torn jeans and the lack of hygiene told her he wasn't their kind of client. Therefore she may as well get right to the point. Hopefully politely scare him away.

"Well, then, let me tell you about our membership packages," she started.

Something swirled in his eyes, the same something she thought she'd seen the other day when they were coming out of Noah's apartment. Then his eyes went blank. Something about the transformation made her uneasy, yet it never paid to be judgmental. She'd been wrong in the past—look at the thing with Noah—i.e., the pickpocket thing—and for certain there would be times in the future when she was wrong.

"Our cheapest membership is fifteen hundred dollars and entitles you to six matches and access to our monthly events for six months. The next package is the three-thousand-dollar membership—"

He held a hand up. "Whoa. Stop right there." He scrubbed a hand under his nose. "Is that the cheapest you got? Fifteen hundred dollars?"

She stared at him, saying nothing.

"Oh, wow. That's a lot of money. See, I been married twice..." His hand returned to his nose to rub again. "Neither one of them worked out—guess I'm simply a lousy picker—so now I want to find a girl that I can settle down with and have kids with and be happy, you know? And I thought if someone else did the picking. But…" His voice trailed off. "No way can I afford those prices, not right now anyway." He sniffed and scrubbed a hand under his nose for the third time.

If he couldn't afford her, there was no way he was right for any of her clients. She delivered her best professional smile to soften the blow. "I'm sorry to hear that. Maybe in the future."

He paused for a moment and simply frowned at her, his eyes hooded. "Yeah, sure, maybe I can… if my br…" he said, his tone bitter before continuing with, "I mean, Noah… He and I… He hasn't always…uh, been the kind of guy you should…oh, shit, I shouldn't say anything. Still, just be careful, okay?" He sent her an assessing look from under his furry brows.

Be careful? What, in case Noah overwhelmed her with cookies and ice cream?

"I'm sorry. I shouldn't air dirty family laundry to strangers but I may as well say it. See, it's that he's got these issues and I don't want you to get hurt, you know?" Bret added even though she hadn't asked for further details.

Issues? What issues? She clamped her teeth over all the questions she wanted to ask. Noah's issues were none of her business, however, Bret had hit upon one of her basic fears, that she would get emotionally involved with the wrong man—oh crap, she was already emotionally involved—which meant she would be hurt.

"Hey," he laughed with a roll of his eyes. "It's not like he's a serial killer or anything. It's only, you know, you saw how he was the other day." He fidgeted for a moment. Another, louder sniff. He cleared his throat loudly. "So you're not dating him or anything, are you? I mean, seeing as he said… well, I kinda thought…"

Dating? It was too soon to call it dating. She wasn't sure what she would call it. Certainly not a relationship. Maybe more along the lines of sex buddies.

Not that it was any of Bret's business. "No, definitely not. I gave him a lift to work, that's all," she said, for some reason deciding to stick to the lie Noah told.

Another sniffle. Reaching into his jeans pocket, he pulled out a wad of Kleenex and blew his nose. He stuck the tissue back into his pocket. "Well, good, 'cause I'd hate to see you dating him. I mean, he is my little brother, and all, and

I've always protected him, but I'm kind of tired of his problems. It seems like no matter what I do, he's never happy."

That didn't sound anything like the man she was beginning to know. In fact, she'd have to say, he'd been pretty darned happy the last time she saw him.

Bret heaved an exaggerated sigh. "No matter how much I give him, it's never enough. He always wants more. It's like he's got this hole inside him that he thinks money will fill. I feel bad my parents didn't want him and dumped him on our crazy grandmother, but that's no excuse for not paying me back the money he owes me."

First of all, she'd met that 'crazy grandmother,' and Tess didn't seem crazy at all. A little eccentric, but certainly not crazy. Secondly, Noah dressed nicely and had just set up a new business next door. He was an attorney, a successful one from what she'd read. Why would he borrow money from his brother, who looked like he didn't have a pot to pee in? Although, there was that ten-year-old car parked in his driveway.

"See, the thing is," Bret continued. "He makes more money than me so I can't figure out why he's always broke. Sometimes I wonder... I mean, I hope he's not... Well, he did enjoy a joint or two way back when, but he swore he was done with that." He sneezed, pulled that tissue from his pocket again and blew his nose. Stuffing the tissue back in his pocket, he shot her a look from under his heavy brows. "That's what he told me and I believe him, you know?"

Drugs? She didn't believe it. She'd been in Noah's home, spent the night with him, and she'd seen no indication of drugs.

At last Bret stood, preparing to leave. "So, listen. If the guy ever pays me back, maybe I'll come back, okay?" With that, he waved goodbye and left.

Bret's conversation was full of innuendos and hints of possible problems yet everything she'd learned of Noah so far belied Bret's comments. What was she supposed to believe? The whole thing left her with an unsettled feeling.

At her feet, Trike groaned, stretched and woke up with a snuffle. The mangy mutt shook her head, flinging gross dog slobber all over Jenn's new dress. Lifting up, she farted.

Jenn stared down at her dress. It was covered in goo and leftover dog food. Darn it. She would have to change clothes. Leading the dog out to her car, she drove the twenty minutes to her mother's house, dropped off the dog, went home and changed into slacks and a nice blouse. She returned to her office and continued to obsess over Noah's continued absence.

The end of the day rolled around and still nothing from the guy next door. To say she was disappointed was an understatement. It was after five and Megan had already gone home. Shutting off her computer, she left her office and locked the door behind her. Reaching her car, she pulled out her keys, prepared to open the door when suddenly something was wrapped around her head, blinding her. Hard muscled arms went around her, trapping her arms next to her body.

She squeaked. Her heart leaped.

"I am the Dread Pirate Roberts," said a voice in her ear in the worst English accent she'd ever heard. "And you are being kidnapped, my sweet Princess Buttercup."

Oh my God, bad English accent or not, she recognized the voice immediately. She giggled. "Oh, oh, please don't hurt me, Mr. Pirate."

"As you wish, my Princess." Against her back, she could feel his manly chest shake with laughter. One of his hands stroked across her arm and edged over to her breast. He cupped her, squeezing gently, sending a lightning strike of desire straight to her lady parts. Her legs wobbled weakly with lust. Apparently this was his version of revenge. Luckily, his version was way better than sending dead, smelly fish.

"Come with me." Holding her elbow, he drew her away from her car. She still couldn't see, yet she trusted him to guide her carefully. The smooth pavement under her feet gave way to the grassy space between their driveways then became pavement again. The snick of a car door opening echoed. Placing his hand on her head, he guided her inside and snapped on her seatbelt. The door slammed shut.

She reached up to remove the hood. The driver's side door opened, and he slid inside. "No, no, no, do not touch zee blindfold," he said, his words inexplicably sliding into a French accent.

She snickered but left the blindfold alone.

"Here, open zee mouth." Something was placed between her lips. She crunched into it. An M&M. Yum.

"Where are we going?" she said, still laughing, however, underneath the laughter was the buzz of excitement. She was waiting for him to touch her again. She wanted him to stroke her, fondle her, light her fire. Being unable to see his touch coming made it even more titillating.

Instead of a touch, she got, "Quiet, wench." The English version of the Dread Pirate Roberts was back. "I'm trying to kidnap you. Hostages should not ask questions."

This had to be the most bizarre kidnapping in history. "How long is this kidnapping going to take?" she asked next, because the longer the better. Still, there was one small, drooly problem. "Because Trike is at my mother's place. If this kidnapping is going to take very long, I need to tell my Mom I might not be there to pick the dog up for a while."

"You vill call your mutter, ja?" he said, his accent now German. He slid her purse off her arm and rooted around inside. "Vas ist her number?"

She was laughing so hard now she could barely speak, but she managed to give him the number. Several moments later, a phone was placed in her outstretched hand.

"You vill speak," said the pirate.

"Mom?"

"Jenn?" she heard loud and clear. "Where are you? You were supposed to be here half an hour ago."

Still shaking with laughter, she had to make several attempts before she managed to answer. "Um, Mom? I'm probably not going to be there soon. Maybe not till late. Hard to say... since I've been kidnapped."

"What!"

More laughter spilled out. "It's okay, Mom. I'm being kidnapped by a friend."

"What friend?" her mother asked, her voice suspicious.

"The Dread Pirate Roberts. You remember him, right? Because, apparently, I'm Princess Buttercup."

The silence went on so long, she was sure they'd been disconnected. Her mom sighed. "What did I ever do to deserve this?" she muttered and continued in a louder voice, "I have a patient coming over at nine so you need to pick up Trike by then. When you're done being kidnapped, make an appointment to see me. I usually charge two-fifty an hour and you're going to need every minute of it." She hung up.

"Wunderbar," the Dread Pirate said, took her phone from her hand and slipped her another M&M. He started the engine, and the car rolled off. "Ve go now."

She laughed for ten minutes without stopping, and every time she was sure she was done, the Dread Pirate would say something, each time in a different, ridiculous accent, that set her off again. Every time she laughingly tried to ask a question an M&M was popped into her mouth. She'd rather it was his tongue, yet for now, the chocolate tidbit wasn't a bad substitute.

Thirty minutes later he slowed to make a turn. She could tell by the motion of the car that they had left pavement and were now on a dirt road. They wound around for a few minutes before he stopped. Turning off the engine, he opened his door, got out and came around to get her. Still wearing her blindfold, she hung onto his arm when he led her on a dirt trail before stopping. He was silent until they reached their destination. He let her stand for just a brief moment before he gently removed the blindfold.

"Behold, my princess," he said in his natural voice. "Your ship awaits you."

She inhaled sharply at the sight of a gorgeous multi-colored hot-air balloon swaying gently against the sky.

"Oh, Noah." She turned to look at him. His lips sketched a smile, however, it was uncertain, maybe because he wasn't sure if she'd like it, or maybe it was because all she said was 'oh Noah' which told him absolutely nothing and now he was confused.

"Noah," she repeated. "This is amazing. Thank you. I love it. Thank you." She didn't know what else to say because she was so filled with something—joy, gratitude, excitement—she didn't know what the feeling was, she only knew it was overwhelming.

"Come on, I'll help you in." After grabbing several wicker hampers from the backseat of his car, he led her to the balloon, and with the assistance of the balloonist, helped her climb into the gondola and handed her the hampers.

Once she had set the hampers on the floor of the gondola, she turned and smiled at him. "Come on."

He put a hand on the edge of the basket. His eyes closed. His face was pale. He took a deep breath, and another and his hand dropped away from the rim of the gondola. "I... Uh... give me a minute. I'll be... I thought I could... Or I wouldn't have... Geez, I thought I was over this." He swallowed.

"Noah?" She could see the indecision, the anxiety in the rigidness of his shoulders. "Is it like with the Slingshot ride?"

He drew in a breath and exhaled in a hard gust.

"Are we going or not?" the balloon pilot asked impatiently.

"Oh, be quiet," she answered sharply. "You're being paid by the hour."

"No, by the ride," he muttered. "And I'd like to get going, otherwise we'll run out of daylight."

"Well, you're going to have to wait." With that, she climbed out of the basket. Stepping close to him, she put her arms around him. She could feel his slight tremble. "You did the ride. How is this any different?" she asked, but even though she asked, she understood, like before, this was not about a fear of heights, it was about his need to be in control. Nothing said losing control more than turning your life over to a man in a balloon that was drifting thousands of feet in the air going wherever the wind took them.

"Well, before, even though I was a hundred feet up in the air, I was attached to something. And also, the ride was over quick. This thing—" He cast his eyes skyward with a grimace.

"Noah, you can't control the wind."

He blinked, not understanding.

"You can't control how high the balloon goes."

He frowned.

"You can't control what direction we go or where we land... or even if we land. We could crash, and you couldn't control that."

He slammed his eyelids shut.

"You can't control life. Shit happens, whether we want it to or not. Trying to control every little thing? There's no joy in living life like that."

He scrubbed a hand over his face. "I know, I know. I don't want to be afraid. Fuck that. I want to take risks, let things happen. Before, the Slingshot? I could do the ride because... because you held my hand and told me that I could do it and I felt free for the first time in my life."

After doing the ride, it seemed as if he'd conquered his fear. Apparently not. Apparently, overcoming fear was an ongoing thing that might have to be conquered every time a new challenge appeared.

She studied his face. "Is this a ploy to get me to hold your hand?" she asked with some suspicion on her voice.

He huffed another sigh. "No. Yes. Maybe?"

"Noah," she said quietly, trying to keep her voice even, neutral, not to plead with him, but a little pleading leaked through despite her efforts. She wordlessly held her hand out. "Here's my hand. Take it."

For a moment he stared at her hand. Glancing up, he locked eyes with her.

"See, Noah," she said. "I'm here. And I'll always hold your hand if you want it. I'll support you, to help you through the fear if you need me. I'll always believe in you."

Another moment passed before he inhaled a deep breath, took her hand and clambered into the gondola, landing on the wooden floor with a thump. Joy filling her heart.

The pilot handed them helmets, and activated the burner, the flames burning blue and yellow. One of the ground helpers released the tethers holding them earthbound.

They soared up, up, up. The ground receded beneath them. The wind caught them and they moved across the landscape. A muted groan escaped from him. Taking a step closer, she wrapped her arm around his waist and leaned in. His jaw was clenched and she could feel him trembling.

Below she could see the shadow of their balloon as they traversed the length of the pasture and drifted skyward over a residential area. Cars the size of toys traced up and down a four-lane road, houses with red and dark green and black roofs passed underneath. Above, puffy white clouds hung like cotton balls floating in the azure sky.

From the corner of her eye, she peeked at him. His hands had clamped tight to the rim of the basket, his knuckles white, yet unlike the Great Adventure ride, his eyes were wide open, staring down, a look of awe, and yes, fear, on his face.

"Oh," he said.

Yeah, oh. A burst of emotion filled her so intense she wanted to shout, to throw her hands in the air and dance until exhaustion claimed her, but more than anything, she wanted to make love to this wonderful man who had given her this gift. Reaching out, she wrapped her fingers around his hand which was gripping the basket rim. He closed his eyes briefly, rolled his hand over and squeezed her hand. She squeezed back.

With an uncertain smile, he bent to open a wicker picnic basket from which he removed several wine flutes and a bottle of wine. Pulling a corkscrew from the basket, he used it to tug out the cork and poured a bubbling white wine into each of the glasses. He handed one to her. The glass trembled in his hand. Still afraid but dealing with it.

"To joy, and a life without fear," he said, his voice raspy. He took a sip. Jenn tilted her glass and drank some of the sparkling white wine. It was sweet and tart and fruity. Divine.

Bending again, he pulled out a small box that he opened, revealing enormous strawberries. He held one to her lips and waited while she took a bite.

Sweet, succulent juice dribbled down her chin. He leaned down and lapped it off with his tongue. A shaft of pure desire darted through her, burning between her legs, tightening her breasts, wrapping her heart in warm hands.

They drifted on the winds of the world.

Periodically, the pilot would fire the burner again to keep them level, but other than the roar of the burn, it was silent. Even nighttime wasn't this quiet. Nighttime always included the distant sound of cars passing by, of dogs barking,

TVs blaring in people's living rooms, crickets chirping, even the muted hum of the streetlights.

Up here, several thousand feet in the air, it was so quiet she could almost hear her heartbeat in her chest. She could still feel Noah's tension as they leaned against the wicker side of the balloon's basket and watched the world pass below, but his tension was lessening with every minute that passed. The picnic basket emptied, he reached into his shirt pocket and pulled out a small pack of M&M's. He doled them out, one for her, one for him. She let each small tidbit sit on her tongue until the candy coating was gone and sweet chocolate tantalized her taste buds.

Neither said a word, the silence too precious to break. It was like being in another time, a time before the cacophony of the modern world.

At some point during the ride, he gave her back her phone. She checked it out to see he'd entered his own phone number. He smirked and gave her another M&M. She tucked her phone into her pocket.

Too soon, they approached another field, and the balloon began to descend. Noise returned, the sound of the wind in the trees and the distant hum of cars on the highway. The shadow of the balloon on the ground grew larger and larger, until they landed with a thump, a bounce and another thump. Several people ran closer and grabbed the tether lines.

Waiting for them on the verge of the pasture was Noah's car, driven by one of the balloonist's aides who was asked to meet them at the arrival spot. The balloon was quickly tied to the ground, and they were helped out onto terra firma.

It was over. Her magic carpet ride was over. She was sad it was over, but the happy feelings were carefully tucked into her memory, so she could recall them again and again.

He walked her to his car and helped her inside without saying a word. Starting the car, he pulled out of the parking lot and drove down the road for ten minutes, still not speaking, but his eyes turned in her direction every few minutes, and a smile would shine, making goosebumps break out on her skin.

"Will you come home with me?" he asked, his face expressionless, yet his voice gave away his anxiety.

She shook her head. "You heard my mother. She said I need to get the dog by nine."

After asking for directions, he began the drive north. Nothing was said during the trip. Her hand lay in his, her arm stretched across the car's console. It wasn't the most comfortable position, however, she wouldn't have traded it for anything. Soon they pulled up in front of her mother's house.

Getting out, she jogged up to the front door which opened before she got there.

"I see the Dread Pirate freed you."

She grinned. "Nope, I'm still being kidnapped." She pointed at the car sitting on the curb.

Her mom turned her head to look down at Trike who was sitting in the foyer, leash in her mouth. "The crazy person wants to take you home," she told the dog.

As if she understood, the mangy mutt ran through the open door and scrambled into the car through the door that Noah held open.

Jenn turned to leave.

"Let me know if you need ransoming," her mother added sarcastically. "I might be able to spare a buck or two."

Giggling, she ran back to Noah's car. Getting inside, she directed him to her own house. Minutes later, he parked outside her home. Cutting the engine, he slid his hand through her hair to the back of her head and kissed her. It was sweet, and gentle, and, oh so, wonderful. The tip of his tongue touched hers. She responded by locking his lips with hers. More kisses. A little heavy breathing. A lot of tingles and blood rushing through her veins, hot and urgent. His hands roamed, tickling her cheek, stroking her eyelids, sliding down to caress her breast. His breath sounded in fits and starts, harsh and heavy. He mumbled something. She mumbled something back. She had no clue what he said. She didn't have any clue what she said back.

After nearly sucking her lips off, he leaned back. Wearing a questioning expression, he searched her face, saying nothing.

"Well, come on. Don't stand there, let's go have some fun," she said.

A huge, rather lascivious, grin spread across his face, but he didn't waste time debating it. They climbed out of the car in a flurry of grunts and groans and laughter. They reached the front door. The dog galloped through the door the minute Jenn got it open and streaked off for rooms unknown. It took less than a minute for them to reach her bedroom.

Gazing around the room, her heart thumped in her chest, her breath came in shallow spurts. Her gaze focused on her bed. It beckoned her.

Heat rose in her chest, making her tremble. She knew what was going to happen, and she wanted it with all her being. She wanted this wonderful man. She remembered how his hands felt on her breasts, on her waist, on her ass. She recalled what his tongue felt like when it tickled the inside of her ear, darted into her navel, tasted her between her legs. She knew what he felt like inside of her and she wanted it again. She wanted him.

He smiled down at her, his smile slow and intimate and promising good things to come. Carefully threading his hands through her hair, he gripped the back of her head and kissed her.

Thoroughly. Passionately. Lovingly. Gentle lips, and gentle hands and soft moans of desire.

While he kissed her, he unbuttoned her blouse and slid it, and her bra, off her arms, the slither of silk sliding over her body sending bolts of lust through her. Her slacks came off next. He let them fall to the floor while she trembled and shook and burned inside. Her panties followed. She stepped out of them. He walked her to the bed and pulled back the thick comforter to reveal pristine white sheets. Picking her up like she was nothing, instead of being this long, awkward thing, all arms and legs, he laid her down.

He stepped back and stripped out of his clothes, watching, his eyes hot, his breathing shallow. When he was down to nothing but glorious, gorgeous skin, he climbed into the bed with her. And made love to her. Unlike before, this time it was sweet and gentle and took a long, long time.

TWENTY-TWO

♥

NoahMaitland@noahmaitlandesq

The balloon ride was terrifying. Falling in love is even scarier.

He woke up to find her leaning over him, staring at his face. "What in the—? What are you doing?"

"I'm counting your eyelashes. You have a lot of them."

He burst out laughing. "I've got the usual amount."

"No, you have way more than most people."

What a weird conversation to be having first thing in the morning before he'd had breakfast, when he still had morning breath and needed desperately to pee. Whatever. "Okay, how many do I have?"

"Oh, at least a hundred." She grinned and laid a hot, sweet kiss on his mouth. "You have gorgeous eyes."

He rolled his gorgeous eyes then turned over to face the warm furry thing that was sleeping on his other side. The furry thing opened its one eye and peered at him. It grinned and drooled. Jeez.

"You know this is the ugliest dog in the world, right?" he said, shaking the goo off his hand.

She poked him in the back. "Hey, she understands you, and that's insulting. Apologize to poor Trike."

He craned his neck to gaze over his shoulder. "How in the world did you end up with a dog that is missing half its parts?"

She shook her head. "She isn't mine. I'm dog sitting for my partner who got married a few weeks ago and is on her extended—very extended—honeymoon. When they get back, they'll repossess her. I can't wait. Even though she's only half a dog, she's managed to eat my bedspread and my dining room chairs.

He frowned. That was an interesting wrinkle. He'd thought that she liked dogs. Okay, maybe not so much. Yet, the minute he came to that conclusion, she reached over his shoulder and gave the ugly thing a scratch under the chin and stroked her one long ear.

He smiled to himself. Such a liar. He also gave the animal a scratch then rolled out of bed. He did need to pee. "'Scuse me. Gotta go." Dashing into the bathroom, he did his business. While he was there, he took the time to peruse all the bottles lined up on the shelf hung over the vanity. The usual toiletries were there, however, there was also an almost full bottle of jasmine-scented bubble bath. Hmm. He took it down. Taking the top off, he gave it a sniff, turned on the hot water in the tub and poured in a dollop of bubble bath liquid.

Sticking his head out of the door, he gestured her inside. A frown crossed her face, but she slid out of the bed, dragging the sheet to cover her naked body and joined him.

"Oh, how lovely." Within two seconds she had dropped the sheet and climbed into the tub. "Thank you," she sighed, sliding down so the bubbles covered her. "You're a very nice man. Now go away."

He went away but, after dressing, he only went as far as his car which he drove to a nearby diner, ordered coffee and scrambled eggs and the biggest, most scrumptious home-made muffins he'd ever seen. While he waited for his order, he glanced around and saw a rack of picture postcards and t-shirts with a variety of messages, all arrayed for sale to the tourists that stopped by. He picked through them. One particular shirt made him smile. He bought it and stuffed it into the bag on top of the food the waitress handed him and drove home.

By the time she was finished with her soak, and had dressed and come down-stairs, he had her dining room table set with placemats underneath her simple white dishes, and on top of the plates, cloth napkins pleated into the shape of a swan (grandmothers were good for more than just hugs). He poured the coffee out of the paper cups into mugs and laid out the array of muffins he'd bought—bran and cranberry and blueberry—onto another plate.

"Oh. You got breakfast." She slewed a glance at him from under her bangs. A shy smile graced her lips. "How nice."

He pulled her chair out for her and spooned the eggs he'd kept warm in the oven onto her plate.

"So tell me about your early years in Colorado," he asked, hoping she'd trust him enough to tell him about the robbery and her father's part in it. Without trust, he wasn't sure their love stood a chance.

But trust was a two-way street. "Before you do, I'd like to tell you about my Gram," he said, and told her how his Gram and his grandfather had end-ed up raising him. Still, there were things he wasn't willing to share yet. His relationship with Jenn—which might not be a relationship at all as it was so new—hadn't progressed to the point where he wanted to share his shame. Because shame is what he felt, along with anger and regret and helplessness at his inability to fix his problems with his parents and Bret. So he cut his narrative short.

Deciding to ease into the topic of Colorado and her father, he asked her about her mother.

She rolled her eyes. "You know how most people complain their parents don't understand them? Well, I have the opposite problem—my mother understands me too well." She paused. "She's a psychologist."

He chuckled. "I figured that out when your mother said to make an appoint-ment with her," he responded. "So I bought you this." He reached into the bag he'd left sitting next to his chair and handed her the t-shirt he'd bought at the diner.

She unfurled the bright red t-shirt and read, '*I know I'm not crazy, my mother had me analyzed*. After she got done laughing, she started to push away from the table then stopped and met his eyes. "Thank you, Noah. This whole thing...it's been wonderful. The Dread Pirate Roberts. The balloon ride. The bubble bath. The breakfast. Everything. I lo—" She stopped, took a deep breath and gave him one of those smiles that celebrities practice in front of their mirrors that were supposed to convey how delighted they were to meet their fans yet gave nothing away. "I had fun. Thank you."

Disappointed, he stood and helped her clear the table. He wished he'd been able to book the balloon ride for Saturday so they would have all of Sunday to spend together, however, on such short notice a weekday was all he could get.

Now, sadly, his glorious day with her was over and they both needed to get to work. However, his determination to win her heart was not over. He didn't only want her, he needed her. More importantly, he knew she was the One. Sex, desire, didn't always last, but love could.

And he was certain now that he was falling in love with her. Deep lifelong love that would grow and grow if given a chance. He wanted that chance, but it was a scary proposition. Taking a chance meant being a different person than the one he'd been in the past. The old Noah would have never dared lose control. The old him would have never dared to feel, to experience, to just be. The old him did what he had to do to keep himself safe. Noah no longer liked that guy, he didn't want to be that guy ever again. Still, that unlikable Noah lurked in the background like a threat.

The idea of staying the old Noah scared the shit out of him.

The idea of not being the old Noah scared the shit out of him.

He was going to have to become something more than he ever was before.

JennGoodwin@MyHeart-2-Heart

I think I might sorta, maybe, possibly, be falling in love with you.

'*I know I'm not crazy, my mother had me analyzed.*' She'd read the words emblazoned on the t-shirt a dozen times, but they still made her laugh.

It would have been smarter not to wear it—it didn't exactly scream professional—yet she wanted to keep it on. Even though she was sure he'd bought it as a joke, it was a tangible, vivid reminder of the last eighteen hours spent gorging herself on his presence.

What wasn't a joke were her memories of his hands on her breasts, her face. Her body still hummed with tiny aftershocks from making love. It felt amazing—good golly, what a wimpy word to describe something that had rocked her to the core—but she wasn't sure there was a good enough word in the English language to describe how their time together felt. What happened in her bed was miles better than doing it on her desk.

Aftershocks or not, it wasn't the memories of how he'd held her, how he'd driven his hard body into hers, that had her head spinning. It was the laughter they'd shared over his foolish impersonations of the Dread Pirate Roberts, and the feel of his warm hand gripping hers as they soared over the southern farmlands of New Jersey, and the thoughtfulness he'd exhibited by preparing a bubble bath and going out to get breakfast.

And the trust. More important than the kisses, the hugs, the silly games, it was the trust he'd placed in her to be there for him when he climbed into the gondola basket of that balloon.

She turned on her computer, however, her mind was still in her bedroom, thinking of making love again. Her office door opened, and Megan appeared. "Hey, you've got three appoi—" Her assistant's voice stopped short before she completed the question. Her eyes zeroed in on the inappropriate-for-the-office t-shirt.

"What is that?"

Oh boy. "A t-shirt."

Megan glowered. "I can see that. I'm not a dummy. Why are you wearing it instead of real clothes?"

If there had been a good response for that question, one that didn't include the words Noah or making love and, oh, God, she was falling in love with him and was pretty sure she didn't want to continue their feud, she would have answered, however, there weren't, so she didn't.

She gave a half-hearted shrug and a weak smile instead.

Megan's eyes widened. "You slept with him," she howled. "You caved. After all your talk about revenge and standing up for yourself and attitude, you caved!"

Okay, maybe now was the time to explain. "Yeah, well, see, there was, you know, a kidnapping and the Dread Pirate Roberts, like the Princess Bride thing—did you ever see the... no, maybe not? Anyway, great movie plus there was the balloon, and these cute little sandwiches, and wine, and also, the bubble bath, and muffins and he's pretty convincing besides being kind of adorable..." She stopped. Megan wasn't buying it.

"You've been lying to me," her assistant said in a low voice. "I thought you trusted me. I thought we were in this together. I thought you realized he wasn't to be trusted." She stared at Jenn, her eyes sad.

Having delivered her accusation, she left, quietly shutting the door behind her.

Jenn didn't move for a minute because all the previous hurts came rushing back. Was Megan right? Would Noah hurt her like the others? He didn't seem the type, but neither had Keith nor her high school boyfriend.

She so wanted him to be different, but it was too soon to tell. For the first time since college, she wanted a relationship, one that included the hotter than hot sex she'd had with him, yet also included the laughter and the handholding and the knowledge that her heart was safe.

The question was, how was she going to manage the issue with Megan? In retrospect, she should have told her assistant about her change of heart the minute she realized she no longer wanted revenge. In fact, now that she contemplated it, she couldn't even explain to herself why she hadn't simply confessed. Something to do with not wanting to be embarrassed when it didn't work out.

How dumb was that? Whether she liked it or not, she was going to have to tell Megan. The explanation would have to include a suitable amount of abasement too.

Leaving her office, she approached Megan. Observing her assistant's closed expression, she sighed. She owed the girl an explanation.

"Hey, I'm sorry. I didn't mean to hide anything from you. This thing..." She paused, not sure how to describe something she barely understood herself. "It just happened. I don't know what else to say except... I think..." She could feel hot blood rushing to her cheeks.

Megan made a face. "You're embarrassed. You're embarrassed because you changed your mind." Tears appeared in her assistant's eyes. "I don't care if you changed your mind. I don't care if you like the guy. It's only that..." She stopped and took a shuddery breath. "I was having so much fun plotting with you. It was like you were my friend, not just my boss."

The teary comment took Jenn by surprise. She'd had no idea Megan felt that way. "Okay," she said because she didn't know what else to say.

This got a shake of Megan's head. "No," she said sadly. "You aren't my friend. You're just my boss."

Studying Megan's face, she got the feeling that this was about more than being left out of the fun. She remembered some of the things Megan had said in her job interview, how she didn't speak to her family anymore because of her choices—choices that weren't really choices, but a fact of life—and how she had moved away from her ultra-conservative small town in the South for the same reasons, and why she was excited about adding a LGBTQ service to Heart-2-Heart in hopes of meeting someone for herself. The girl was lonely.

A surge of compassion swelled. Opening her arms, she gave Megan a hug. "I'm so sorry. I won't leave you out anymore. I may not be plotting revenge, real revenge, anymore but..." She smiled ruefully. "It's weird, yet for some reason, we're still playing this silly game. So I still need help coming up with fun ideas to make him 'come' see me." She wiggled her eyebrows with lascivious intent. "Get it?"

Megan giggled. "So...is this the guy? Are you in love with him?"

The words popped out of her mouth without hesitation. "Yeah, I think I am." She blinked. "Maybe?"

A slow grin spread across Megan's face. "Cool," she said and put her glasses on. "Then we need to do something more so you can be sure. And...I have this really cool idea," she said, leaning towards Jenn so she could explain.

Wow. Why had she ever decided to leave Megan out of her plans. The girl was a genius.

"I'm going to go get what we need," she told Megan. "Keep an eye on the dog while I'm gone." Megan waved a hand, agreeing, and shooed Jenn on her way.

Reaching the store, she bought the items she needed and drove back to her office. After parking, she walked across the driveway to Noah's bungalow and climbed up the stairs and stopped. She ripped open the large bag and put a red M&M on the welcome mat. Backing up, she dropped another tidbit, added another on the stairs while she continued to back towards her own entry. She ran out of candies two feet before she reached Megan's desk.

Megan looked up then looked down at the trail of candies that dotted their carpeting. "I hope there are no hungry squirrels or snoopy kids out there right now."

"Fingers crossed," she said, and retreated to her office, took out her phone and sent a text. She waited. Minutes later she heard the front door open and the sound of footsteps.

"Hold the calls, Megan," she heard through the closed door. "In fact, hold everything." Her office door opened. He walked in and shut it behind him, a sly grin tilting one side of his mouth.

Taking her time, she rose and walked to stand in front of him. His eyes held hers when she unbuckled his belt. He unhooked the catch on his gray slacks. Next came the zipper. A second later he was in her hand. His breath hissed out, his eyelids slid down to half-mast, hooding his eyes. He looked hungry. After digging into this pocket, he handed her a condom. She did the honors.

Then he did the honors, this time in her chair.

Done, with a kiss on her nose, he put an angry frown on his face, stalked past Megan, still maintaining their fictitious feud, yelling, "That'll teach you," and returned to his office. And when the coast was clear that evening, he followed her home.

She woke up early. Rolling over in bed, she perused Noah's face, appreciating his slightly stubble-covered jaw, the sharp angles of his cheekbones. The swelling was completely gone, and the bruises were just a faint tinge under his skin. She noted the tiny scar above one brow—she'd have to ask about the origin—and the lush lower lip.

Her body still thrummed from his attention the night before. Her heart still felt full of some weird emotion that she hesitated to put a name to.

Noah's hand came down to rest on her side. It felt right there, warm and large, possessing yet not possessive. "Mmmm. Morning. It's Saturday. I want to do something special today," he murmured.

She closed her eyes, drifting in this feeling of content.

The contentment suddenly disappeared to be replaced by a feeling of guilt. She didn't deserve to feel contentment, happiness...maybe even loved. She was lying to him.

She bit her lip. "I need to tell you something," she said. "The truth about why we left Colorado." Immediately, the smile on his face disappeared. He sat up, tucking the sheet around himself.

"Okay."

"My father did something..."

He nodded.

She'd never told anyone about what happened, too ashamed to tell people her father not only robbed an armored car, but that the guards were shot in the process. It was so hard talking about it. Still, she wanted him to know.

"My dad and a friend started a company." She stopped, this bit of telling bringing back all the pain.

He said nothing, only waiting patiently, his eyes focused on her.

"Both of them were mechanical engineers, a very specialized type of mechanical engineer. But the recession was going on. So his company went out of business. He lost everything. And his job was so specialized..." She took a shaky breath. "He couldn't find anything else. He looked for over a year..."

Oh, God, she didn't know if he could do this. She hated that time in her life. She hated her father and all her friends and... she had hated life in general. If there was any possibility that she and Noah could build a life together that was more than just sex, he needed to know.

"For a smart guy, my dad turned out to be really stupid," she continued bitterly. "We needed money and he decided—he and this stupid, dumbass friend he met somewhere, I have no idea—that there was an easy way to get it. They decided to rob an armored car."

Slowly, the rest of the story got told, all the gory details, including how their friends and neighbors didn't believe Leah wasn't involved, the harassment that forced them to move out of Colorado. While she talked, the hurt returned, a hard, burning lump in her chest that made it hard to breathe, made her voice tremble, made tears run down her cheeks.

Arm wrapped around her shoulder, he murmured things—not words, but comforting sounds of solace. Using a thumb, he wiped the tears from her face. Finally there were no more words, no more tears, left. She let out the breath she'd been holding.

He kissed her, softly, tenderly and said, "Someday I'll tell you the full story about how my father tried to shoot one of my mother's boyfriends and almost went to prison for assault." Laughter underlay the tone of his voice. "He chased the guy around the parking lot of his apartment complex three times before he had to stop to catch his breath. My dad's not in very good shape, you know, so the guy got away."

She giggled wetly. "Very funny, but it's not as bad as robbing an armored car."

"No." He kissed her again. "Jenn. I don't care about what your father did. You didn't rob anything, your father did. You didn't shoot someone, he did. You didn't benefit in any way from what he did, but you paid for it anyway. Don't ever believe I'll think badly of you for what happened. It's past, it's irrelevant, it doesn't change who you are, which is a wonderful, caring woman with a zest for life."

He was so nice, so sweet, so understanding. He was also crazy-sexy and hand-some. She loved his broad shoulders. She loved his lips—loved kissing them. She loved how strong he was and how he held himself back from coming until she had.

Somehow, telling him about her father, and her hurt, had eased a lot of the pain. She took a quick, tremulous breath, holding back the tears, her throat too tight to speak. The words *I love you* trembled on the tip of her tongue even though she couldn't make herself say the words out loud yet.

"Okay, now?" he asked, wrapping an arm around her.

She sighed.

After a few minutes of silence, he said, "It's Saturday. I have to go home and feed Iggy but after that, I'm free. What should we do today?" he asked, getting up to visit the bathroom.

His question elicited her groan. "Nothing. I have to go to work."

He poked his head out of the door, toothbrush in hand, toothpaste still gracing his luscious lips. "Oh. Okay. So tonight?"

She shook her head. "Sorry. I have this thing tonight. A mixer."

He wrinkled his brow. "A drinking party?"

"No, a mixer is like a party where everyone is looking for a match. We invite—"

A cell rang. He made a face. "Shit. My phone. Sorry." He grabbed it and swiped the call.

"Hello." He paused. His mouth tightened. "Hey, Mom." Pause. "Yeah, I heard through the grapevine you were home." Another pause, this one longer than the first, one where Jenn could hear the raised voice coming through the phone while Noah's mouth got tighter and tighter.

"Yeah, I know. I'm sorry. I forgot."

She tried not to listen—this was family business—however, it was hard not to when he was only feet away. More yelling while he listened then, "Mom, no, I can't."

More listening. She could see his face getting red. "I know I owe you the money—"

A long explanation came over the phone, the female voice rising and falling. His eyes closed. His lips moved. She could see what he was repeating over and over. Fuck. Fuck, fuck, fuck.

"No, I can't do that. I told you before, I don't have the money right now."

He took a deep breath. "Mom," he said, his voice tight. As usual, her tirade continued. "Melanie! Stop. God damn it, I told you! I'm broke. My car broke down and it cost a fortune to have fixed. You're going to have to wait."

A protest came over the line.

He pressed several fingers to his forehead. "Yes, I know. I'll try to get the money to you as soon as possible." He closed his eyes, and the words that followed were softer, and contrite. "Please, Mom. Don't apologize. Really, don't worry about it. I'll work something out. We'll talk about it later, okay? I love you too," he said, and hung up.

She simply waited while he took a deep breath, rubbing a finger across his forehead.

"Sorry." He took another deep breath. "That was my mother."

She rolled her eyes. It went without saying.

Walking to his pants he'd draped over a chair, he tucked his phone inside a pocket. "I'm sorry," he said again. "I don't want to get you involved in my problems, but she's my mom."

She watched him, frowning. There was nothing she could say. Families. They were complicated. Hers certainly was. His didn't sound much better.

Coming up behind him, she wrapped her arms around his waist and leaned against his back. They stood silent for a minute until she felt his muscles begin to relax a little. Eventually he turned.

"So. Tomorrow?"

She shook her head. "My mom's birthday is tomorrow and my sister is coming in from out of town. I need to be there."

He gave her a half smile, yet she could see in his eyes that he was disappointed. She was disappointed too, in fact more than disappointed because somewhere during the night while they'd had mad, crazy sex, something had happened to her heart. It was almost like, for the last ten years, her heart had been this enormous bird trapped in a cage meant for a canary, its wings beating, beating, beating uselessly against the bars in an effort to escape. And suddenly someone wonderful named Noah, opened the door and set her free to soar among the clouds... if that's what she chose to do.

When she'd told Megan that maybe she was in love? She was wrong. There was no maybe about it. She *was* in love. How had it happened? When had it happened?

She remembered their day at the amusement park. She thought about Noah and his fear of heights, and how she had teased him and pushed him to face his fears. And he had. That was the definition of a brave person, someone who was afraid and still did what needed to be done.

Unlike Jenn. Not telling him of her feelings was the definition of cowardice. She was nothing but a big scaredy cat, and the result was that she was depriving herself of something precious. It was time to stand up and be a man...woman...whatever. It was time to claim her right to love and be loved, however, she didn't know if she had the fortitude to have another emotional discussion about her feelings. She needed time to figure out a way to tell him about her revelation.

Feeling uncomfortable with her decision, yet not knowing what else to do, she finished dressing, said goodbye to him at the front door and headed off to work to prepare for the mixer that night. Usually she loved the mixers but today all she wanted to do was crawl back in bed with him and make love to him. And to think, she wouldn't see him tomorrow either.

Bummer. Super bummer.

TWENTY-THREE

JennGoodwin@MyHeart-2-Heart

Dogs: a man's—and a woman's—best friend.

By the time Monday afternoon arrived Jenn was going crazy with frustration. "Help," she whined to Megan.

"What? With what?"

"Have you seen Noah? I haven't seen him all day, so where is he? Why hasn't he come over to do what he needs to do?"

Megan snickered. "So what you actually mean is, do you."

"Yeah, that. I need him."

A look of exasperation crossed Megan's face. "Then call him, for heaven's sake, and ask him to come over."

Okay, Jenn guessed she could call him and ask him those questions, but that wasn't supposed to be the way the game was played. She needed a good idea.

"Come on, you're the creative one around here, come up with an idea, something that will have him hotfooting it over here asap.

"Let me think," Megan said. Within minutes she rushed back into Jenn's office, pulling the dog by the collar behind her. "I have an idea." She outlined it.

With a nod of approval, Jenn grabbed Trike's collar, took the paper Megan held out, tucked it under the dog's collar and turned her over to Megan. "Just take her to his front door and knock. Trike can take it from there."

Megan wiggled her eyebrows in excitement. They traded a high-five. Leading the dog, her assistant left. Within two minutes, the girl returned. "All set," she said with a grin.

Jenn returned to her office and sat, determined to be prepared. She pulled a mirror out of her desk drawer and combed her hair.

Hmmm.

She pulled out a tube of mascara and swabbed that on.

Ooo-kay.

She added lipstick, a nice deep rose color that went well with her complexion.

Hmmm, not quite. She readjusted her blouse to fix the sagging neckline, readjusted it again so that the neckline sagged even further and hiked up her bra so her boobs were pointing the direction boobs were supposed to point.

All right. She was ready. Now where was he?

Ten minutes passed then, the moment she had decided her ploy hadn't worked, a dark form appeared. Next to him stood Trike, drooling happily on their pristine hardwood floor. She gave Jenn a woofy greeting.

"Looks like you lost something," he said, his eyes narrowed, roving up and down her body.

Cocking her head, she studied the dog at Noah's side. "Huh. Are you sure that ugly thing is mine?"

One corner of his mouth tipped up. "Well, I'd say so. She has a note attached to her collar that says, 'My name is Trike. If found, please immediately return me to Jenn next door.'"

"Ahh, then, of course she must be mine." She reached into her drawer and pulled out a dog biscuit. "Good dog, Trike. Treat?" With a doggy grin, Trike gently lipped the treat into her mouth.

"Megan?" Jenn said, holding Noah's gaze. He stared back, his eyes hot with desire.

"Got it." Megan popped into Jenn's office, almost like she'd been waiting for the call. Which she had. Grabbing Trike by the collar, she led the dog away.

Noah shut the door. "Sorry for not communicating. I had appointments all morning." He licked his lips, then, strolling around to her side of the desk, he kissed her. Once he was done kissing her, he lifted her on top of her desk.

The next fifteen minutes were among the best fifteen minutes of her life. When he left, she retrieved the tube of Chapstick she kept in her purse and slathered it on her lips, applied some heavy-duty cream to her cheeks (razor burn), her neck (razor burn) and her backside (plastic laminate skid marks).

Over the next few days, Trike got *lost* a bunch more times. Megan got crazy into the game. Instead of thinking up ways to take revenge on Noah, she came up with several clever messages to attach to her collar that were guaranteed to lure him into rushing over to Jenn's office.

By Wednesday afternoon Trike realized that making the trip back and forth between the two houses meant she got lots of treats and made the trek without being led. She and Noah also enjoyed their treats.

They did a lot of laughing, a lot of kissing and occasional other stuff, and getting to know each other better. Thursday afternoon, it all came to a screeching halt.

He informed her he had to meet a client down in Philly so he would be gone most of the day. With her afternoon free, she decided to use the time to run some errands. She was exiting the house when she saw Noah's brother Bret next to her bike, bending over with his hand groping up under the steering forks.

"What are you doing?" she demanded.

He jerked upright, his mouth falling open, an expression of shock in his eyes. "Um." He snapped his mouth closed and replaced the shocked look with that coaxing smile she remembered from their interview, the one that had made her uneasy. She glanced at the street, checking for his big red truck. Nada. Turning back, she crossed her arms over her chest, waiting.

"So, here's the thing," he blurted. "I was thinking about getting a motorcycle for myself, you know, 'cause it's gotta be cheaper than that gas guzzler I drive, so I decided I'd check out your bike to kinda see what I want to buy. Do a little pre-shopping, you know?"

Sure, like you're going to buy a motorcycle with all that money you told me you don't have, she wanted to say. What she said instead was, "If you want to check out bikes, I'll give you the name of my dealer."

"Oh, right. Yeah, guess that's a better idea." He scuffed his feet, his eyes not meeting hers.

Using her key fob, she started Harley's engine.

"So how much did this baby cost?" he asked. He reached out one hand to stroke the gas tank and yanked it back at the blazing look she sent him.

"A lot."

His eyes narrowed as he stared at her. "Uh huh, I bet, but I guess you can afford it, right?

What nerve. What she paid for her Harley was none of his business. She stifled the comment before it could be uttered, and instead said, "I guess I can afford it as much as the next person," politely even though she wanted to kick his butt.

He rocked back and forth on his heels, still staring. "Yeah. Yeah, I bet you can, being rich and all." A smile spread across his face, sly at first then morphing into that 'aw shucks' smile he seemed so good at.

"Must be nice to not have to worry about money," he mused quietly. "We never had enough, you know. Gram and Grandpa always had their hand out, saying they needed money if my mom and dad expected them to raise Noah. Guess not much has changed only now it's Noah asking *me* for money."

The comment didn't even deserve an answer. Having gotten to know him, and Tess, she was sure it was a lie. Retrieving her helmet, she buckled it on and mounted.

Bret stepped back. "Hey, who knows, maybe he'll start paying me back what he owes me now that he has a rich girlfriend. Or maybe you can pay me directly. What do you think?" he asked, the tone of his voice suggesting he might be joking. She knew he wasn't.

"Bye, Bret," she said, revving the motor.

He hesitated before walking off and heading up the street. She waited until he'd disappeared before riding off in the opposite direction.

Anger coursed through her. He wasn't shopping around. He was on foot, the easier to hot wire the bike, get on and ride off. It wasn't something she wanted to do, but she was going to have to tell Noah his brother might be a thief.

Returning from her errands, pulled up behind the house, and parked. Then she inserted the disc alarm on the front wheel to be on the safe side. After catching Noah's brother this morning, she didn't think he'd be stupid enough to return a second time today but she wasn't taking any chances.

She spent what remained of the afternoon half working and half going to the window near Megan's desk to see if Noah had returned from Philly. He'd said he planned only to be gone until three o'clock, yet the afternoon had come and gone and now it was six o'clock, still no Noah and she began to worry that something had happened to him. On top of that, the issue with finding Bret messing with her bike was like an itch she couldn't scratch, adding irritation on top of her worries.

Megan left, so she finally packed it in. Trike was with her mother today and needed to be picked up.

Striding to her bike, she heard the roar of a motorcycle engine right behind her. The bike swept by her and stopped abruptly a few feet away. The rider turned off the engine and pulled his helmet off.

"So, how do you like it?" Noah said and patted the gas tank between his legs.

Her worry boiled into anger. "Where have you been?" she demanded from between her teeth.

His face fell. "I told you I would be busy, but yesterday I took the last one of my motorcycle safety class so I could get my motorcycle license, so today I went to dealer and bought this bike. I figured now we can ride together. I thought you'd be happy."

She turned her gaze to the bike, a nice Yamaha XRS 900 listed for around eleven thousand dollars when new, but this bike had a missing fender which meant it was used. With depreciation, it was probably worth a few thousand.

"Very nice. However, I wouldn't let your brother know you have it if I were you."

Dismounting from the bike, he hung the helmet from the strap from one handlebar. He frowned. "Bret? Why's that?"

"He was here this afternoon. I caught him messing with my bike. He got this guilty look on his face when he saw me."

"What do you mean, you caught him messing with your bike? What was he doing? What did he say?"

She shrugged. "Some stupid thing about wanting to buy a bike, but he couldn't because you owned him money. However, with me being your *rich*—" She emphasized her comment with air quotes. "girlfriend, maybe I should pay him directly instead of you paying him back because, of course I can afford it because I'm *rich!*"

He shook his head. "What are you talking about? None of that makes sense. I don't owe him money."

"Of course it makes no sense. All I know is I caught him messing with my bike, like he had his hand up under the fairing like he was feeling around for the wiring, but he had this cockamamie excuse that he was looking to buy a bike like mine. Like I believe that. If I had to guess, I'd say it was more he was about to steal it."

"What! That's a out right lie," he spat out, his face turning red.

She gasped, stunned by his response. He was essentially accusing her of lying when for her entire life, she'd tried to tell the truth, not that it had done any damned good. The problem was, like in the past, she had no proof. Even so, if he loved her, he should believe her.

"I'm telling you what I saw."

"There's no way. He would never. He's my brother and I think I know him well enough to know he wouldn't steal your bike."

Like hell. "You're an ass." With that, she turned and walked to her motorcycle. She slipped her helmet on, started the engine, and rode away, to all appearances unfazed by Noah's accusation, but inside she was seething with anger.

Riding down the street, she watched him in her rear-view mirror and saw him running after her. She continued to watch until she turned a corner towards the main road and lost sight of him. So much for being in love. True to her suspicions; love always betrayed.

If only this time it had been different.

From his spot behind a hedge, Bret watched when the woman left the pink and purple house for the second time that day. He'd hung around all afternoon, hoping for another crack at her bike, but realized after a few hours that she'd set a disc alarm on the front wheel which would have alerted her if he even breathed on the bike. Damned bitch.

Like they say in the movies: foiled again.

Which didn't stop him hanging from around for the rest of the day, thinking, mulling over other ways he could get his hands on the money he needed. Rob a bank, like that bitch's father? Nope, too much risk, and anyway, he didn't have the tools, or—he admitted it, the smarts—to rob a bank. Rob a store? Nah, he'd get peanuts. He didn't have a gun, and he was pretty sure he'd need a gun for that. He wasn't much for guns anyway.

No matter how much he mulled it over, he couldn't come up with another solution. Everything he could think of was either too dangerous or would take too long. It was the motorcycle or nothing. There had to be some way he could get his hands on the bike. He already had a buyer for it, but the buyer wouldn't wait forever, and neither would Gary Barbie.

Yeah, Gary Barbie. Just thinking about him made Bret sweat like a pig and his heart race. Gary was running out of patience and Gary Barbie was a scary guy just like the two guys he'd sent to Bret's trailer the other night who weighed over two-fifty apiece. Actually, it didn't matter how much they weighed. They didn't need brawn to break a few of his fingers with a hammer.

He was still lurking in the hedge, fuming over his dilemma and ways to solve it when another motorcycle roared up and drew to a halt.

The rider dismounted and pulled off his helmet.

Son of a bitch. It was Noah. On a fucking motorcycle. He stared at it with a critical eye. When thinking about the girl's motorcycle, he'd done some research about bikes so he'd know what he could get for hers if he sold it without papers. Noah's bike was used, not expensive to begin with, which meant it might only be worth a few thousand. Which didn't mean he wouldn't take it if he could get it, but that her bike was the real prize.

Noah said something to the girl. She said something back that made his brother put his hand on the motorcycle's handlebars and grin.

Bret frowned. How could his brother afford to buy a motorcycle? According to Noah, he was broke, at least that's what he said whenever Bret asked for money. When Bret thought about it, it really pissed him off, Noah going off and spending money on a motorcycle when Bret was living in a trailer scratching to get by. Fuck that, even if Noah's bike wasn't worth shit, he was taking it too. He just had to figure out how to do it. But first, hers.

He started walking back to where his girlfriend had waited in his truck all afternoon, fuming at that blonde bitch's high-handed attitude. What the hell did she care if her bike got stolen? She had plenty of money. He knew that for a fact. It had taken a long time, and a lot of digging because things get buried on the internet after more than ten years, but Bret eventually found the information he needed. Seems her dear old dad was a crook. Big time—like four million dollars big time.

Her schmuck of a father killed himself rather than be captured by the cops, but the money wasn't with him and it was never recovered. Her and her dear old mother could deny it all they wanted, but where else could the money be?

So first the motorcycle, and then he'd work on finding out where the rest of the money was and maybe getting a piece of that too.

TWENTY-FOUR

♥

NoahMaitland@noahmaitlandesq

I will keep saying sorry until you forgive me. So here goes. I'm sorry, I'm sorry, I'm sorry. I'm sorry, I'm sorry, I'm sorry. I'm sorry, I'm sorry.

He stopped running. He should have tried to catch her on his new motorcycle but, without thinking, he'd run after on foot. And now she was gone, out of sight. He'd never catch her. He bent over, hands on his knees and tried to catch his breath. Oh my God, what the hell was the matter with him? Why in the hell had he yelled at her? It wasn't her fault. She hadn't done anything wrong. It was him, him and his stupid family. Them and their demands and their irresponsibility and their constant need, need, need, and him with his inability to cut them loose.

Of course she was right. Bret *would* steal her motorcycle. That was exactly the kind of thing he would do, yet he had automatically leaped to his brother's defense, without thinking it through because that's what he'd always done, which was the problem with his relationship with his family.

His legs trembling from exertion, he walked back to get his new bike, this hard knot in his chest that was a combination of anger at himself, regret at his stupidity, but mostly fear. The idea that he'd messed up so badly that he'd lost her was like a punch to the gut.

It had never been clearer that he needed to do something more, something permanent, to get his family to take control of their own lives and let him live his. If that meant his father had to somehow support himself and all his many ex-wives by himself, so be it. If it meant his mother had to get a job, she'd have to get a job. If it meant Bret ended up in jail or the gutter, that was his problem.

Noah needed to stop enabling them. He needed to come up with a real, workable plan that would accomplish that, however, first he owed Jenn a big fat, sincere, apology. In addition to that, he needed to find out what the hell was going on with this thing about her being rich.

Why would Bret believe she was rich? Noah hadn't said anything. He was certain Gram wouldn't have said anything. Actually, no one would have said anything because Jenn wasn't rich, and she never claimed she was. He knew in his heart that she and her mother had nothing to do with that armored car robbery.

After her confession the other day, he'd gone online to do more research. It had taken him an hour to find a couple of old articles about the robbery buried ten pages deep. How in the world Bret managed to jump to the conclusion Jenn was rich, he'd never know, since Bret wasn't the smartest tool in the shed. What he was, was sly, greedy, and overly motivated by money—and a gamer which meant, despite his limited academic skills, he was great on the computer. Had he found the same articles? Or had he somehow found more detailed information? If so, was there something in those articles that led him to believe she had some of the money from the robbery? Without knowing what Bret read, Noah had no idea what the answers were.

He needed to figure it out.

Mounting the bike, the purchase he'd hoped would bring them even closer, he rode home and parked his new bike next to his old car. Entering his apartment, he went into the kitchen, grabbed some Iggy food and went upstairs to his bedroom and over to Iggy's terrarium.

"Hey, dude. How's it hangin'?"

Iggy poked his head out from inside his log. Seeing a dangling kale leaf, he darted out and curled it into his mouth.

Noah rubbed his chest, like that would rub away the dull pain inside. "So, Iggy, I messed up. I yelled at her. I called her a liar. I'm such a dope."

Iggy stared up at him, masticating his leaf, his eyes thoughtful.

"So what should I do, huh? I love her. I'm going to apologize, but I feel like an apology's not enough. C'mon, dude, help me out here." He cringed, hearing how his voice shook. "I'm in deep shit. And it's all my fucking brother's fault." Clenching his fist, he banged on the wall in frustration. Iggy jumped and scuttled back into his log.

Damn it. He held out another leaf until Iggy ventured back out again. "Do me a favor, dude. If you see my brother, ever, run the other way. Don't listen to a word he says, and don't ever, ever trust him. Promise me."

Of course, Iggy had nothing to say. Lizards didn't have any problems other than where their next bite was coming from, and what they needed to do to regulate their body temperature.

Abandoning his rant, Noah changed into something comfortable, then sat down at his computer and pulled up the internet page he'd bookmarked before, which had a link below that sent him to another article which sent him to a third article which finally led to a long article written by the Denver Gazette several days after the robbery.

The headline said her father had robbed an armored car which he already knew. He clicked on the link, opened up the actual story and began to read. It was all there, everything she had said, the robbery, the shooting of the guard. Her father's turning his gun on himself rather than go to prison.

Taking a deep breath, he read on. And a missing four million dollars. A chill went down his spine. In spite of swearing she didn't have the money or know where it was, the FBI hadn't believed Jenn's mother. And they hadn't believed Jenn's mother, Leah, that her husband's partner in crime must have the money.

The press didn't believe them either and speculated endlessly about where Leah could have it hidden. Even their friends and neighbors said they were lying. The media had had a field day. There were several quotes from neighbors, and even a young man who said he was Jenn's boyfriend and told the press that she had always been all about money.

Fuck. She hadn't shared any of the latter information. It certainly explained her reaction.

It also explained why Bret believed she was rich. If he'd found any of these articles, he would naturally jump to the conclusion that Randy Goodwin's family had the money.

He closed the site and put his thoughts toward two things. How would he be able to forever solve the problem with his family, most specifically, his brother, and how could he apologize to her? He hoped, with enough groveling, she would forgive him.

With that discouraging thought, he picked up the phone. "Gram," he said when she picked up. "Help."

A moment passed. "Okay, what did they do now?" she finally asked, somehow automatically assuming someone in his immediate family had screwed up, although she was wrong in this instance. With a sigh of defeat, he told her what happened.

"Good God, Noah. What an ass."

Where had he heard that before? He gave a weak chuckle, not that it was funny. "Yeah, that seems to be the universal consensus. Now that you've given me your opinion, how about giving me some help?"

She laughed. "Well, of course you're going to have to apologize."

"I know that," he said in disgust. "Of course I will, but saying sorry isn't going to be enough." He hesitated, trying to decide if he should tell Gram about Jenn's history. However, if he was going to marry the woman, and he was determined he would, Gram should know the facts.

"Some things happened in her past. Bad things, that have made her not trust people." He summarized what he'd read online.

"Well," she said after considering the facts. "I read somewhere that for your apology to really mean something you have to do something, or maybe it was give something—I can't remember which—that hurts." She paused. "Or something like that."

Crap. "You mean, like wearing a hair shirt?"

"I don't think that's what they meant, but that does give me an idea," she said and went on to explain.

Propping his elbow on his desk, he buried his head in his hand. He was really, truly going to hate this.

JennGoodwin@MyHeart-2-Heart

Saying "I'm sorry" is saying "I love you" with a wounded heart in one hand and your smothered pride in the other.

Stupid, stupid, stupid. She was so stupid. She hadn't ridden four blocks before she realized what she had done. Rather than calmly and rationally explaining why she believed Bret was stealing her bike, she'd called him an ass and stormed off without letting him even respond.

After avoiding love all these years and finally finding it, she may have lost it all through her own stupidity.

This aching, yawning hole in her chest expanded until it seemed it would engulf her. She was so wrong, so stupid. What should she do? It had been so long since she'd let herself get involved with a man, she didn't know what she should do in a situation like this.

An apology. Well, of course. Would that be enough?

The hole in her chest got bigger.

Riding home, she parked her bike and walked over to her mom's to pick up Trike. After returning home, she fed the dog and ate her own dinner, all the while agonizing over her problem. Her booboo was too big to handle with a text or a phone call. No, what she should do was march herself over to his office tomorrow morning and kiss his feet while saying 'I'm sorry' a hundred times.

The problem was... she was a coward. She needed a little help.

The next morning, she loaded Trike in the car and drove to work, not feeling very positive. She parked the car and led Trike inside.

Megan briefly looked up from her computer. "Morning. What's on the agenda today?" her assistant asked with a smirk, jerking her chin in the direction of Noah's building.

She grimaced. "I need your help. I've fucked up."

Megan's jaw dropped. "Holy crap, Jenn. What did you say?" she asked, her tone stunned because it was well known that Jenn didn't curse.

"You heard me. I fucked up. Royally. I called Noah an ass."

Megan pushed her glasses further up her nose and sat back in her chair, biting her lip in concern. "What happened?" she wanted to know, so Jenn told her, not sparing herself in the slightest.

"Oh, boy. That's not good." Her assistant mulled that over for a moment. "Okay, it's not good, but it's not irredeemable. Apologies can work wonders. We just have to find the right kind of apology." She paused, her mouth quirked up in a hesitant smile. "I know you said you wouldn't do it, but I don't suppose you could, you know, that thing that isn't on a 1040 form?"

"No." She narrowed her eyes at Megan. "That's not an apology, that's manipulation."

"Yeah, but guys love that kind of manipulation."

After thinking about it for a moment, she rolled her eyes. "Okay, you're right. I'll include that in my apology. Much better than offering cookies or ice cream, but first the apology. The words need to be right. Can you help me craft something?"

"Well, of course, although maybe you should apologize in person?"

Of course she should. Right after she figured out if he was going to kill her. There was also the fact that she was a big coward, which is what she told Megan.

"Got it," Megan responded with a smile. Together, they worked out an apology that was short and to the point yet also sincere and heartfelt, one that promised that a honest conversation would follow if Noah still wished to speak to her. It also promised a reward that would have him erupting with pleasure if he forgave her. Nothing wrong with a little sexual bribery, right?

She handwrote it, believing that something typed out on a computer wasn't as meaningful like something handwritten. They attached the note to Trike's collar, opened the door and pointed her in Noah's direction. They waited.

A half hour passed. Jenn bit her lip and glanced at Megan, trying not to let her concern show. Megan gave her a hopeful smile back. "He'll answer. He's probably thinking about what he wants to say."

Another half hour passed. An uneasy feeling was sitting low in her stomach, almost like she was sick, but she never got sick. It was nerves. Megan gave her a reassuring pat on the hand, but now she looked concerned too.

Another twenty minutes passed. The nausea that had waylaid her stomach had now wrapped itself around her lungs and her heart until she felt like she would die.

He wasn't going to answer. He wasn't going to forgive her. Tears burned at the back of her eyes. She had spent the last ten years denying love, telling herself love wasn't important, that love could only betray, only to realize she needed that love, and that the love she needed was Noah's.

Ironically, after all those years, after all the denials because of her fear and lack of trust, she was the one who had been the betrayer. She had betrayed him and betrayed their love because she hadn't trusted him enough to discuss the problem.

She stood. "He's not coming."

Megan looked at her, commiseration in her eyes. "He's thinking about it," she said, however, her voice was weak and unconvincing. "I mean, he hasn't sent Trike back, right, so he must be."

"Megan. How long does it take a guy to make a decision about the offer of a blow job?"

Not an hour and a half. Attitude, she told herself, pulling her shoulders back. She needed some attitude. It was the only thing that would save her. She turned, preparing to enter her office, when there was a knock on the front door. Her heart leaped. Pivoting on her heel, she marched to the door and opened it. On the porch stood a boy about thirteen years old holding out a folded slip of paper.

"Here, lady," he said. "Some guy said to give this to you."

Once again, her heart leaped in her chest. This must be Noah's answer. Thank God. Yet when she reached out to take it, the boy turned and pointed over his shoulder. "Lady, do you know that guy there on the sidewalk, 'cause he's been walking up and down in front of your place for like twenty minutes?"

Jenn's gaze followed his pointing finger. Oh my God. Just like the day she'd hung the rat banner, a crowd of people had gathered on the sidewalk watching the show. Pacing back and forth in front of Heart-2-Heart was Noah, wearing one of those sandwich board things that crazy people in aluminum foil hats used to wear back in the day to announce the Martians were coming to take over the Earth and that the world was doomed.

Only he wasn't announcing the arrival of ET. In big red capital letters, the front placard said, NOAH MAITLAND IS AN ASS. He turned and walked in the other direction. She let out a snort of laughter. On the back placard was a large picture of a horse's backend.

"Did he give you that?" she asked.

At the sound of her voice, Noah abruptly stopped his pacing. Turning to face her, he lifted a hand in a tentative wave. She met his eyes. Oh, thank God, he smiled. It looked like he'd accepted her apology. Hope filling her, she took the note the boy still held out. "From him?"

The boy shook his head. "Nah, some other guy. A sort of fat guy, he gave me five bucks," he said. "Gotta go. My mom's expecting me. See ya." Turning, he ran off.

Noah still stood on the sidewalk, surrounded by the neighborhood crowd who were laughing and pointing at his sign. He ignored them, his eyes focused on Jenn. Even from thirty feet away, she could see the open longing on his face.

Her heart melted a little. So, yeah, he'd said something stupid yesterday, like her, but he was doing everything he could to apologize by embarrassing himself in front of the entire neighborhood. What had she done? Sent him a note. Not good enough. Maybe it was time to dump her attitude. She had developed it to protect herself, however, maybe she didn't need that shield any longer. Stepping down off the porch, she began walking towards Noah, her mind busy trying to come up with a way to say what was really in her heart. As she walked, she unfolded the note she still held in her hand. The handwritten words jumped off the paper.

I have your dog. Your going to pay. Instrucktions to follow.

She gasped. "Noah!" Stricken, she held the paper out. "Noah, someone kidnapped Trike."

His jaw dropped. Tearing off the sandwich board signs, he threw them to the ground, leaving him in jeans and a t-shirt that made the most of his gorgeous chest. He took the note from her hand and read it.

"Who in the world would kidnap Trike? I mean, she's only two-thirds of a dog."

She glared at him.

"I know. I'm sorry. I didn't mean it that way. I only meant, she's not some pedigreed dog worth thousands." His mouth tightened. "When did you notice Trike was missing?"

"I didn't... I...uh..." Heat rushed to her face. "I sent her over to your place around nine-thirty with..." Her face got hotter. "...uh, an offer."

The grim expression slipped away to be replaced with one of speculation. "An offer?"

The rat. He was trying to make her say it, but not if she could help it. "You know. An offer. An *apology*. A *big* apology. An eight-inch apology."

"The kind that involves a little sumpin' sumpin? That kind of apology?"

"Yes!" She jabbed him in the shoulder. He grinned.

"Stop it. I have a kidnapped dog, and it's not even my dog and Amy is supposed to be back in a day or so. If her dog is gone, she'll kill me."

The grin disappeared. "I'm sorry. I came in late this morning because—" He pointed to the sign lying on the grass. "I didn't go into my office, just put that on and started walking the sidewalk, so I didn't get your note. Although, you know what? You don't owe me an apology. The whole thing? My fault. I was stupid. I spoke without thinking. And you know what else? You were totally right. I'm pretty sure my brother was trying to steal your bike, and this note kind of seals the deal in my mind. This is definitely his handiwork. He never could spell."

Taking her hand, he pulled her down the porch steps and dragged her toward his house. "Come on. I have an idea... I hope I'm wrong but..."

Together, they pushed their way through the people gathered on the lawn and entered Noah's bungalow.

His assistant jumped up from her seat, her expression one of alarm. "Hey. What's happened? Is everything okay? Did those maniacs out front do something to you?"

"Trike's been stolen," Jenn blurted out and explained how she had sent the dog over the way she always did, but Trike had disappeared in the short distance between the two houses.

"I want to check the security cameras. If someone did take Trike, it should be on the tapes."

They followed Debra into the kitchen and waited while the woman opened a cabinet to reveal a computer panel and a screen. She pressed a few buttons, and a video appeared. They watched for a moment before Debra mumbled, "Too early," and fast forwarded a few times.

"Around nine-thirty," he told her.

"Got it." She fast forwarded again and hit play. On the screen, she could see the side of the Heart-2-Heart house and the driveway separating their two houses. Nothing appeared for a few seconds then, "Stop," she exclaimed. "There." She pointed at the screen. Around the corner from the back of the bungalow, Trike hopped into view. The dog got as far as Noah's driveway when a big red truck pulled into the driveway. A man got out. He left the truck door open. The dog stopped. Her head lowered, her shoulders hunched defensively, but it did no good. The man rushed toward Trike, scooped her up and threw her into the truck.

He growled. "Son of a bitch. That's definitely Bret." Pulling out his cell phone, he used his contact list to make a call.

"Gram, something bad has happened and I need your help."

The outer door opened, and a teenage girl walked in. "The girl next door said Jenn was over here. I got a message for her."

"Gram, call you back."

"So which one of you is Jenn?" the teenager asked, holding out a note.

Jenn took the note and opened it. "I want mony. a million dollars. Instruckons to follow," she read aloud. She stared at the note. "A million dollars? Is he nuts? Why would he even dream I would give him a million dollars for a dog that's not even mine?"

He opened his mouth to respond, but at that moment, his phone rang. He answered it. "Gram," he said. "Oh, geez, Gram. I... Sorry to interrupt your day, but that God damned effing Bret. I'm going to effing kill him." He related the events of the morning.

"Yeah, yeah, okay," he said, and hung up. Almost immediately the phone rang again. "Hey, Zach, what's going on?" Noah asked. There was a pause, and the muted sound of someone speaking on the phone. Noah's eyes closed in despair. "Shit. I'm sorry. Something happened and I totally forgot about our session."

She waited, needing him to hang up and talk to her. She needed answers. She needed him to hold her and hug her and tell her that thing—that thing that started with a big capital L—that she'd been avoiding since forever, however, he continued to talk, rapidly describing the dognapping and how they had seen Bret take the dog.

When he still didn't hang up, she heaved a sigh of resignation, then she started to walk out.

"Wait!" he yelled. "Hang on, Zach," he said into his phone before rushing to her side and saying, "Listen, go back to your office. I'm going to figure this out, I promise. The minute I do, I'll come over and tell you. Just wait for me, okay?"

He gave her a slow, heartfelt kiss.

Smiling to herself, she returned to Heart-2-Heart, for the first time believing that the name of their business also applied to her.

TWENTY-FIVE

NoahMaitland@noahmaitlandesq

Violets are blue, roses are red. Better run, Bret, you're about to be dead.

T he only good thing Noah could say about this morning was that it proved he had good people on his side. His grandmother and Zach were both on their way with offers to do anything they could to help, however, the truth was, all they could do was offer their support. What he needed was someone to get the dog back, and that someone would need to be someone with a badge and legal authority.

"Now would be a good time to call your trooper friend," he told Debra, massaging his temple because a headache was beginning to develop.

Picking up her phone, she scrolled through her contact list and tapped the screen. She had a short conversation and hung up. "On his way," she said.

Trooper Swenson arrived in ten minutes. Way to go, Debra. Who needed 911 when his assistant had a state trooper on speed dial?

Minutes after Swanson's arrival, Zach appeared with Gram right on his heels, her new boyfriend in tow.

"Noah," Gram greeted him, a shit-eating, *I've-been-laid-and-yum* look on her face. The guy responsible for the look had an arm draped over her shoulder, a similar expression on his face.

"Bruce," she said. "This is Noah, my smart grandson. Noah, Bruce. Shake hands like good boys." As ordered, they did. "Now that's out of the way, explain what's going on with the stupid side of the family tree."

Despite the seriousness of the situation, he had to smile. It was nice she still considered him the smart one, although he wasn't feeling very smart right now. He'd let Bret outsmart him, and that was painful and more than a tad humbling.

He turned to the trooper who'd been lurking in the shadows, all stony-faced and Sasquatch tall. "Gram, Bruce, this is Trooper Lance Swanson. He's hopefully going to help us recover the dog."

Gram's eyes lit up perusing the man's long, muscular body. "Mmm, mmm, mmm. If I didn't already have my man, I might take a stab at you, young fellow."

Bruce rolled his eyes then simply patted Tess's hand, his expression one of wry acceptance. Smart man, he'd already figured out his woman had a lot to say, however, that none of it was necessarily true.

Lance grinned at the older woman. "Yes, ma'am. Just say the word."

Leading the group to a small conference room, Noah asked Debra to queue up the video of the dognapping while he passed around the ransom notes that had been delivered this morning.

Trooper Swenson scratched the side of his neck. "Well, based on that tape, we know your brother stole the dog, but we don't know where he is. If I knew that, it would help."

Gram snorted. "I've got a pretty good idea where he might be," she announced and turned to stare at Noah, one eyebrow cocked.

Well, fuck. It was so obvious, it was amazing he hadn't come up with it himself. "Of course, where else would he be?" he said, shaking his head in disgust. He turned to Swenson. "Dollars to donuts he's at my mother's place.

That's where he always goes when he's trying to hide from me. And my mother always hides him. Partners in crime from way back."

"Certainly worth checking out," the trooper said. "If he's there, I can retrieve the dog."

"Wait. What?" Noah objected. "That's it? What about arresting Bret for theft?"

"Sure, I can arrest him. Not that much is going to happen to him, though. The law doesn't care all that much about a dog getting stolen, unless it's a valuable pedigree, which this one clearly is not. At worst, he'll get a fine and probation." One corner of Swenson's mouth went up in an ironic smile.

"At least we'd have the dog back," Gram said.

"Yeah, that's all well and good, but what about the ransom part? Surely that's a crime."

"Maybe. I'd have to check. Again, we're talking about a dog, not a person. The law doesn't like spending resources on things like this. I have a friend who recently became a judge, though, so I'll ask her."

Noah banged his fist on the wall. The headache from earlier now was a vice gripping his entire head. "God damn it, enough is enough. I've had it with this bullshit. I want him to pay, and while I'm at it, I want to do something about the rest of my family. I can't take it anymore. They're ruining my life. Their shit has possibly effed up my relationship with the girl I want to marry. This garbage needs to stop, and it stops right now."

Gram did a little jig. "Yahoo!" she shouted. "He wants to get married. It's about damned time."

"The question is, how can I do that unless I fix this shit with my family?"

His question got a humph and an eye roll from his grandmother.

"Not you, Gram. The other part of my family."

"I knew that. The answer is, apparently, you haven't watched enough of those old Dr. Phil shows," she said. "If you did, you'd know the answer. Stop enabling them. Make a plan and stick to it. It's time your family grows up. And it's time you did too."

He looked at her, a sick feeling swirling in his stomach. He'd agonized and stressed and told himself a hundred times that he needed to do exactly what Gram said, but every time he hadn't been able to make himself do it, and he wasn't sure he could do it now even though it needed to be done.

Then he remembered his nearly empty bank account and his father's five expensive weddings, and the resulting alimony, and his mother's aborted trip to Vegas, never mind Bret's recent felonious activities, and his resolve hardened. He wasn't doing his family, or himself, any favors by allowing them to remain dependent on him.

More importantly, the image of Jenn was vivid in his mind. If she was going to be his future, he couldn't continue this way. How long would they have a future if it were being constantly invaded by the demands of his family?

Speaking of which. "Where's Jenn?" he asked, scrutinizing the room.

Debra crossed her arms over her chest and gave him a look. He recognized that look. It was the look his grandmother frequently gave him, the same one she was giving him now. It was the look that said he'd fucked up.

"Oh crap," he said. "What did I do?"

"You ignored her. She got tired of waiting and went back to her office."

Well, shit. And after all this morning's humiliation. He walked outside. The crowd was gone, but his sandwich board still lay on the porch next door. He stared at it for a moment, smiling. Picking it up, he opened the door to Heart-2-Heart and walked in.

Jenn and Megan stood at her desk, both of them staring at her computer. Jenn's eyes lifted and met his. She straightened. Her eyes darted down to look at the sign hanging over his chest. He saw a smile tug at the corners of her mouth. She crossed her arms over her chest and gave him one of those looks, the same one Debra and Gram had leveled on him.

He took a deep breath. He wasn't a lawyer for nothing. He knew when to cop a plea. "I'm sorry for telling you to leave," he said in his most contrite voice. One of her eyebrows went up. Okay, so it wasn't quite enough.

He pointed at the sign, the one naming him an ass, and smiled. He'd been told he had a charming smile, so he hoped it would do the trick. Her other eyebrow went up. Damn, she was going to make him say it. She wanted his heart on a platter. She wanted total capitulation. She wanted his balls in a vice. The fact was, he was willing to give her all of that...except his balls. Those he wanted to keep. He might need them something in the not-too-distant future.

Taking a step in her direction, he rested his hands on her shoulders and stared into her eyes. "I'm sorry," he repeated. He shook his head and gave her a rueful smile. "I said I would come up with a plan and I did. I can't tell you all the details, but I'm going to fix this so that you get Trike back and we never have to worry about my miserable, greedy, felonious family again. I want you to know, I'm doing it for you. For us. I just need a bit of time to make it work."

He paused, his eyes searching hers then, without another word, he pulled her tight up against the sandwich board, the one declaring him an ass, which seemed appropriate, and kissed the shit out of her. In the background, Megan hooted her approval.

"And if it's okay to say it now, I love you."

With one last long look at her reddened lips and her stunned expression, he left and walked back to his house to join his fellow conspirators who were waiting to help him craft a plan to get his family out of his hair once and for all.

TWENTY-SIX

♥

JennGoodwin@MyHeart-2-Heart

Roses are red, violets are blue, from now on, I belong to you.

She touched her lips. They felt scorched from the heat of his kiss. It was too bad that was the only thing she'd been able to touch. She sighed and glanced over at Megan. The girl was smirking.

"Shut up," she said.

Megan's hands went up in surrender. "I didn't say anything."

"No, but you were thinking it."

More smirking. "What do you think he meant when he said he had a plan?"

Huh, good question. She went to the window and peeked out. There were oodles of cars in his driveway. She recognized his car and Debra's car, and gulp—there was a police car—but there were several others that she didn't recognize. What the heck was going on?

With no appointments on her calendar that day, she had nothing to do but pace around the confines of the reception area and obsess about the answer to that question. And whether he was going to get Trike back. And why a cop was there. She wanted to rush over there and ask him. And just to confirm the 'love' part, she'd maybe kiss the socks off him.

Just when she had screwed up enough courage to walk across the driveway, someone left Noah's house and walked across the lawn towards her.

It was her cop! Again? Holy cow and he was coming in her direction. He walked in. His face was stern, his cheekbones sharp enough to carve up a good medium-rare steak.

"Miss Goodwin," he said, his mouth barely moving. "This is for you." He handed her a piece of paper. Turning, he handed an identical one to Megan. With a salute, he made a smart military turn on his heel and left.

She stared at Megan. Megan stared back. They both stared at the papers in their hands.

"What the heck?" her assistant said, then, unfolding the paper, she read it. "OMG," she gasped. "I've been subpoenaed. For tomorrow." She turned the paper this way and that as if that would change the message. "What do you think?" she finally asked.

Jenn opened the paper still in her hand. It was also a subpoena, very official looking, but at the bottom was drawn a little heart with an arrow through it. She smiled.

"I think we better be there," she answered. After sending Megan home, she locked up the office and drove to her condo. She reviewed her wardrobe for the perfect outfit to wear to court because, who knew, she might want to seduce the attorney.

Nine o'clock the following morning, she met Megan outside Noah's place per the instructions in the subpoena. The driveway was already filled with cars so obviously whatever he had planned was a go.

"This is so weird," Megan said. "I wonder what's going on."

"I don't know, but knowing Noah, it's sure to be fun. We won't know unless we go in."

Together, they climbed the stairs to his front door and entered.

"Jenn. Megan. We're glad you're on time," Debra said, and led them towards the back of the bungalow and ushered them into a good-sized conference room.

They stopped at the entrance and Jenn quickly checked out the room. With a little bit of imagination and a fair amount of squinting, the room could almost look like a courtroom.

At the far end of the room was a wide podium. A few feet in front of the podium were two small tables, each with a single chair behind them facing the podium. Behind the two tables were a dozen chairs lined up in two rows, however, Jenn's attention was focused on Noah, who stood off to the side, his arms crossed over his chest, his face expressionless. Okay. Interesting. She shot him a glance and lifted a brow. His expression didn't change for a minute, and her heart dropped. Then one eyelid slowly went down in a wink.

A shiver went down her spine. Oooh, this was almost better than sex. Okay. Not really, but still plenty exciting.

With one hand, he pointed to the rows of chairs. "Have a seat, ladies," he offered. "In the front row please. Things will get started shortly."

She turned to find a seat and saw the blonde lady in the second row. "Mom! What are you doing here?" she said.

Her mother blinked at her. "I don't know. Your young man came to see me and asked me to attend, so here I am."

Okay. Wow. So weird. Her gaze shifted to the familiar face of the woman sitting next to Leah. "Tess. Hi. Uh, what's going on?"

"You'll see." The older woman rubbed her hands together gleefully. "Just you wait and see what he has in store. Oh, by the way—" She pointed at the man next to her. "You remember Bruce, right?"

She did yet hadn't expected to see him here. Tess pointed at the burly man sitting at the far end of the row. "That's Zach," Tess said. "Noah's friend. Moral support."

He grinned and gave a thumbs-up.

There were a few other people sitting in the two rows. As Jenn didn't know them, she simply nodded and took a seat. A few minutes passed. The room was quiet. The door opened again and Debra ushered in a couple. The man was tall and skinny. Despite the long, hippy-style hair pulled back in a ponytail, and the earring in his right ear, the strong jaw line, and the silvery gray eyes told her this must be Noah's father. Holding his hand was a short, stocky woman with a broad face and short brown hair.

"Dad," Noah said, confirming the man's identity. He pointed at the empty seat at the end of the front row. "Please take a seat here."

Instead of taking the seat, the man blustered, "What the hell, Noah. What's going on? Why are we here? I cut my vacation short because Crystal here—" He glanced at the stocky woman on his arm. "Insisted that we be here."

Noah's lips tightened. "I'll explain shortly, Dad."

"No, you'll explain now, or we're going to leave, right, honey bunch?" he asked.

"Oh, shut up, Roger, and sit down," was her response.

He sat. After a second or two of silence, he inhaled a breath and whined, "Crystal, sweetness, I don't like—"

The woman glared daggers at him. "Roger," she said in a tone that said *defy me and you'll pay*. All the starch left Roger's body, and he slumped in his chair. Done with her intimidation, Crystal settled down in the empty seat next to him.

Noah's phone rang. He answered it, listened for a moment then walked out, shutting the door behind him.

After that, the room was silent except for the sounds of people shifting impatiently and Roger grumbling under his breath.

Bang!

The sound of the front door slamming penetrated the room and everyone jumped. Bedlam erupted in the outer room.

"What the fuck! Let me go, you fucker. Who the fuck do you think you are?" More banging, and the sound of a woman's voice shrilling over the rest of the noise. Underneath the shrieking and shouting, Jenn could hear Noah's low, calm voice of reason telling everyone to calm down and the sound of loud barking.

The conference room door slammed open, and a woman, tall and elegant with sleek dark hair, stormed in. "Noah, what is going on? This policeman arrested Bret. I don't understand. Why has Bret been arrested? What did he do?

And why am I here? Am I under arrest? That horrible policeman made me come too. I don't understand." Based on her loud demands, this was Noah's mother.

Taking his mother's hand, Noah led her to the front of the room and pulled out the chair sitting behind one of the tables. "Mom, stop talking and sit down." The woman's eyes widened in shock. "Noah!" she gasped, however, her son ignored her.

From behind, Jenn heard Tess utter a quiet, yet heartfelt, "You go, Noah!"

"Sit, Mom," he repeated. Reluctantly, with a sour look for her son, the woman sat.

The door opened again and Debra entered. At her side stood Trike, her long pink tongue lolling out and her one yellow eye dancing with glee. Spotting Jenn, she let out a little woof. Her stub of a tail wagged so hard that her entire back end wiggled like a metronome.

"Trike!" Jenn exclaimed and held her hands out. With another woof, Trike launched herself at Jenn, nearly knocking her out of her chair. She wrapped her arms around the animal and buried her nose in her fur.

"I'm so glad to see you." She'd been nearly frantic at the idea she'd never see the dog again. Who would have thought? The dog's entire body wriggled in ecstasy. Rearing up, she gave Jenn a long, juicy slurp with her tongue. "Ugh. Sit, Trike," she told the dog at the same time wiping the slime off her face. To her shock, the silly mutt actually did.

Noah walked back to the conference room door, opened it and poked his head out. "You can bring him in now," he said to whoever was on the other side of the door.

Trooper Lance Swenson appeared in the doorway. He took a deep breath, his jaw rigid and his pale blue eyes flashing. "You wanted him, you got him." Having said his piece, he dragged a cursing, struggling Bret through the entrance and shoved him forward.

Bret staggered, caught his balance. Spying Noah standing off to the side, he let loose a stream of curses before spitting out, "Fuck you, brother!" He thrust a hand inside his dirty t-shirt and scratched madly. Seeing Trike sitting nearby, he continued with, "And fuck you too, you stupid fucking mutt. I hate you!" at the same time he raked his nails up and down his neck, turning the skin bright red. He reached up under his shirt and scratched some more.

Jenn clapped her hand over her mouth. Not because of the foul language, she'd heard plenty of that before. And not because of what he said to Noah either. No, what made her gasp was Bret's blotchy, reddened face, the snot running out of his nose that made him sniff and snort and hack every two seconds, and the swollen red eyes that leaked water down his blotchy cheeks in a steady stream. A rash covered his checks and trailed down his neck into the collar of his t-shirt. The sniffing and snorting and the crazy scratching told her one thing.

Oh, my God!

Bret Maitland was allergic to the dog.

TWENTY-SEVEN

♥

JennGoodwin@MyHeart-2-Heart

All's well that ends well. Don't you just love it?

Trooper Swenson dragged Bret to the front of the room and pushed him down in the chair behind the second table.

Jenn held back the chuckles that threatened to escape while watching Bret alternate between scratching his neck and wiping the crap dripping from his nose and eyes. Karma was a bitch, and in this case it was an actual bitch—bitch dog, that is—that made sure Bret paid for his crime.

One last time, Noah opened the door. A young woman entered, early thirties, tall and slender with short dark-hair, a black judge's robe hanging open over a pantsuit.

"Judge Tatum," Noah said. "Welcome."

The judge looked around as she entered the room, her bright blue eyes filled with amusement.

"Oh, wow," Megan said hoarsely, and grabbed Jenn's hand in a grip so tight it made her turn to look at her assistant, thinking something bad had happened. Instead, Megan was staring at the woman, her mouth half open, her eyes wide.

Hearing Megan's loud exclamation, the judge looked around until she spotted Megan in the crowd of people. Her eyes locked onto Megan's as a flush spread across the judge's cheekbones.

What in the world? Jenn swiveled her gaze back to Megan. Megan was staring at the black-robed woman, a dazed expression on her face as if she'd seen Katy Perry or Beyonce.

Tess poked Jenn in the back and whispered, "And who says there isn't such a thing as love at first sight?" followed by a snicker.

The judge blinked. Straightening her shoulders, she turned and nodded at Noah. He cleared his throat. "Ladies and gentlemen, please rise for the Honorable Judge Jane Tatum."

Everyone rose while the judge walked the length of the room until she reached the podium. Behind the podium was a stool. She boosted herself up to sit. "You may all sit now," she said in a sexy, contralto voice.

Megan's hands rose to her chest. "Oh, my God, I may faint."

Jenn stared at her. *Good God, please tell me I'm not that sappy about Noah.*

Debra retreated to the back of the room leaving Trike to settle down next to Jenn. Noah shut the conference door and walked to the front of the room.

Turning, he addressed his small audience. "Ladies and gentlemen, let it be known this is not an official trial. It's simply a hearing to determine whether to remand Bret Maitland over for trial. This is also a hearing for Melanie Maitland versus Noah Maitland, Judge Jane Tatum presiding."

Bret jumped to his feet, curses spilling out of his mouth. "What the fuck, man. You can't do this. It isn't legal. I don't have a lawyer. I'm entitled to counsel. I haven't had time to prepare a defense, and what am I being accused of, anyway? What the fuck."

Noah leveled a steely stare on his brother. "You should thank your lucky stars it isn't legal. I'm giving you a chance to make restitution without the possibility of prison. Now, unless you actually do want to go to court and face criminal charges for theft and extortion which is subject to prison for up to—" Cocking his head, he turned to Judge Tatum.

"Ten years," she responded.

"Ten years. I suggest you sit down and shut up."

Bret snapped his mouth shut and sat.

"Judge Tatum, this is a simple case, in which the defendant, Bret Maitland, kidnapped Jenn Goodwin's dog, Trike—" He pointed to the back of the room. Trike, hearing her name, woofed, making the judge smile.

"The defendant kidnapped the dog and attempted to extort a million dollars from the victim, Jenn Goodwin..." He pointed at Jenn who raised her hand to acknowledge her presence. "For the return of the dog. With your permission, I'll present Exhibit A," he said.

The judge nodded.

At his words, Debra turned on the recording machine and played the video. In the tape, everyone could see Trike exit the pink and purple Heart-2-Heart house, hop down the steps of the porch on her three legs, and lurch across the lawn in the direction of Noah's house. Ten seconds into the tape, a red pickup truck backed into the driveway. A man, who was clearly Bret, jumped out of the truck, leaving the door open. He ran around to the other side, briefly out of sight of the camera. Seconds later, he reappeared holding the dog. He tossed the animal into the passenger side of the truck. After slamming the truck door, he jumped into the driver's seat and within thirty seconds of his arrival, he was gone. And so was the dog.

Bret jumped to his feet. "I never stole that dog. It jumped in all on its own. He's my pal."

"Really?" Noah asked. He crooked a finger at Jenn who rose and led Trike forward. The dog hip-hopped eagerly to Noah, but when she got close, her big shaggy head turned towards Bret and a growl rumbled in her throat.

"See, he's my pal," Bret said, reaching out a hand. *Snap* went Trike's teeth, barely missing Bret's fingers.

"Shit!" he yelled. "Someone should shoot this fucking dog. He's dangerous."

"Trike's a girl," was Noah's response.

Clapping her hand over her mouth, Jenn covered the snort of laughter that erupted and led the dog back to her seat. Her only regret was that Trike had missed. Maybe if Bret had a few less fingers, he'd be less able to steal.

"Sit down, Mr. Maitland," the judge ordered. Reluctantly, his lip jutting out, Bret did, but not before a loud honking sniffle and wiping his dripping nose on his arm.

A similar smile hovered on the judge's lips. She returned her attention to Noah. "Even if Mr. Maitland stole the dog, in the State of New Jersey, that's a misdemeanor. What evidence do you have of the extortion?"

Reaching into a folder, Noah pulled out the first note that Jenn had received and handed it to the judge. "Exhibit A. The ransom note."

She read it. "How do we know this note was written by Mr. Bret Maitland?"

Noah shot Jenn a glance over his shoulder, a sparkle in his eyes before turning back to the judge and laying one more piece of paper in front of the judge.

"This is the second ransom note. Notice the handwriting and the spelling are the same as the first note." He waited a second while she skimmed the second demand. "Please turn it over."

The judge did. She blinked, frowned and turned to stare at Bret, her expression one of astonishment.

"So, you can see, Judge Tatum, the note was written on the back of a bill from Dr. Basil Shepard, addressed to Bret Maitland for medication for a... uh.... well..." He shot a sideways glance at his brother. "I guess you can see what it was for. If necessary, we can always verify this with Dr. Shephard."

Aw, come on, please tell us why he went to see the doctor. I hope it's something heinous like leprosy or elephantiasis.

The judge chuckled. "No, no need. I can clearly see what he was treated for." She shot Bret a glance. "I hope, for the sake of your lady friends that it's cleared up now?"

Megan snickered which is when Jenn realized what was ailing Bret. Of course. Served the scumbag right.

"Thank you, Attorney Maitland. I believe I have seen enough. Bret Maitland, please rise."

Reluctantly, a scowl on his face, Bret did.

"Mr. Maitland, I have a choice. This is not a real court of law, however, given the evidence presented to me, I *can* remand you over to Trooper Swenson to be charged with theft of the dog, a misdemeanor, but also with extortion, which can be subject to a maximum of ten years in prison."

Bret licked his lips, still looking defiant, yet Jenn could see his hands shaking at his side.

"Or there is another solution which I believe Attorney Maitland would like to suggest."

Noah turned to face his brother. "Bret, all I want is for you to get your life straightened out. I want you to stop hanging around with low-lifes. I want you to get a job and support yourself. I want you to stop living off my income."

Bret's shoulders hunched. "Yeah. Okay. Whatever," he said, however, even Jenn could see he was already thinking of how he could say yes, then turn around and return to the way things had been before.

"I'm going to give you three months to find a job, during which time I'll continue to support you. At the end of that, I'm done, and whatever happens, happens. If you don't have money for food, that's not my problem. If you can't pay your rent, I guess you'll be homeless. If you can't make your payment on the truck, I guess you'll walk. If you get in trouble with the law, you'll go to jail because I won't bail you out any longer." He stopped.

His gaze shifted to meet Jenn's and she could see in his eyes his need for strength and support. Silently, hoping he understood, she lifted one hand and held it out the same way she had at the balloon site, letting him know that she would always be there for him.

A smile burgeoned on his face, telling her know he understood. They may have had a rough start, she may have initially avoided what he had to offer, his love, but there was no doubt in her mind now that she loved him, and she would help him through what was obviously a horrible time.

"Whatever," Bret repeated.

"And if you don't think I mean it, you are going to sign this full confession right now—" He laid a paper in front of his brother. "—that I will keep, and if you don't keep your word, I will give it to the cops to arrest you."

Fury radiated off Bret when he realized Noah was serious and that this was the end of his free ride. Throwing himself back into his chair, he yanked the pen

Noah held out from his hand and slashed his name across the page and thrust it back at his brother.

"Fuck you, asshole," he spat out.

The trooper took him by the arm and led him towards the exit. They passed Trike, who snapped at him. Bret let out a loud yelp and dashed through the door.

Noah closed his eyes, his shoulders dropping. Jenn wanted to rush to him and throw her arms around him and hug him so that he'd know he'd done the right thing, but she waited, knowing he needed a moment to gather himself before continuing with the next item on his agenda.

After a moment, he turned to face his mother. She looked terrified, probably wondering if someone was going to send her to prison for allowing Bret to hide out in her apartment.

"Now, Mom, let's talk about you," he said. "I have a few things to show you. Debra, can you turn on the projector?"

The lights dimmed slightly and what appeared to be a tax return shone on the back wall. Most was blacked out, however, the number at the bottom was highlighted.

"That was my income for last year. Debra, please show the next slide."

A spreadsheet appeared with line after line of numbers. "Mom, this is an itemized list of what I gave you last year. It's been about the same each year for the last five years."

Melanie's lip trembled.

"Next," he told Debra. The spreadsheet was exchanged for a new one. "That's what I gave to Bret. Next." Another spreadsheet. "That's for Dad." His gaze traveled from Melanie and over her shoulder to Noah's father sitting slumped in his chair in the back of the room, saying nothing. "I've had to start over, rebuild my business. This means, if I'm lucky, I might make half of what I made last year."

Silence greeted his words. She didn't know if anyone else had done the math, however, she did and it was obvious that, even though he'd earned an extremely healthy income last year, there had been very little left for Noah to live on. As for this year, the numbers would never work.

"Oh, Noah," Melanie finally said in a sad voice.

"Relax, Mom," he said in a gentle voice. "I'm not sending you to the big house. I want the same thing from you that I want from Bret. I want to stop supporting you, which means I want you to get a job..."

Tears filled her eyes.

"And I'll help with that, but more importantly, I want you to be happy. I want you to stop relying on other people, most especially men, to make you happy. You said yourself that there's something wrong with you. I want to help you fix it, so that you can live a fulfilling productive life." He turned and beckoned towards Jenn's mother, Leah, who rose and walked to the front.

"Mom, this is Leah. She's a psychologist, but she's also Jenn's mother. Because she's Jenn's mother she can't work with you—it would be a conflict of interest—" He smiled at her and Leah smiled back. "She's agreed to work with you at no charge to find another psychologist to help you figure out why you always need to have a man in your life, and why you're so stuck. I'll pay for the psychologist for a year. She's also going to find a life coach who will help you put together a plan to find a good job. You have a degree in teaching so it should be very doable."

Melanie heaved a sigh, her bottom lip trembling. She frown. "Yes, but what about your father?" She turned to look at Roger sitting behind her. "He's as big a mooch as I am, so why are you picking on only me?"

"Hey!" Noah's father snapped, starting to jump up out of his seat, however, the woman next to him yanked him back down into his seat.

"Pipe down, Roger," the woman said. Roger subsided, looking sulky, but obedient as Crystal stood to answer the question. "Melanie, I'm Crystal Borden. Like I told Noah on the phone, nobody needs to worry about Roger from here on out." Her lips curled slyly. "I'll pay his bills and he'll have a comfortable life that I'll provide. I've settled a small sum on all the previous Mrs. Maitlands in lieu of the alimony they are each supposed to get, but mostly so they don't ever come begging for money from Noah. Apparently, Roger rarely paid them even though it was a pretty pitiful amount so they were thrilled to get it. Once we leave here, we're going back to my island, and Roger will never leave there again, at least not without me. I'm going to be wife number six, however, I can promise you, I'll be the last."

"Sweetie pie," Roger protested.

Crystal winked at the crowd who had turned to watch her. "FYI, I can promise that because there are no other women on my island under the age of sixty."

Melanie stared at Crystal. "Um, I don't understand. How did this happen? How did he end up with you?" she ventured. "Didn't he just marry someone named Connie something or other?"

This elicited a smug smile from Crystal. "Nope, the most recent, number five, was named Kitty, poor thing, but you know how that goes. Very young. Very dumb. Very greedy. Now, also about to become very divorced. That's the nice thing about Nevada. A short waiting period for the divorce, and even shorter one for the wedding which will be in about a month."

Jenn hid her smile. Roger's new fiancée appeared to be a real ball buster.

"Now that this circus is done..." Crystal said and turned to the man cringing at her side. "Come, Roger," she ordered and snapped her fingers. "We have a flight to catch to Reno. Hurry up."

Looking like a beaten dog, Roger followed the woman out the door.

The room was silent for a good minute after they left. No one said anything, no one looked at anyone else.

Melanie snickered. "Looks like Roger finally got the woman he deserves."

Laughter broke out.

Still chuckling, Leah gently laid her hand on Melanie's shoulder. "I couldn't agree more. However, let's talk about you now. You and I need to figure out some next steps so you get what you deserve." She led the confused-looking woman out the door.

Noah turned to the remaining participants. "I want to thank all of you for coming here this morning, taking time out of your busy lives to help me bring some resolution to my life." He waited a second for a few people to mumble their replies before turning and following his mother.

The action over, the rest of the crowd trickled away until only Jenn, Megan and the judge remained.

Jenn threw a side-eye at Megan, who stood with her head bowed, yet was sneaking glances at the judge from under her bangs. After a second, Jenn gave Megan a nudge. "Go on, go introduce yourself," she told her assistant.

A look of panic crossed Megan's face and she started to shake her head. "Out of my league," she muttered which was why Jenn gave her a shove in the right direction and quickly exited through the door, shutting it behind her and leaving them alone.

The front room was empty. Except for Noah. He stood in the middle of the room, his stiff shoulders showing his tension, a look of trepidation on his face.

She didn't say anything, simply waited for him to speak.

He sighed, and his shoulders sagged. "I meant to tell you...uh, what I wanted to tell you...the other morning when I showed up wearing the sandwich boards. I had it all planned out how I was going to abase myself and apologize—"

"You didn't need to—" she interrupted.

"Yes, I did. Gram said I needed to find a way to let you know how sorry I was, and that I had to do something that really hurt. Uh, me, not you."

She snorted. "Well, I don't know if you needed to do that. A simple sorry would have been sufficient, you know. I realized the minute I left that I was being stupid...but, you know...so stubborn."

"Got it. I still want to say I'm sorry my family has put you through so much shit," he responded with a faint grin, holding her gaze, his beautiful steel-gray eyes filled with yearning.

She ducked her head, a smile tugging at the corners of her mouth. In spite of her amusement, she kept her lips locked over the words because she wanted to hear what he had to say, and it was kind of nice knowing he cared so much.

He continued with his speech. "Well, still, I'm sorry I accused you of lying about Bret. I'm so used to making excuses for him, the words just flew out without me thinking."

Her smile widened before she got control and put on her stern face. "Okay. Apology accepted." She tapped her chin. "I need to say I'm sorry too. I'm sorry for storming off and not letting you finish."

"No, actually, you were entitled. I should have listened. I'm sorry I didn't," he said next, reaching out and taking her hand.

"Well, I should have explained better so really it's my fault," Jenn responded, twining her fingers with his, gripping them hard, as if those fingers were the only thing keeping her tethered to sanity.

"No, don't say that. I should have believed you, so it's my fault," he said, the words rasping out hoarsely.

"I should have explained about how everyone accused us of lying when we lived in Colorado made me super-sensitive. When you said I was lying, it was like being back in Colorado again, with everyone saying we knew about the robbery and the money."

"Oh, God, I'm so sorry. I never meant to bring up bad memories. I'm sorry you got caught in my idiot brother's schemes."

She smiled. "I'm sorry you have an idiot brother."

He grimaced. "Yeah. Unfortunately, sometimes I'm an idiot too. Sorry."

Crossing her arms over her chest, she gave him a mock stern look. "You're never going to be an idiot again, right?"

"Of course not. Never." He rolled his eyes. "But I might. Because I'm a guy."

Her mouth dropped for a second. Then she giggled. "Okay, I can't top that. You win," she said.

One side of his mouth curled up in amusement, then turned serious again. "Yes. I do win. Because I got you." He paused. "Right?" he asked in a tentative voice.

This overwhelming feeling clenched in her chest, this huge bubble that was this combination of love and sympathy and exaltation at his declaration but mostly love.

"I want you to know, what I did in there—" He gestured at the closed conference room door. "I did for you. I did it *because* of you. I've tried for years to fix this situation and I've failed every time. I was too afraid. Afraid of losing…"

He shook his head. "I don't know what I was afraid of losing. It's not like any of them love me." Pause. "Maybe my mom, but I was still afraid. Until I met you. You gave me courage. You showed me that it was okay to be afraid. You showed me that I could conquer that fear. You made me see that sometimes taking a risk is worth it, that I might not be losing something, but actually gaining something. I love you. I love your courage, and your daring and your joy in life. You make me want to live life to the fullest."

Tears filled his eyes, along with a look of pleading. His hand tightened around hers. "Show me how. Stay with me and show me how to live life. Please?"

The bubble in her chest burst, filling her with happiness, and a little guilt. She threw her arms around Noah's neck and kissed him. "Yes! Yes, yes, yes. I love you too. You make me believe in love again."

"So you'll stay with me?"

"I will," she said, almost like she was saying her wedding vows. Then a thought occurred to her. "Let's go skydiving!"

His eyes widened in alarm. "Do we have to?" he whined. This got another stern look. "Oh, all right. Someday," he said. "I promise. For our wedding day?" He paused, giving her a look that said he might think about it, yet he'd put it off if he could. "Or possibly for my eightieth birthday."

"No," she said. "Next week."

He blanched. After taking a deep breath, he said, "All right. I will," and the deal was sealed. All that needed to happen now was the wearing of a white dress and the walk down the aisle.

TWENTY-EIGHT

JennGoodwin@MyHeart-2-Heart

That happily-ever-after thing? I bet you thought we'd never get there.

It was official; Jenn Goodwin was crazy.

She zoomed into the parking lot, desperately hoping to find an empty parking spot in the crowded lot. Yeah, yeah, of course she realized she was zooming. So what! Right now, the heck with the no-zooming rule. The heck with her mom's fears. Her mom would simply have to learn to deal. Just like her mom would have to ignore that Jenn was massively late.

Speeding around the lot, she saw one lonely little empty parking spot way in the back and quickly zipped into the spot, barely beating out a slower car whose driver rudely gave her the finger.

Well, thank God. At least one thing had gone right today. Well, not the rude digit thing...

Because anything that could go wrong today had. First it had been her alarm. It didn't go off, and she overslept. By two hours. Then there was the toilet. Someone—who shall remain nameless—had dropped a towel into it and it overflowed, so when she finally got up this morning she was greeted by a mess that took her almost an hour to clean up. Her car wouldn't start. She always kept a battery tester on hand at home and at work. What she didn't have on hand was an extra battery so she was forced to take her motorcycle which would have been fine except that there had been torrential rains in the last few days so not only did she have to ride twenty miles below the speed limit, but the bridge over the Raritan River—stupid Raritan River, always flooding—had washed out so she'd had to backtrack fifteen miles and find another route.

However, at last she was here.

Dismounting, she set the kickstand, then twisted her backpack around to her front. Yanking up the hem of her long dress, she galloped through the parking lot then over the grassy lawn, around the side of the building and across the length of the stone terrace until she reached the small group of women standing there.

She skidded to a halt, her breath wheezing in and out of her chest.

"Oh, my God, woman," Megan burst out, her eyes wide behind her glasses. "We thought you weren't coming."

Her partner, Amy, narrowed her eyes in a glare. "You are late," she ground out. "No excuse. I told you to stay over night in the hotel but you ignored me and now look. You're late."

So much for the actually showing up. "I know," she gasped. "Overslept... bathroom flooded...car battery... Raritan River...another flood."

Her sister Emma, who had flown in from Colorado, shook her head. "See! Even Amy knows better so. You should have stayed here last night, but nooooo, of course not. You never listen. I don't know why you don't listen. You haven't changed a bit since you were a kid."

Giving her sister the kind of look she deserved, Jenn removed her backpack and carefully handed it to her mother, who set it on the ground and reached inside to retrieve the cargo she had stowed inside.

"Emma," Leah scolded as she cuddled the contents of the backpack in her arms. "Don't pick on your little sister. It doesn't make the situation better to make her feel bad. It is what it is."

In response, Emma curled a lip. Leaning closer, she repeated, "You should have stayed here overnight like I told you too," under her breath.

Jenn shook her head. "You know I couldn't," she said.

"Humph," was Emma's answer.

Still, Emma was right. Yes, she should have stayed overnight. Yes, she should have already had her hair and makeup done. At the very least she should have driven here in her car several hours earlier with her dress and other precious cargo in the back seat in order to achieve all the aforementioned things but, of course, that hadn't happened.

Instead, she'd had to ride her Harley dressed in her wedding gown, wearing sneakers—because even she wasn't crazy enough to ride her bike wearing heels—and arrive at her own wedding with her hair mashed flat by her helmet and her wedding dress wrinkled like a crushed Kleenex. Too late to fix that now.

Because in front of her were fifty guests seated on white wicker chairs waiting for Jenn to walk down the aisle. Amy's husband, Nick, was in the front row with Trike, who had insisted on coming to the wedding. Clustered around Trike's paws were four puppies. It seemed that, somehow, despite a previous oopsie, Amy and Nick still hadn't gotten around to getting Trike spayed.

Under Jenn's feet was a long narrow red carpet that had been unfurled down the three short steps of the terrace and across the grass ending at a flower-bedecked cupola. Her mind briefly made note of Noah's friend Zach and a short, older man with a fringe of white hair to the side of the cupola, yet it was Noah, hands loosely clasped in front of him, wearing a morning suit, gray jacket with tails, dark pants and a silver vest that matched his eyes, where her gaze returned to.

He was tall and lovely and masculine—broad in the place a man should be broad, and slim where a man should be slim. His light brown hair shone in the sunlight, and his smile was incandescent. Altogether a gorgeous hunk of man. Her man. Her soon-to-be husband. The man who had taught her that love wasn't conditional, and that love could be trusted.

And she had taught him that, with love supporting him, there was nothing to fear.

One hand lifted in a slight wave. She waved back, her heart so full of love she felt like she could float into the sky.

"Don't forget this," her mother whispered in her ear and handed her the braided cord made up of blue and white ribbon, the colors for their wedding.

Music rose from the three musicians seated next to the cupola. Emma in her blue dress stepped down the stairs followed by Amy then Megan.

Leah threaded her hand through the crook of Jenn's arm and turned them both to face the crowd. Jenn took a deep breath to steady herself, tugged on the braided cord she held then she and her mother, along with a fuzzy orange and brown puppy named Quad, stepped onto the red carpet and walked slowly down the stairs.

Because, somehow, perversely, she had fallen in love with the smallest of Trike's five puppies and couldn't resist adopting her.

The puppy gave a shrill yip, thrilled to be finally on the move. The crowd laughed and rose for the wedding march. Together, she and her mother walked slowly down the aisle until she reached her love. She could see the joy she felt reflected in his eyes and on his face. As her maid of honor, Emma took the bouquet from Jenn's hands and the other women took a small step back, allowing Noah and Jenn to take center stage.

He took her hand. He bent and whispered in her ear, "I love you. Thank you for marrying me. Thank you for helping me find a way to really live life," and kissed her cheek before straightening to face the minister.

Her job done, Jenn's mother took her seat in the front row.

"Dearly beloved, we are gathered here today," the minister began in a deep voice, and continued the vows till he reached, "Jenn, Noah, do you take each other in sickness and in health till death do you part?"

"I do," they both responded at the same time, repeating the words that would meld their futures together for the rest of their lives. Quad yipped her agreement.

"You may kiss the bride," the minister finished, but Noah had already bent her over his arm and was kissing her, this time delivering a kiss that involved tongue and groping hands and elicited whoops from the groomsmen standing beside her newly minted husband.

"At least wait for a bed," someone yelled.

With a laugh, Noah pulled Jenn upright, and they began walking back up the aisle towards the reception hall, and a future that included Noah, Jenn and Quad, and maybe someday a child or two, as they became one big happy family.

In spite of the flooded bathroom, the non-starting car, and the crushed dress and hairdo, it was the happiest day of Jenn's life. But what made her the happiest of all was that not one of the dogs peed on her dress.

THE END

If you enjoyed this story, check out the last book in the series;

Heart Burned coming in 2026.

Heart Burned

Chapter One

I t was a dark and stormy night.

Okay, it wasn't. As usual, the butthead weatherman was wrong. There wasn't a cloud in the sky, and it was a full moon. So bright, it lit up the yard like it was frickin' daytime, which was bad, very bad.

Because Emma had to run across that brightly lit back yard to reach John Henderson's ugly monstrosity of a house, the one with—get this—freaking stone turrets like a castle. Regardless, brightly lit yard or not, that's where she needed to go. It wasn't like it was that far, right? She could do it. She had to do it because, in the house, she hoped to find something that could change her life forever.

She mentally calculated the distance.

Uh, no, actually, damn it, she couldn't. Because, despite her long legs, Emma didn't run that fast and security was due to drive by any minute.

Her phone vibrated in her pocket. Oh, crap, she'd forgotten to turn off the ringer. What a dodo. She pulled it out. A text from her sister, Jenn. *Call me. I have news.*

She hit reply to answer her sister's message, but another text caught her eye. And a text under that, and the next one. And the next one. Oh crap, it was actually ten texts. Ten texts? Did someone die? Her heart in her throat, she read the most recent one.

Emma Goodwin! Where the hell are you!!!!!! You were supposed to meet me for drinks. I've waited and waited, and you aren't here. I had a surprise for you, but now I don't. I'm not waiting anymore! I'm going home. FU.

Oh shit! Was tonight the night she was supposed to meet her best friend, Laurel, for drinks? She quickly clicked on her calendar. Yep, shit, there it was. Damn it, she'd completely forgotten about their date when she'd learned that John Henderson, who never went anywhere overnight, *ever*, the effing weasel, would be in the hospital overnight to have his tonsils removed—at forty-eight years old. This is what happened when a girl put all her usually excellent brain towards planning a criminal act; it forgets to set a reminder.

Emma wavered for a minute, asking herself if she should call Laurel back now, or chicken out and send a text? She checked the time on her phone. Three-fifteen a.m..

Brawk!

Big sorry. Stuff happening, important shit. About my dad, she typed, then paused. Laurel was going to be mega pissed. She'd need to do some major ass-kissing to make up for it. *Explain tomorrow. Eight am. Waffles, my place*, she added and hit send.

She stuck her phone into her pocket and returned to studying the wide expanse of lawn. Sadly, the brightly lit space hadn't gotten any darker while she'd been busy dithering. And she was still on the wrong side of that wide-open space.

She checked her watch. Two minutes till security did their next drive-by, and two hours till sunrise. She needed to be in and out of the house before the sun rose, so it was now or never, and never wasn't an option. She bounced on her toes. Hopefully, limbering up would help. She extended one leg, stretching the hamstring, then the other. Why risk a muscle tear, right? And since running so wasn't her thing, she sucked in a few deep breaths because a girl can never have too much oxygen, right?

She eyed the lawn. One minute until the drive-by. "Well, fuck it. I'm going in." Taking a deep breath, she ran. She stopped when her foot caught a protruding root, sending her flying. "Ooof! Son of a bitch!"

Rolling over, she stared at the stupid moon that was responsible for this whole effing problem and took a minute to catch her breath, flexing all her various limbs to make sure she hadn't broken anything. A scraped palm, a banged-up elbow, and a rip in the knee of her jeans. The good news was she was only a few feet away from her goal.

After getting to her feet, she tip-toed to the side of the house. Once there, she leaned back against the wall and surveyed the stretch of lawn she'd just run across, making sure there weren't two big burly security assholes running hell-bent-for-leather in her wake. Nope, she was good. Except for the shaking of her hands. And the pitching and rolling of her stomach, making her want to hurl. And her wobbly knees. Yep, nothing to worry about here.

She took a deep breath. Now for the entry. She edged along the wall and around the corner until she came to the garage door. She knew the door only had one camera focused on it instead of the six bazillion pointed at the main entrance. Why in the hell John thought any reputable thief would enter through the front door versus the garage door in back was a mystery, still, whatever. It all worked in her favor, so who was she to complain?

She picked up a rock and tossed it between her hands a few times, gauging the distance and the amount of force she'd need to knock the camera askew without breaking it. Breaking it would be bad. Using the nice controlled over-hand pitch her dad had taught her, she threw.

Whannnng!

Hot damn! The camera slewed sideways a few inches and was now focused on that stupid effing hot tub where John thought he could get Emma naked and Emma thought different. With that success, her nerves settled a bit.

Her back against the wall, she slid sideways, making sure she was out of camera range, until she was at the garage door and the control panel next to it. She lifted the lid to expose the keypad and keyed in the five-digit security code she'd memorized.

Beep.

See, here's the thing; Mr. Security Conscious Henderson had a fatal weakness. He loved tall blondes. And Emma was a tall blonde. She had long, slim legs, boobs that belonged on a woman thirty pounds heavier, and eyes that seemed to take up half her face. All in all, she was like a freaking Barbie doll on steroids, and men loved that.

Emma, on the other hand, had never liked her appearance very much, yet it came in handy sometimes, as with John. A few deep sighs, a little ass wiggle and a bit of *Oh John, you're so strong,* and the man couldn't wait to invite her to his home.

Of course, he'd made her turn her back when he typed the code into the keypad; however, that's what makeup mirrors were for. A girl had to powder her nose, right, and if she happened to see the code as she doing it...well...

She entered, closing the door quietly behind her. Her heart pounded like it wanted to break through her ribs, but she ignored it as she made her way past John's Mercedes and the Jag, the ATV and the snowmobile and opened the door into the ginormous kitchen. She wondered if he'd paid for this big house and all his toys with her father's ill-gotten loot.

"Okay, now. Office, office, where's the office?"

John hadn't let her explore the house the one time she was inside. His plan was a direct walk into the bedroom. Since that didn't work for Emma, he'd taken her to his office instead, where he'd spent the next half hour showing her all his toys, including his fancy security system, which is how she knew all about the bazillion cameras. And how to turn them on and off. She wondered if he'd paid for this big house and all his toys with her father's ill-gotten loot.

After tiptoeing through the house, she reached his office out front, but crap, this was taking too much time. Sweat broke out on her forehead at the thought of getting caught by the security team if she took too long to leave.

She plopped onto the desk chair, opened drawer after drawer and perused the contents. This breaking and entering was a new thing for her, and majorly nerve-racking. She much preferred her usual way of getting the answers she needed. It was amazing the information men would divulge when it was a dumb blonde asking dumb questions. Unfortunately, John had been cagier than her other suspects, so she'd had to resort to these desperate measures.

She opened the last drawer. Nothing. Well, crap. That left the safe. She knew he had a safe because he'd bragged about how he wasn't one of those idiots who were stupid enough to keep his important documents in a desk drawer. Fingers crossed he used the same security code for the safe as on the doors. A lot of people did—lazy people—so they didn't have to memorize or write down multiple codes. If the code were different, she might have to come back and actually visit John's bedroom. Ugh.

After a brief search, she found it embedded in the back wall of the built-in bookshelf, poorly hidden behind a stack of encyclopedias. Picking one up, she opened it to the copyright page. Nineteen-eighty-two. Good lord. A lot had happened since nineteen-eighty-two. She set it aside. "Okay, Mr. Safe, let's give this a try." Holding her breath, she tapped a key. Then another key, and another until she'd entered the same five numbers as the outside keypad.

Click.

"Eureka!" she said under her breath. She swung open the door and peeked inside. An accordion folder holding papers, like she expected, all filed neatly by year. Very nice, very organized. Very suspicious, because why would someone keep their bank statements in a safe? Quickly thumbing through the tabs, she found the year she was searching for—ten years ago, the year that her father robbed an armored car, the year he died—and pulled everything out. Statements in hand, she made herself take a few slow, calm breaths because she was having trouble breathing. Keeling over from lack of oxygen wasn't part of the plan.

Her dizziness under control, she found the tab labeled *Provident Union Savings* and pulled all the statements. The question was, would these statements prove that John was the man she was searching for? There was no guarantee because what kind of dope would deposit a large amount of cash into their bank right after the news that four million dollars was stolen right in front of the Denver National Bank? Any halfway smart crook would know better. Of course, that didn't describe John.

She wiped the sweat off her forehead. Or maybe he was smarter than she thought, and he'd used a fence to launder the money. A fence would layer the money into different bank accounts gradually over time. As a financial advisor, she knew more than the average person about money laundering. If that was the case, she might never be able to find proof. She needed that proof. She'd spent too many years living with the feeling that her father's actions were all her fault.

Hopefully, though, the proof was right here, in her hands. She'd have to go through the statements page by page to see if they revealed anything. Unfortunately, there wasn't time for that now. She couldn't take the pages with her either. If John realized they were missing, the first thing he would do was move the money elsewhere—that is, if he had the money. At this point, she had no idea. That's why she needed to peruse the statements further.

Time for some handy-dandy modern technology. She loved modern technology. Most of the time. Sometimes it was a pain in the ass, like when people put security alarm systems on their doors or texted you when you were trying to break into someone's house.

One at a time, she laid the statements on top of the humongous walnut desk until the desk top was covered with about thirty pages, making sure to layer them bottom over top so that the account numbers were all hidden. Possessing the account numbers would make her an actual thief, not simply someone trying to get to the bottom of a mystery. The transaction history was what she would need if she decided to go to the police.

Next, her phone. She turned it on and selected Camera. And the screen turned black. What the eff? She pressed the power button. Nothing! Damn it. All that time her phone was stuck in her pocket with the power on, and now it was dead. Damn it, damn it, damn it.

This is what happens when a girl spends sixty hours a day obsessing about the stock market instead of learning the ins and outs of espionage. She forgets to plug in her phone. No wonder so many crooks ended up in prison. Being a criminal was really hard.

Aggh. Now what?

Peering around the room, she found a copy machine. Perfect. She stacked the statements on the feed tray and pushed copy. Click, click, clickety-click. Whoosh. Paper slid out in a steady stream. See, sometimes lower-tech was better.

A minute later, the whooshing stopped. Gathering the originals up, she put them back in the accordion file, careful to file them exactly the way she'd found them, put the file back in the safe and relocked it. She picked up the printed copies and tore off the part bearing his name, address, and, more importantly, the account numbers off each page.

She fed the torn tops of the statements into the shredder, folded the rest of the papers in half, tucked everything into the waistband of her jeans and allowed the tails of her tee shirt to cover them.

Okay, one last thing, just to be on the safe side. Crossing her fingers that this worked, she tapped the space bar on his computer and held her breath as she waited for the screen to activate. Yes! Okay, now, crossing her fingers, her legs and her toes, she typed in the password she'd used for the safe and keypad outside.

Yes! Thank god. The last thing she needed was to leave any trace of her midnight visit. She quickly clicked on the security system icon and waited another few seconds for the program to load. There, finally. Reaching into her pocket, she pulled out the instructions she'd written down. First, delete the last thirty minutes of the recording. That done, she went into the menu, selected the scheduler and set it to automatically start recording in one hour, giving her plenty of time to vamoose. Closing out the system, she stood.

After a quick glance around the room to make sure she hadn't forgotten anything, she left the office and tip-toed through the kitchen, into the garage and around all John's toys, his ode to vomit-inducing wealth, and edged open the garage door. She peered outside. Oh, look at that. It had clouded up. Maybe the weatherman wasn't such a dumb fuck after all. Still, the darker, the better. She exited, shut the door, and reset the alarm. God, she couldn't wait to get out of here.

"Good evening. Find anything?"

"EEEEEEEEEKKKK!" she shrieked. Backpedaling a step, she lost her balance, tripped, and fell for the second time that night. "Son of a bitch!"

"Do you need help getting to your feet?" the man asked, staring down at her.

A shiver slithered down her spine. He was big and broad, and scary. Very scary. Yet attractive...in a scary kind of way. He crossed his arms over his broad chest and cocked a brow.

"Are you going to murder me if I do? If so, I'd rather not waste the energy by getting to my feet. You can murder me when I'm lying down just as easy, right?" She scrunched her arms over her chest to protect herself. Not that her efforts would stop him.

Sighing, he shook his head. A lock of mahogany brown hair fell over one of his eyes. He brushed it aside. "I'm not going to murder you. Do you want up or not?"

Like a murderer would tell her the truth. Although, it was possible he wasn't a murderer. He seemed too handsome to be a murderer. Still, you never knew. Look at Ted Bundy.

She peered at him. Gray dress pants, dress shoes, and a tweed sports coat, all immaculate. Okay, maybe not a murderer, because what kind of murderer dressed up when he was hunting someone to murder? Although, again, Ted Bundy.

"Come on, do you want help or not?"

The cement patio was cold, and her back had begun to hurt. "Okay, then, yeah." She held out her hand. He took it and hoisted her to her feet. She brushed the seat of her black jeans, then her knees, trying not to look at him to give herself time to think. Who the hell was this guy? What was he doing here? And was he simply biding his time before he threw her into the trunk of his car, only to have his wicked way with her later? A little tingle riffled through her. Would that be so bad?

"Done dusting?" he asked with a lift of his eyebrows. He seemed harmless. Then again, so did Ted Bundy.

"Only one more speck." She flicked a nonexistent bit of dirt off her shoulder.

A little huff, part laugh, part snort of disbelief, sounded.

Jerk. "What, you have a problem with cleanliness?"

"I have a problem with thieves."

Smart ass. Maybe he was part of John's security team. If so, he must be new because she didn't remember him from either of her two visits. But who else could he be? "Hey, I didn't steal anything. You can check me out, and you'll see I didn't take a thing. I don't even have a bag or anything to put stuff in. See, here's the thing: when I was here last week, I lost—"

"Stop talking and empty your pockets."

She stopped talking. And glared at him. He glared back, only his glare was fiercer. Gulp.

"Never mind. I'll just empty my pockets." Digging into her jeans pockets, she pulled out her cell phone, a wadded-up tissue, a cherry lifesaver covered in lint, a dime and two pennies, a couple of bobby pins, her cell phone, her wallet, and oh yeah...oops. A lock pick—something she'd acquired from her friend Anna's locksmith husband—in case she needed it for the desk drawers.

"Tsk, tsk," he said and reached towards her. She took a step back. His rather warm brown eyes turned steely. "If you know what's good for you, you won't move," he said.

She froze. "Fine, whatever. Not moving. Definitely not moving." Yep, because she was a girl who always knew what was good for her. Check out her last name. Goodwin. She'd be good; she always tried to be good; however, for the moment she was relying on the *win* part of her name.

Before she could stop him, he reached over and took her wallet out of her hands. "Hey!"

"No talking."

"Who do you—"

His glare was as lethal as a Luger pistol. She clapped her mouth shut, but still, her heart leaped in her chest as she waited for the axe to fall. He flipped her wallet open, pulled out her driver's license and read. His eyes widened, then lifted to stare at her. Taking a cell phone from his pocket, he typed something in, then waited as the screen populated. He read it. A grin lit his face. "Emma Goodwin. My, my, my."

Uh oh. She wasn't sure she liked that look on his face. It didn't indicate, *say, aren't you that babe Mr. Henderson entertained in the hot tub the other day?* It said more, *I'm onto your dirty little secret.*

Hands behind her back, she stared up at the stars as she considered how to respond, however, before she could decide, he slid a finger under the hem of her black long-sleeved t-shirt and gently lifted it to bare her midriff.

"Dear me. What have we here?"

She blinked at him, hoping she looked innocent.

"Take them out and hand them to me."

"Uh..."

"Now."

Before she could stop herself, she did. Oh, geez, what a dope.

He perused the first document. "This appears to be a statement from Provident Union Savings. Month of January." He flipped through several pages before stopping. "February...Oh, and March, April. ..." He paused and held up a single sheet. "And here's Ma—"

She yanked the piece of paper out of his hand. "Okay, okay. I get it. You can stop."

He shook his head. "You have been a busy girl, haven't you? But your little raid is over. It's time to go." After tucking the folded papers into his jacket pocket, he wrapped a long-fingered hand around her upper arm.

Her pulse skyrocketed. Was this the end of her? Was all that reading of the statements, and the tsk, tsk, and all the other stuff nothing more than a ploy to get her to relax so he could murder her later without her resisting? Well, it wouldn't work on her. She was smarter than that.

Although forgetting to recharge her phone said otherwise.

"Wait, stop. Hold on, buster. Who are you?" So far she wasn't dead, but that could change at any time. "I'm not going anywhere with someone I don't know."

"Hmm. You're right. Better safe than sorry—that's what I always say. Okay, not a problem." He unclipped something from his belt and held it out for her to see. "Agent Hammond."

Her heart plummeted. Damn it all to hell. A frickin' badge. She touched it, wanting to make sure it was real. It wasn't unheard of for bad guys to buy fake badges for obviously nefarious reasons. This badge was heavy-duty, solid, and it seemed real. She leaned over and peered more closely at it.

CBI—the Colorado Bureau of Investigation. Oh, fuck. "You're from the CBI? Where's Bill?" Agent Bill Porter, who, for the last ten years, had dropped by every six months to see if she'd managed to find the money her father and his unknown partner stole. The first time Bill interrogated her was when she was in high school. He'd intimidated the shit out of her, but over time, his visits became nothing more than an excuse for a friendly chit-chat over coffee and donuts. "What are you doing messing in his case? He won't like you stepping on his toes. Bill's touchy that way."

The guy, the policemen, the agent, whatever he was, smiled. "Bill retired last month. He turned the case over to me. Said he hoped I could do what he hadn't been able to do in ten years. Seems like I'm off to a great start, doesn't it?"

Emma ground her teeth. Aw, crap she was so fucked.

Also by Katy Berritt